D0449548

RHIANNON

My life could not possibly suck more than it does right now.

I try not to cry.

And to let it go.

I don't want to be this totally depressed person, with a heart so broken it hurts every time I breathe.

I still love Steve. And here's the worst part.

I want him back.

NICOLE

Danny was my first real boyfriend. He just came right up to me with his cute smile and customized Vans and his yellow rubber bracelet that says MOMENT OF ZEN and his radical attitude and picked me to be with out of everyone else.

And it was great at first. But then there was that night. So I had to break up with him. I couldn't deal with it then and I still can't deal with it now.

JAMES

I don't like the way he's looking at her. And I definitely don't like the way he said, "If you ever feel like hanging out . . ."

Whatever. It's her life. I don't know why, but it's like I go into this hyper protective bodyguard mode whenever some dude tries to hit on Rhiannon.

"Oh," Keith goes. "Are you two . . .?"

"No!" Rhiannon yells. "We're just friends."

Dude. Why'd she have to yell like that? Is the thought of us together so horrendous? I mean, it's not like I want to be with her, but jeez.

OTHER BOOKS YOU MAY ENJOY

Take Me There

SUSANE COLASANTI

speak
An Imprint of Penguin Group (USA) Inc.

SPEAK
Published by the Penguin Group
Penguin Group (USA) Inc., 345 Hudson Street, New York, New York 10014, U.S.A.
Penguin Group (Canada), 90 Eglinton Avenue East, Suite 700, Toronto, Ontario, Canada M4P 2Y3
(a division of Pearson Penguin Canada Inc.)
Penguin Books Ltd, 80 Strand, London WC2R 0RL, England
Penguin Ireland, 25 St Stephen's Green, Dublin 2, Ireland (a division of Penguin Books Ltd)
Penguin Group (Australia), 250 Camberwell Road, Camberwell, Victoria 3124, Australia
(a division of Pearson Australia Group Pty Ltd)
Penguin Books India Pvt Ltd, 11 Community Centre, Panchsheel Park, New Delhi - 110 017, India
Penguin Group (NZ), 67 Apollo Drive, Rosedale, North Shore 0632, New Zealand
(a division of Pearson New Zealand Ltd)
Penguin Books (South Africa) (Pty) Ltd, 24 Sturdee Avenue, Rosebank, Johannesburg 2196, South Africa

Registered Offices: Penguin Books Ltd, 80 Strand, London WC2R 0RL, England

First published in the United States of America by Viking,
a division of Penguin Young Readers Group, 2008
Published by Speak, an imprint of Penguin Group (USA) Inc., 2009

5 7 9 10 8 6 4

Copyright © Susane Colasanti, 2008
All rights reserved
The lines from "i carry your heart with me (i carry it in". Copyright 1952, © 1980, 1991 by the Trustees for
E. E. Cummings Trust, from *Complete Poems*: 1904–1962 by E. E. Cummings, edited by George J. Firmage.
Used by permission of Liveright Publishing Corporation. The lines from "Rebel" copyright © 2004
by Tatyana Fatima Cabrera. All rights reserved. Used by permission of Tatyana Fatima Cabrera.

THE LIBRARY OF CONGRESS CATALOGING-IN-PUBLICATION DATA
Colasanti, Susane.
Take me there / by Susane Colasanti.
p. cm.
Summary: Three New York high school students try to sort out their emotions as they deal
with relationships, crushes, their families, and planning for the future.
[1. Interpersonal relations—Fiction. 2. High schools—Fiction. 3. Schools—Fiction.
4. Dating (Social customs)—Fiction. 5. Emotional problems—Fiction. 6. New York (N.Y.)—Fiction.] I. Title.
PZ7.C6699Tak 2008
[Fic]—dc22
2007037119
ISBN: 978-0-670-06333-8 (hc)
Speak ISBN 978-0-14-241435-4
Printed in the United States of America

Set in Fairfield, Korinna, and Century Gothic
Book Design by Sam Kim

PUBLISHER'S NOTE
This is a work of fiction. Names, characters, places, and incidents either are the product
of the author's imagination or are used fictitiously, and any resemblance to actual persons,
living or dead, businesses, companies, events, or locales is entirely coincidental.

Except in the United States of America, this book is sold subject to the condition
that it shall not, by way of trade or otherwise, be lent, re-sold, hired out, or otherwise
circulated without the publisher's prior consent in any form of binding or cover
other than that in which it is published and without a similar condition
including this condition being imposed on the subsequent purchaser.

The publisher does not have any control over and does not assume
any responsibility for author or third-party Web sites or their content.

FOR PIERRE,
who proves that true love
is something real.

☽

Acknowledgments

FINDING MY WAY into the light would not have been possible without the guidance and encouragement of the phenomenal support team at Viking Children's Books. Anne Rivers Gunton, my spectacular editor, has an incredible talent for shaping a story until it sparkles brighter than I ever imagined. Your patience and dedication are invaluable. Regina Hayes is an amazing source of inspiration. Thank you so much for believing in me. Sam Kim created an absolutely gorgeous cover and Nico Medina is the best copy editor ever. You guys rock.

I would also like to thank my agent, Gillian MacKenzie, for her determination and attention to detail. Can't wait to hear the soundtrack.

My life would be a darker world without these contributions of glowing genius. Authors Laurie Halse Anderson, Blake Nelson, Judy Blume, and S. E. Hinton have sparked an eternal flame with their brilliance. All of my students over the past decade have challenged and influenced me in countless ways. The fascinating Tatyana Cabrera let me share her fierce talent with the world. And Jonathan Rubinstein created a neighborhood coffeehouse that always feels like home.

My friends are the most dazzling family I could ever hope for. I would be lost without all of you. Laila, your awesome daily e-mails of encouragement kept the fire burning. Allison, you increased the luminosity of all those mornings.

Intense thanks to Pierre, for being my number-one fan and totally devoted to taking excellent care of me. You give me the strength to keep going. Feel the gluons.

To everyone who reads this book, infinite thank-yous. You are pure sunlight to me.

PART ONE
May 20–23

☽ ✿ ☗

To move the world,
we must first move ourselves.
—Socrates

RHIANNON
CHAPTER 1
Saturday

MY LIFE COULD not possibly suck more than it does right now.

I try not to cry.

And to let it go.

I don't want to be this totally depressed person, with a heart so broken it hurts every time I breathe.

I still love him. And here's the worst part.

I want him back.

☽

The homework pile on my desk is laughing at my pain. *I'm not laughing with you,* it says. *I'm laughing at you. You pathetic idiot.*

The homework pile is right. I am pathetic. I am an idiot.

I vaguely remember remnants of my normal life. They're

like a dream. These detached, blurry images that may belong to someone else.

I hate being like this.

And then other times I'm like, *Okay, Ree. Enough already. Get over it.* Because how can I let someone who doesn't love me anymore turn me into this person I don't even recognize?

Being awake sucks.

My Persian cat Snickers, aka Snick-Snick, jumps up into bed with me and purrs. He curls up in a fluff ball, pressing against my ribs. I pet his long, soft fur. He feels sad, like me.

Question: When does the pain go away?

I reach over to my nightstand for the remote and my glasses. I turn on the TV. Here's the agenda: I'll watch a gazillion movies, read the huge stack of magazines I've accumulated because I never have time to read them, and snarf horrifying amounts of junk food until it's time to get up and go to school on Monday.

Getting dumped is crazy times. Like . . . what? You're supposed to instantly turn off all your emotions just because he says it's over? You're supposed to go on with your life like nothing happened?

Garden State is in the DVD player. I press PLAY even though I just watched it a week ago.

I wish Steve were here so bad, watching the movie with me. We had this way together. I would lie against him with my cheek on his chest, feeling his heartbeat. And he would hold my hand with my fingers folded in between his. He had this way of making me feel so good by not really doing much of anything. Just by being him.

Question: Where did all that love go?

☽

Last week I went through the motions of school on automatic. I cried at the most random things. Someone would be pouring a glass of water and I'd suddenly feel tears running down my face. But the absolute worst was when people asked if I was okay. Because then I had to admit that it was real, it happened, and we weren't together anymore.

And yeah, it got better. My stomach eventually went back to normal. I didn't cry every day.

But my heart. My heart will always be broken.

☽

Just when Zach Braff is screaming into the rain, Brooke comes barging in with Cinnabon.

Brooke's hair is wrapped in a towel because she's in grad school and on break and it's two in the afternoon and that's what time she gets up. Brooke is ten years older than me (I'm seventeen), so you have to wonder what my parents (who are over fifty) were thinking. She's in this endless PhD program for art history. Dad's always ranting how she'll never find a job after. But it's just what she's into, and she's not changing her mind. That doesn't stop Dad from trying to change it for her, though. He's an international currency trader, and he's all about the big bucks. As in he wants us to get paid the big bucks when we grow up. Which is highly unlikely, considering the types of careers we want.

But Dad is really stubborn. So he got this summer internship all set up for Brooke with a broker at Citigroup, where he works, hoping that she'd see the light and become someone she's not because that's what responsible adults do. But she was like, *I'd rather eat dirt than expose myself to the corruption of impressionable minds.* So Dad was like, *Okay fine, be like that, but don't expect me to keep paying for it.*

Anyway, Brooke has an apartment in this sketch neighborhood uptown near Columbia, where she goes, but she always stays here for breaks since the downtown nightlife is where it's at. She works the bar-and-club scene something fierce. Like she's nineteen and just having fun instead of twenty-seven and interviewing potential husbands.

So she's been home for a week, but she's going backpacking through Europe on one of those *Europe-on-Thirty-Dollars-a-Day* plans. She's leaving Friday.

"Extra icing!" Brooke reports. She sits on the side of my bed and puts the Cinnabon box on my stomach. I haven't moved since I woke up. Or whatever you call it.

Brooke glances at the TV. "Oh! I love this movie!"

I sniff at the box.

She goes, "But how can you watch it again?"

"It's the best."

"But you already know what happens."

"So?"

"So then how . . . ? Whatever." Brooke looks me over. "And FYI? This is the last day we're letting you sulk. No boy is worth wasting a gorgeous weekend over. It's really nice out, by the way."

"How would you know?"

"I've been out, he*llo*."

I pop open the box. This intense cinnamon smell wafts out. "So?"

"So you have to get up and get on with your life." Brooke rubs her hair with the towel. "He is *so* not worth it."

"It's only been a week."

"Yeah! Exactly!" Brooke rubs furiously. "Which is more than enough time to recuperate. News flash! You live in the best city in the world! There are endless possibilities out there!"

I peel open the container of extra icing.

"And plenty of guys who will treat you better than Steve ever did."

"He treated me great."

"Please. The boy couldn't get a clue if they were giving them away on the street."

It's not like I'm agreeing with her or anything. But if your boyfriend, out of nowhere and with no advance warning whatsoever, dumps you for no apparent reason, is it really about you? Or is it all him?

☽

When the phone rings, I have no idea how long I've been in bed. All I know is I'm on my third movie, I've read two *People* magazines and one *Teen Vogue*, and I'm most of the way through a box of Vienna Cremes. The Cinnabon is long gone.

"Hello?" my voice cracks into the phone.

"Hey," James says.

"Hey."

"What's wrong?"

That's the thing about James. He knows when something's

wrong, before you even say anything. He's so not a typical straight boy.

It's impossible to describe my agony. And I'm sure my friends are sick of hearing about it. So I just go, "I'm still . . ."

"Still?"

"Yeah."

"Drag."

Everyone says that it gets better with time and that time heals all wounds and blah-di-blah-blah.

Question: What if they're wrong?

"Tell me about it," I mumble.

"Sounds like you could use a change of scenery."

I wait for him to try. It's not going to work.

He goes, "Nice how Keith's party is tonight."

"I already told you. I'm not going."

"Um-hm, yeah. So when am I picking you up?"

"No way."

"Come on."

"Not going."

"You have to go."

"I'm not leaving this bed."

"Distraction is your friend."

"Not leaving." I so don't want to deal with people right now. Plus, there's a chance Steve will be there. But still. Somewhere in the back of my mind, a voice is screaming at me to get up, brush myself off, and go. So it's complicated.

"Steve is such a dumbass," James informs me.

"I knew it!" I always knew James had a problem with Steve, even though he never said anything. James has been my best friend since seventh grade, when I lost my notebook on the first day of school and he helped me find it. It's awesome that we ended up going to the same high school, too. "But why?"

"You deserve someone better."

"Better like how?"

"Better like not a dumbass."

"Yeah. He was overrated." Not like I believe what I'm saying. I'm just trying to convince myself that out of me and Steve, I wasn't the one who did anything wrong.

"Exactly," James says. "So what time should I pick you up?"

☽

Top Five Things I Miss About Steve

5. Cracking up together over old *SNL* reruns of Mr. Bill.

4. When we'd double with Nicole and Danny to see bands at The Elbow Room.

3. The way he'd surprise me by finding out where movies were being filmed around our neighborhood in Greenwich Village. And then we'd go watch.

2. He always remembered that I like extra sprinkles when we went out for ice cream.

1. How it felt to be loved.

☽

"Hey!" James yells at Keith, who almost dumped his beer all over my shirt. "Watch it!"

"Sorry, man," Keith grumbles, not looking sorry about anything.

James turns back to me and goes, "Freak."

Which is what I usually think every time I see Keith. So I'm trying to pretend that even though we're at Keith's house, I won't have to see him again. Because he's totally obnoxious. But he lives in this huge loft in SoHo, which is, like, this ultra-ritzy neighborhood one over from the Village, and he throws these incredible parties. So of course everyone goes. And if you just avoid him while you're there, it's a total blast.

We drool over the enormous living room, the balcony, the high ceilings. My house is nothing compared to this. This is ridiculous.

"Did you see the flat-screen TV?" James pants. "It's gotta be a fifty-inch. I'd never leave the house."

"Sign me up."

The music is so loud my bones are shaking with the beat.

"So," James says.

"So," I say.

"Are you okay?"

"No."

"Maybe after, we'll do Magnolia?"

The Magnolia Bakery is this place in our neighborhood that has the most amazing cupcakes ever. The thing about these cupcakes is they have icing in all these sweet pastel colors and old-school sprinkles. My favorite combination is pink icing with blue flower sprinkles. Serendipity determines if you'll get the icing-sprinkle combo you want.

"I think this party is enough excitement for one night," I tell him. Another thing about Magnolia is that it's open really late on weekends. The line at midnight is outrageous. "How about tomorrow?"

"You're on."

"You guys having a good time?" Keith butts in. He holds out a beer for me. As if I'm interested in drinking something that tastes like Drano.

"I don't drink."

"Oh." Keith nods, acting all serious. "And doesn't that make you thirsty?" Then he laughs like that was the funniest thing anyone's ever said in the entire history of the world.

"I mean I don't ingest toxic substances."

"Well, then I guess I didn't have to hide the rat poison after all." Keith laughs hysterically again. "Yo!" he gasps. "I crack myself up!"

We stare at him.

"Anyway," Keith continues smoothly, as if we all have a sense of humor in common. "That sucks about you and Steve, but . . . if you ever feel like hanging out . . ."

"Um." I can't believe he's actually asking me out like this. I glance at James.

"Oh," Keith goes. "Are you two . . . ?"

"No!" I say. "We're just friends."

"That's what I thought." Keith inspects me. He actually does that sleazy guy thing where they slowly rake their eyes up and down your body.

Gross.

Then Keith's like, "Well . . . you know where to find me." And he slithers away like the snake that he is.

James mumbles something.

"What?"

"Nothing." He looks bothered. "I'm getting a Coke."

Standing there with the party swirling all around me, I get this really intense alone feeling. Even with James here and Nicole coming later, being at a party with friends instead of a boyfriend is always sort of sad. Especially when you thought you'd have a boyfriend to do couple things with for the rest of junior year. And maybe even longer if Steve came back from college to take me to the prom and stuff. Before The Incident, this year felt like it was going by really fast. Now it's taking forever, even though we only have four more weeks left.

I'm itching to check my voice mail, but James made me leave my cell at home. He knew that if I brought it with me, I'd be checking to see if Steve called like every three seconds.

"Hey, Ree," Nicole says, suddenly here. She hugs me.

I hug her back, clinging to her like Velcro. Nicole is the type of person that's great in a crisis. She can figure out your problem before you're even done explaining it. And she always knows exactly what to say to make you feel better.

"Are you okay?" Nicole is worried about me. She knows it's too soon to be over it. She knows I think about him all the time.

"Yeah," I say. "I mean . . . no. You know."

She knows. She's been here.

Nicole bites her lip. "If it makes you feel better, we can go over it again."

That's another thing about Nicole. She comes off all wild like with how she dresses, but she's not really like that. She's actually super sensitive and sweet.

But still. It must take an enormous amount of strength for her to say that. We've analyzed the whole thing to the point of exhaustion, until there's nothing left to say. But why he dumped me is the most annoying unsolved mystery *ever*. So of course I want to go over everything he said for the millionth time.

I'm like, "Only if it's truly okay with you and you're not just saying that because you feel sorry for me because—"

"It's okay."

"So . . . well, at first he seemed the same as always . . ."

The whole thing was so strange. The entire four months we were going out, I thought we had this amazing connection, right from the start. No, I *knew* we did.

But then.

☽

"I, um . . . I don't think we should go out anymore."

"*What?*" He couldn't be serious. There was no way. "What are you talking about?"

"I just don't feel it anymore," Steve said. All casual. As if he was saying, "I don't feel like going to the park."

"Why not?"

"I don't know."

"How can you not know?" I kept expecting the joke to be over.

Steve just shook his head, looking at the floor.

"What happened?" I said. My eyes filled with tears.

"Nothing. I just . . . I'm leaving for college anyway, so—"

"But that's not until August!"

"Yeah, but . . ."

"So that's why?" I wiped my cheek. "I thought you said you wanted to try a long-distance relationship."

"Look. I know this is hard to hear, but . . . I just don't think it's a good idea."

I watched Steve. He didn't even look sad. How was that possible? This is a boy who said he loved me. Who stayed in my room all day when I was sick, playing cards and making me smoothies in the blender, even though he didn't know how and the blender got jammed. The same boy who put his hands all over my body, kissed me for hours . . .

And then suddenly it was over. It was the worst feeling I've ever felt in my entire life.

I cried harder.

Steve got up.

"Where are you going?" You could hear how scared I was. I was like, *This is it. He's leaving already. He can't even stand to be in the same room with me. I'm that repulsive.*

Steve sat back down on the couch with the tissue box. He held one out.

"Here," he said.

I wiped my nose. "Do you still love me?"

"Yeah, but—"

"Then why are you doing this?"

"It's not you. It's me. I'm . . ."

"You're what?"

"I just have to do this, is all."

"But I still love you."

Steve cracked his knuckles. I always hated when he did that, but now I would give anything to be back together with him. If he would just take it all back, he could crack his knuckles all he wanted and I wouldn't care.

I sniffed.

"I was wondering," he said, "if . . . we could maybe . . . like, be friends?"

Was he serious? In what twisted universe would a girl who's just been dumped still want to be friends with the boy who dumped her?

"I don't get this," I said. "I thought you were happy with me."

"I was."

"So why are you doing this?"

Steve got up.

"Don't go!" I yelled. I was crying so hard.

"I'm sorry. . . ."

"Please don't go!" I wanted him to sit next to me and hug me and say that he was still mine. That I'm the only girl in the world who could make him happy. That we belong together.

But Steve just walked away. He walked right out of my house.

And then I was completely alone.

☽

"I want him back," I reveal to Nicole.

"Huh?"

"I'm getting him back."

"How?"

"I was hoping you'd know."

Nicole stares.

"I can't do this," I say. "I'm not this strong. I still think about him all the time. It's driving me insane."

"You'll get through this. And I know it's impossible to believe right now, but it gets better. Trust me."

It's so weird how Nicole and I always go through the same things at the same time. So of course both of our relationships just ended. Nicole and Danny broke up three weeks ago. And Steve dumped me last week. Or seven days, nine hours, and twenty-three minutes ago. Not that I'm counting.

Before Danny, she was seeing this guy Jared. And Jared dumped her so hard she wouldn't get out of bed. So I would go over to her place after school with all her favorite snacks. Butterscotch Krimpets (which you can only get at this one deli nowhere near either of our neighborhoods). Lemonheads (candy section, middle shelf, Rite Aid). Entenmann's Ultimate Crumb Cake (available everywhere). Chocolate-covered cherries (strictly Godiva, no discount type allowed). Nicole was totally destroyed. And then one day she decided that she was completely over Jared. And she started dating Danny the next day.

Nicole thinks the same thing will happen to me. That once I start liking someone else, this will all go away. But I'm still in love with Steve. And I'll never feel this way about anyone else. He just needs me to remind him of what he had.

Has.

"Don't you think I can get him back?" I panic.

"No, it's just . . . why would you want to after what he did?"

"Because I still love him. You can't just turn love off. You still feel it."

"But that'll go away and—"

"But I don't want it to go away," I interrupt. "I want to be with him."

"Hello, sexy ladies," Sheila says.

"Hey," I go.

Nicole's like, "Where's Brad?"

"He's coming later. I'm going up to see the pool. Want to come with?"

"Sure," I tell her. I assume Nicole will also come, but then I notice her watching Danny. Who's walking over here. "Let's go."

Sheila's talking about Brad and this problem they're having, but I'm not being a good friend. I manage to steer the conversation back to me and Steve by doing one of those sorry-ass moves where you take something the other person just said and go, "Oh, yeah! That's just like what happened with me when . . ." When, really, the two things aren't even related. You're just using it as an excuse to talk about yourself more.

I want to get Sheila's advice. So I'm about to tell her about the whole Steve dilemma when I notice Joni. She's standing really close to our lounge chairs. Too close. All pretending not to listen. When it's totally obvious that she's majorly listening.

The conversation shifts back to Sheila's stuff. I don't say anything else about Steve. I don't really need the whole school knowing my business.

☽

The first thing I do when I get home is zoom to my room to check my messages and e-mail. Snick-Snick follows me in. I close my door and peek at the answering machine. The red light stares back at me defiantly. Not blinking. There's nothing on my cell, either.

I press the start button on my iBook and go to the closet. I take out a soft white tank top and pink pajama bottoms from my dresser. I watch my screen saver of Topher Grace come on while I change. James always teases me about it whenever he comes over. He's all like, "Where's the screen saver of me?"

I click my Gmail widget and see that I have five new messages. I get this adrenaline rush of anticipation.

But none of them are from Steve.

I can't wait anymore. If I wait around for him to realize how lame he's being, I'll probably be waiting forever.

I click on "Compose Mail." Here's what I write:

> **To: steve <richthecopyguy>**
> **Subject: us**
> **Steve,**
> **I just have to tell you that I don't know how to do this. I still have feelings for you and I think**

I click the DISCARD button.

I start again.

> **Steve,**
> **I've written this e-mail a thousand times in my head, all different versions, trying to think of the right words that will make you come back to me. I never stopped loving you**

I click DISCARD.

I start again.

> **Steve,**
> **How's it going? I thought I would see you at Keith's**

party tonight, but no. Were you there? It was fun
times, as usual.
So, I was wondering if

DISCARD.

Again.

Steve,
Can you just tell me why you did this?

I don't send that one, either.

CHAPTER 2

Sunday

AWAKE.

I push the covers down to the bottom of my bed. Snickers meows and leaps away onto the floor with his legs sticking out in all different directions. It's those negative vibes of desperation I keep giving off. They're repelling everyone and everything around me.

I go over to my desk to check my e-mail. Still nothing from Steve. And my cell's been on all night, so I know he didn't call.

This is torture. It's just torture.

Question: If you were happy with your boyfriend but he wasn't happy with you, was that happiness real?

☽

Sundays blow. There's never anything on. But I have to kill time so I can get to the part where I feel better faster. So I go over to the DVD shelf and pick out *13 Going on 30*. I just want to lose myself in a fantasy that I'm still hoping will come true.

When I'm at the part where Jenna and Matt get Razzles, Brooke strides into the living room. She goes, "God!" and flings herself dramatically over the other couch. "New York guys are such . . . *children*."

I don't know what it is with her and interrupting my busy movie schedule. I press PAUSE on the remote. This won't be short.

"There's this total manwhore phenomenon happening, where even the geeks are players now. It's like Manhattan is this giant playground and guys want to keep playing forever."

I gaze at the TV wistfully.

"They're all totally neurotic and miserable. Working these eighty-hour weeks to pay for a bunch of stuff they don't even have time to enjoy."

The sad thing about all this is that Brooke won't meet her soul mate in a bar. He'll probably be standing next to her in Walgreens, getting toothpaste or something. Or maybe he's been living next door this whole time. Like when Nicole liked this guy she kept seeing at the Barnes & Noble café? She'd go back to Barnes & Noble around the same time every Saturday and he was there a lot of the times. But after all that stalking, it turned out that he lived in her building right above her.

But it's hard to find your soul mate when everyone's so anonymous and living in their own private bubble worlds. It's not like you can just go up to a boy you like and say, "Are you my soul mate?"

Brooke is oblivious that some of us are trying to watch a movie here. She keeps ranting about how unfair it is.

I pick up the remote, hoping she'll take a hint.

"Even if you're pretty, it still doesn't matter." Brooke sinks back against the cushions, deflated. "They'll buy you a drink, but they'll be looking over your shoulder the whole time they're talking to you. Looking for something better to come along. Because you know. Angelina Jolie might be just around the corner."

"And she might actually like them."

"I just want a boyfriend," Brooke says miserably.

I press PLAY. If I keep listening to Brooke complain, all that hope I was feeling might start feeling more like desperation.

☽

The thing about New York weather is that lots of times it's too cold or too hot or too humid or too something. We don't get a lot of absolutely perfect weather, where you just want to be outside all day. But now it's the last week of May and gorgeous out.

I'm chilling in the park near my house, waiting for James. This is a really cool park because it's right on the Hudson River. There are piers sticking out over the water and paths to ride your bike and it's the ultimate place to come at night and do moon observations. I have three whole journals with moon sketches. Or sometimes I just sit and think about stuff, watching the city lights glitter across the river in New Jersey.

There's still some of my granita left. It's the best, most refreshing drink in the world, and I get them from my fave coffeehouse, Joe the Art of Coffee. I love being there, just sipping my granita and reading. Everyone thinks it's named after the owner, but his name is Jonathan. He's this super friendly guy who comes around and talks to you. This one time we had a really intense conversation about when he started Joe. He said it never occurred to him that he would fail. I wish I felt that confident now.

My iPod is playing a really cool song by the Watchmen, this random Canadian group James told me about. I'm lying on my back on the grass with my eyes closed. I found a spot in the shade, so it feels like the air and my skin are exactly the same temperature. Like I'm completely blended in with the environment. Maybe this is what it feels like to get reincarnated as a flower, the way Nicole wants to.

But I can't really appreciate how good this should feel. Because every place I go, it's like I can still feel the energy of being there with Steve. Just like in the movie *Serendipity*. And I can't stand it, because every time I think I'm improving, I realize there's no way to completely get my life back. If I were a flower, none of this would be happening.

The last time Steve and I were here, it was on my birthday. He gave me this huge present. But it actually wasn't. Because when I opened the box, there was another box inside. And another box inside that one. There were, like, six boxes altogether, and each one was wrapped in a different type of paper. It must have taken him forever.

When I finally opened the last box, there was this superball inside that lights up when you bounce it. And it wasn't just any old superball, either. It was this special one we saw at the MoMA Design Store when I was bouncing it all around and yelling about how awesome the lights were. Which totally made the security guard come over and guard my area, like I was going to start bouncing the ball against people instead of the floor or something. Anyway, Steve remembered all that, and he went back and got the exact same superball.

A breeze blows over me, smelling like summer. Summer is almost here. I should be happy.

I open my eyes and look up at the sky and there's James, looking down at me.

"Hey," he says. "Did I scare you?"

"No."

"Sorry if I scared you."

"You didn't."

"Ready?"

I hold out my hand. And he helps me up.

☽

"Did you see if they have pink ones?"

"Oh, come on. They always have pink ones."

I point at James. "But did you *see* pink ones?"

"Not exactly," he admits. "But don't worry. It's all good."

The line at Magnolia isn't too long today. We're almost up to the window. That's where you can look in to see what cupcakes they have and with what color icing.

"So," he says.

"Yeah?"

"Keith was so random last night—"

"I know! It's like, *Hello! My boyfriend just broke up with me!*"

"What's up with that?"

"Seriously."

We move up a few steps in line. I still can't see in.

"As if I'd ever go out with him," I add.

James smiles. "What's so bad about Keith?"

"Like he's anywhere *near* my type."

"And what's your type?"

"Oooh!" I can see in the window now. "*Yes!* They have the pink ones! Plus your green ones. Bonus!"

"What sprinkles?"

"I think yours are . . . yeah, yellow circles."

"Nice."

"And mine have blue flowers!"

We slap a high five.

We always walk to the pier and eat our cupcakes there. It's amazing how you can do something like this a million times and never get sick of it. As usual, James inhales his cupcake in three bites while I'm still peeling the paper off mine.

He's like, "You never told me." Some crumbs fly out of his mouth.

"Told you what?"

"What your type is."

"You've been my best friend for four years. How can you not know this?"

"Um, maybe because you never told me?"

Which is true. We've both dated a few people since middle school, but Steve is the first boy I've been serious about. And James never takes the risk of asking a girl out unless he knows she likes him first. He does pretty good for a computer geek, though. He's even dated a couple hotties. But for some reason it never lasts. And he always has the lamest excuse for why it didn't work out. He was going out with Jessica for a while, but I don't know what happened with that. If he wasn't such a good person, I'd suspect that he's a closet manwhore. But James is way too sensitive and deep for that. It must be a standards thing.

"Okay, well . . . you know I like Topher Grace."

"Ah, yes. Of the infamous screen saver."

"Jealous much?"

"Not to negate my heterosexuality, but he doesn't exactly seem like the most attractive candidate out there."

"He's not," I explain. "That's the whole point of him."

"Obviously."

"I mean, it's something about him that's the attractive part. Like, I think he's cute and all, but it's more about his personality. Something in his eyes." I take a huge bite of my cupcake. Sprinkles fall off.

"I hate to be the one to tell you this."

"What?"

James leans over and whispers, "You don't actually *know* Topher Grace."

I throw a flower sprinkle at him. It bounces off his nose.

"You know what I mean," I say. "There's something about him that's—I just know what I like."

James is watching the skyline sparkle as more lights blink on. My favorite thing is how the pink sunset light reflects off all the building glass. I try to concentrate on this, on being here. I don't want to think about Steve anymore. Somewhere underneath it all, I know he doesn't deserve to take up space in my brain.

☽

One way I know James and I are going to be friends for a long time is that we both love board games. And who else loves board games anymore? All my other friends switched to video games or being glued to the computer sometime around fifth grade. But James never changed. And neither did I.

So now we're at his place, playing Parcheesi. I always feel really comfy when I'm over, because it's so colorful and warm and cluttered with his mom's pottery and knickknacks. This is what a home is supposed to feel like. Not like mine, which feels too empty. And big. You could probably fit this whole apartment in my living room. I used to feel really guilty about it when I came over, like I don't deserve to live in a brownstone while James doesn't even get his own room. But now I just feel relaxed. We sometimes have these sweet family dinners with his parents and little brother and real comfort food. Not gourmet cuisine like the complicated, exotic stuff my mom always gets. And then we sit around after, playing games or talking or watching TV. Or just doing our own things, together.

But I know James doesn't feel the same way about living here. That's why I hope he becomes a super successful software designer and gets the house he's always dreamed about. I know he feels cramped here. It's not like he's the one just visiting.

"Oh, man," James mutters. I have a blockade set up, and he wants to pass.

"Sucks to be you."

"Somewhat." He's trying to figure out a way to save himself.

"There's no way out."

"Maybe not." He inspects the board, configuring all the possibilities.

"Admit it. You're screwed."

"Not yet."

"James!" his mom yells from the kitchen. "Could you give me a hand, please?"

"Not now," James says.

"What?"

"Not now, Ma!"

Mrs. Worther comes into the living room. "It'll only take a second."

"It never takes a second. And in case you haven't noticed, I have company."

"Well, of course I noticed!" his mom huffs. "I just need—"

"Okay. Ma? If I help you, do you promise I can have the rest of the night free to hang out with Rhiannon?"

"Jeez! You act like I'm always bothering you."

"That's because you *are* always bothering me."

Listening to James and his mom, I miss not having that kind of relationship with my mom. Not that I want her to always be bugging me to do stuff, but it would be nice if we did things together once in a while—the way we used to when I was younger—and if we talked more. Mom's always so tired or busy when she gets home from work. If we're eating together, it's mostly in silence.

"Don't touch the board," James warns me.

"Who, me?" I flutter my eyelashes innocently. "Whatever do you mean?"

"Knock it off. I'm on to your cute act."

"Hmmm?"

"Yeah, yeah . . ." James mutters on his way out.

I examine the board. I'm definitely winning, so there's no point in moving any of my guys. Not that I ever would.

Okay, except sometimes? James is too good, and I have no chance of winning without a little intervention. It's like when we play Monopoly. We both have very different strategies. He's always like, "Why do you even bother with Baltic Avenue?" Meanwhile he has a zillion hotels on Boardwalk, so there's really no point in playing him. Sometimes not even being the lucky wheelbarrow helps. So I might take a few five-hundreds from under his side of the board when he gets up for a drink or something. But he always figures it out right away when he comes back, so it's not really cheating. It's more like teasing.

Brian peeks around the corner. Brian is five and too cute for words. He has his stuffed Prickle with him. Prickle is his favorite Gumby character, and the stuffed Prickle was his mom's when she was in high school.

"Hey, Brian," I say.

"Hi."

"Come here."

Brian runs over with Prickle's arms waving all around. He almost crashes into the Parcheesi board. "What are you doing?"

"Playing a game with James."

He looks around for James. "But James isn't here."

"Yeah, he is. He's helping your mom with something."

"So you're playing by yourself?"

"No. I'm just waiting for him to come back."

"Is waiting boring?"

"Kind of."

"Reading's more fun, right?"

"Right."

"Wanna read?"

"Sure."

So Brian runs to get *Lafcadio*, which is this cool Shel Silverstein book we're currently reading. And the TV's on and the ceiling fan's whirring and the neighbors are laughing through the wall. And his dad is in the little office space he converted from a closet, working on an article and listening to National Public Radio. And I can smell dinner cooking and James and his mom are talking in the kitchen and Brian comes running back with his book.

This place definitely feels like home to me.

☽

I usually have this horrible feeling in my stomach on Sunday nights. I call it the Sunday Night Dread. Because tomorrow I have to go back. And there's all this homework I promised myself I would do Friday night so I wouldn't be doing everything totally last-minute the way everyone else does. And now it's already Sunday night and where did the weekend go?

Back in my room, I get out my binoculars and try to see Mars. It's close to Earth right now, which means you're supposed to be able to see it with the naked eye. It looks like a red star. But, as usual, it's not clear enough to see much of anything besides the moon. Still, I like this routine of trying.

Steve always hated routines. He complained that I wasn't spontaneous enough, that I always had to plan everything in advance. I could tell he wanted me to be more exciting, but it's just the way I am. I love routines. Like how James and I have our Magnolia routine. Or even when we play Monopoly, he's always the top hat and I'm always the wheelbarrow. It's our thing. It's just the way we are together.

But Steve wasn't like that.

Maybe that's okay, though. Maybe it's impossible to find

everything you want in one person. Maybe everyone in your life gives you certain things you need. And your friends give you the rest of what you can't get from your boyfriend.

Question: Is it unrealistic to believe that one person can be your everything?

CHAPTER 3
Monday

THE THING ABOUT first period is that it starts at eight o'clock and my brain isn't working yet. No one's is. Except for the teachers'. But they get paid for that. And even then you can totally tell that some of them are still hungover from partying too late. Or maybe that's just true about Mr. Farrell. He looks like he might be fun to hang out with.

My brain's still asleep. Plus my contacts were all dry and irritating yesterday, which means I had to wear my glasses today. And it's not like I have cool retro glasses like James or anything. I have these boring ones that I picked out freshman year and never bothered updating because I thought I wouldn't have to wear them again.

Question: Did I pick out these glasses because I was trying to make a statement that dorky glasses are in?

Anyway, I have Earth Science first period, and today's a lab day. Which means that instead of going to gym second period, we have science for twice as long. Which would be excruciating enough for most kids in here under normal circumstances. But lab in this school is not normal circumstances. And that would be because our school is retarded.

First off, we don't have enough lab stools. So it's first-come-first-sit. But even the prospect of standing for two periods hunched over the lab table the whole time isn't enough to make me get out of bed ten minutes earlier. I usually slide in just as the bell's ringing. So I'm standing and bending over and my back is killing me. You'd think Eliezer or Miguel would have the skills to be a proper gentleman and let me sit. But no.

We go to Eames Academy of Design. It's a magnet school for kids who want to be things like interior designers or urban planners or architects. When I first told my parents I wanted to apply, my dad was like, *No way.* He was hating Brooke's decision to reject the joys of capitalism and wanted me to make up for it. So we had this whole heated argument about how it's more important to do something you love than to make a lot of money (my side), versus you have to be a responsible adult and support yourself because no one else is going to do it for you (his side). I had to throw this whole hysterical screaming fit before he even listened to what I was saying. Which is such a joke, because this school is really selective and lots of kids don't even get in, so it's supposed to be a privilege to even be here. So we agreed that I could go if I got in. If I didn't get in, I'd be forced into some obnoxious college-prep private school horror show. Guess who won that battle?

Kids apply from all over New York City to go here. It's supposed to be one of the best public schools around. But you don't necessarily get in for having good grades in middle school.

It's not that kind of selective. You have to have some special talent. Besides me and James, there are only a few other kids who live close by. Everyone else is from the Bronx or Brooklyn or Queens, or just from other neighborhoods in Manhattan, all spread out.

So you'd think our school would be all technologically advanced and crammed with supplies. Which I guess it is when you see the computer labs and projectors in the classrooms. But not so much with basic stuff, like restocking soap in the bathrooms or having short paper for the copier (so all of our handouts are on long paper until more short paper comes in) or having enough lab stools to sit on.

I stand up straight and stretch out my back. Part of it makes a cracking noise.

Other than lab days, Earth Science is tolerable. Math's okay (I'm a peer tutor), English Lit rocks (mostly because of free-write time), and Web Design blows (completely). I wish I was as smart as James. Then everything would be so easy. Everyone always says how I'm so smart, but they don't know what it's like being me. Always feeling like you could do better. Maybe I'm too hard on myself. But that's part of being a perfectionist.

There are only about three people who know what's going on in this class, because Ms. Parker can't teach. Plus, she always throws in these impossible questions that like maybe Einstein could figure out on one of his good days. So the last fifteen minutes of lab is the worst kind of stressful. It's this frenzy of flipping through notes and everyone getting mad at everyone else because no one knows what to put for the conclusions section.

"What'd you get for three?" Eliezer asks us.

"We just did three," Miguel says. "Weren't you listening?"

Here's Miguel: wicked smart, completely destroys the curve.

"Dude," Eliezer says. "Just what'd you get?"

Here's Eliezer: burnout senior, needs this class to graduate.

Miguel looks at Eliezer like he's the biggest reject ever. Then he starts explaining like he's talking to someone whose last reading accomplishment was *Pat the Bunny*.

"You have to explain that the half-life of Carbon-14 is 5,700 years, so that means after that period of time has elapsed, half of the original C-14 sample is still radioactive element, while half of the sample has been converted into its stable decay product, which is Nitrogen-14."

Eliezer stares at Miguel. He goes, *"Huh?"*

I think Miguel lost him at *elapsed*.

"What part don't you get?" I ask him.

Eliezer snatches Miguel's paper and starts copying.

"Don't!" Miguel panics. "You know if we copy, we'll all get zeroes."

Eliezer keeps copying. "Like she's gonna notice one answer."

Miguel throws me a desperate look.

"She reads everything," I say. I unzip the side pocket of my bag and take out a new pencil. They're lined up in their holders next to my colored pens and regular pens.

Eliezer goes, "Yeah, right."

"Ever read her comments when you get your labs back?"

"No."

"Well, if you did, you'd see that she reads everything."

"She even corrects your spelling," Miguel adds.

Eliezer realizes he's outnumbered. He pushes Miguel's lab back to him.

"Whatever," he groans. "Let's just get this over with."

☽

On my way to math, Steve's across the hall and I want to go up to him. But the hall is crowded and I can't get through, and then he's gone.

Nicole's waiting for me around the corner. She's like, "Did you see Brad?"

I didn't.

"He shaved his head!"

"*Ew.* How does it look?"

"Disgusting. Everyone's saying how his head is shaped like an egg."

"This just in."

"Did you get number thirty-two on the homework?"

"Um." I think I might have tried that one between thinking about Steve and thinking about Steve.

The bell rings.

"Not that it matters," Nicole grumbles on her way to the back of the room. She always sits in the back and I always sit in the front. Unless we have assigned seats. She likes to do that so she can spy on everyone and write down story ideas without them knowing. "I didn't get any of the other ones, either."

"You're coming to tutoring, right?"

"I'm not sure."

I'm a peer tutor for math on Tuesdays. Nicole comes almost every week. I like explaining math to people. I'm into the finite rules and organized methods. I guess that's why I rock at math. Which is weird, because you're not supposed to be good at both math and artistic stuff. But making numbers work has a calming effect on me. Plus, everyone knows that colleges will reject you if you don't have enough activities. It's so they know you're not just some antisocial brain in a jar.

I sit down. Keith is staring at me. He waves.

I wave back. I still haven't told him no. For some reason, I lied to James yesterday and told him I already did.

"Good morning, leaders of tomorrow!" Mr. Farrell shouts. "Who wants to put number thirty-two on the board?"

I look back at Nicole. Her eyes say, *See?*

"Nicole?" Mr. Farrell says. "Thanks."

"But I didn't—"

"And who wants to do thirty-three?"

Nicole sighs this long, dramatic sigh. She pops open her binder. She lifts her homework pages out like they're made of lead instead of paper.

"Okay, Jackson," Mr. Farrell decides. Jackson always looks like he's about to bust a vital organ over the chance to put a problem up.

Then Mr. Farrell sits on top of his desk to take attendance. He's wearing his math tie with the neon numbers and a white shirt and his brown cords. He has this habit of wearing the same pants every Monday for some reason. They look like they've seen better days. And his scuffed brown loafers don't really go with his pants. They're different shades of brown.

Nicole is putting the problem up. Mr. Farrell finishes attendance and turns around to watch her. I catch him looking at her butt for a few seconds. I look around to see if anyone else caught it. But the class is dead. It's always like this at the end of the year. Especially on Mondays. We have these state tests coming up called Regents Exams. You have to pass all of the ones you need or you can't graduate. The Regents are less than a month away, but no one stresses until the night before. Now we're just killing time. Stuck in faux-education limbo.

A police siren screeches by outside.

Nicole puts the chalk down. The problem is only half done.

"Not so fast, Nicole," Mr. Farrell says.

"But I didn't get this one."

"You need to at least try."

"I did. I got half of it."

"You need to try harder."

Nicole sucks her tooth. She picks up the chalk.

Everyone's waiting.

"Like she's ever gonna get it," Gloria informs the room.

Nicole freezes up. She doesn't turn away from the board.

"Can I explain mine?" Jackson begs.

"Not yet." Mr. Farrell holds his hand up in a you-must-chill gesture. "Let's give Nicole a chance to finish." Then he darts an angry look at Gloria.

But Nicole just stands there. I send her a telepathic message to hang in.

"Here's what we'll do," Mr. Farrell announces. "Why don't we start this worksheet—no, stay where you are, Gloria, you're working individually—and that way I can walk you through it, Nicole. Okay, who—thanks, Jackson, you can have a seat, we'll go over that one later—who wants to pass out the worksheet?"

No one raises their hand. Someone yawns rude loud.

"Do we get participation points?" Gloria demands.

"Sure."

Gloria gets up to pass them out. She snaps her gum. The snap sounds like a firecracker.

"Gum, Gloria," Mr. Farrell warns.

She's like, "Sorry." Even though you can tell that she's totally not. "It won't happen again."

"I know. Because you're going to throw your gum out."

Gloria glares at him. He should know better by now.

Gloria is one of those girls whose purpose in life is to give teachers a hard time. And also all of us, for extra fun. Girls are petrified of Gloria, because she's totally gorgeous and can have any guy she wants. And every guy she wants is coincidentally already someone's boyfriend. Not that she cares. If you give her attitude or even look at her wrong, she'll get you back. And it will be ugly. Or sometimes, she'll just decide she wants what you have and there's nothing you can do about it.

Like in ninth grade? Our social circles actually intersected for a little while at the beginning of the year. Back when I thought we were friends. And our mutual friend Sheila was having a movie-night party at her house (it was Reese Witherspoon screening night), where six of us got together to eat pizza and watch movies and do the old-school sleepover thing. So we were playing Truth, and I said how I liked this boy Emilio and I could tell he liked me, too.

I can't even tell you how shocked I was when Gloria totally went after him Monday at school. She seemed completely trustworthy and sympathetic at the sleepover, all listening to everyone's secrets and giving advice. And then she went and did that? I totally didn't see it coming. Neither did the rest of the girls who were there. They all heard me say how I liked Emilio, and they all saw how Gloria stole him away from me. So of course we all iced her. A couple of the girls told the whole school what she did. And even though it was embarrassing, I wasn't that mad. Because then Gloria got this immediate reputation as a skanky boyfriend-stealing chickenhead.

It's not like I didn't confront her. I did. And you know what she said? She was all, "But you never went up to him."

And I was like, "But you knew I liked him."

"You don't even know for sure if he liked you," Gloria said. "You just thought he did."

"Yeah," I said. "Because he *did*."

Then she was like, "There's no law against talking to people. That's all I did. He was the one who asked me out."

Yeah. That tends to happen when you rub your ginormous breasts up against some boy's arm.

I take out my red mechanical pencil that I always use for math. Red goes with math. I click it twice and wait for my worksheet.

Gloria holds a sheet out to me. But when I reach for it, she drops it on the floor.

"Oops," she drawls. "My bad."

She doesn't pick it up.

I reach down to get it. My binder slides off my desk and crashes to the floor.

"Oops," she says. "*So* sorry."

Apparently, Gloria still blames me for when all the girls stopped talking to her. Like her lack of morals is somehow my fault. It's so *stupid*.

I start the first problem. I show my work for cross-multiplying.

I try to concentrate. This is one of the few rooms with ventilation, but there's still not enough air in here.

Steve and I usually sat together at lunch, but I've been sitting with James since The Incident. I wonder if I should try and sit with Steve anyway since he said let's be friends. Or maybe I should wait until after school, when I can talk to him alone.

Mr. Farrell is still helping Nicole with the problem. Which is weird, because he never helps us put up homework problems. It's either sink or swim in here. But maybe he feels bad for her, because even though she works really hard, she's still barely passing this class. Or maybe he feels bad about what Gloria said.

I'm trying to figure out what I should say to Steve later. Should I be like how I miss him and I forgive him? Or would that make me look desperate? Or maybe I should wait for him to come to me instead. . . .

When Mr. Farrell tells us to pass our papers up, I'm still on the first problem.

☽

I hate days like this.

Like when one minor thing happens but it gets all huge in your head and ends up bothering you for the whole rest of the day. I can already tell the thing with Gloria is like this. The entire day is going to suck now.

But then I open my locker. And there's a bunch of flowers sitting there, right on top of my books.

They're not just any flowers, either. They're spray roses. I love spray roses because they're smaller than regular roses, so there are a few different buds on the same stem. And they smell just as pretty.

I lift out the roses carefully and hold them up to my nose. I love this. And I love what this means.

There's only one person who knows how much I love spray roses.

This must be his way of saying sorry. But maybe he's not ready to talk about it yet. He probably just wants me to know that he's thinking about me and that he still loves me and he realizes that he made a huge mistake and he totally misses me.

I love days like this.

$$\text{\textemdash}\,\mathbb{D}\,\text{\textemdash}$$

At lunch, I sit with James.

Steve looks at me from across the cafeteria.

My heart forgets how to beat.

He smiles at me.

I smile back.

And then James shoves his chair back and gets up.

I'm like, "Where are you going?"

He says, "I'm done."

It's obvious something's wrong and he doesn't want to talk about it. And it isn't the first time he's shut down. It's how James deals with stress. Especially when he has a ton of stuff to do and no time to do it. I know he needs space right now.

So I go back to sneaking looks at Steve. He smiles at me again.

I'm so psyched that even the grungy Hot Pockets taste good.

☽

By the time the last bell rings, I know exactly what I'm saying to Steve. I worked it all out during the mind-numbing dreck that was eighth period. And I'm sure he's been waiting for me to talk to him ever since I found the flowers.

I'm putting my stuff in my bag and trying to smooth down my out-of-control curly and out-of-control frizzy dark brown hair. Which is a pointless struggle, but we try. I have a really big Italian last name. Ferrara. I also have really big Italian hair to go with it. Everyone loves my hair, but I hate it. It's wild. It doesn't fit into my ultra-organized life. It extends beyond the borders, freaking out whenever it feels like it.

But my first name is way more interesting. Mom got the idea from an old Fleetwood Mac song, which was this major group in the seventies. Back when my parents were these people I would never recognize today.

The halls are emptying fast. No one wants to stick around for tutoring during the last week of May when it's sunny and seventy out. Maybe Mr. Farrell will tell me I only have to do another week of tutoring. There's Regents later, but the one for this class is a joke. I heard it's not because the test is that easy, but the grading scale is way lax.

I go down the back staircase in case Steve already went to his locker and he's on his way out. I need to tell him this now. When I'm about to walk down the hall to where our lockers are, Nicole comes running around the corner and slams into me.

"There you are!" she gasps.

"What's wrong?"

"Wrong? Nothing! Nothing's wrong." She stands right in front of me, swaying from side to side. "I, uh . . . I just thought you left already."

"So?"

"No, it's just . . . I have a surprise for you."

I smile really big. I love surprises. As long as they don't disrupt my schedule or anything. "What is it?"

"I can't tell you—duh! Okay, so let's go." She grabs my arm and spins me toward the stairs.

"Wait! I need to go to my locker."

"No way. We don't have time."

"Why not?"

"Because of the surprise!" Nicole coughs. "We have to leave *right now*."

"But I need my stuff."

"Like what?"

"Uh . . . review books? And my math book?"

"Oh, yeah! I totally spaced on those homework problems."

"What are you talking about?" Nicole never forgets about math homework. She stresses it every night.

"You know what?" Her voice sounds all high-pitched and anxious. "I have to get my book, too, so why don't I get your stuff for you?"

"What—is Brad dealing weed in front of my locker again?"

"Ha-ha! Right? Okay, so meet me out front!" Nicole zooms off.

"Wait!" I yell after her.

She turns around and walks backward. "What?"

"Get the roses!"

"What roses?"

"Just get them!"

We know each other's locker combinations and we've gotten stuff for each other before. But she's acting weird. If I didn't know her better, I'd think she was hiding something from me.

☽

The cute waiter we always hope we get at Chat 'n Chew puts a huge plate with a grilled cheese sandwich (tomato and bacon) and fries (extra crispy) in front of us.

On the walk over here, I told Nicole about the roses. I wanted her to agree that it was Steve's way of saying sorry. But she looked less than thrilled. She's definitely in a weird mood.

Instead of talking about Steve, Nicole talked my ear off about the Last Blast dance. That's what we're getting instead of a junior prom. Joni's cousin goes to school in New Jersey, where they're having their junior prom next week. So of course Joni's all twarked up into a big snit because she won't have the opportunity to spend hundreds of dollars on a dress she'll only wear once in her life. She took her argument straight to the principal. Plus, her father's this big-shot PR rep who's probably the only parent to donate money to the school every year. Supposedly, when he heard we don't even get a junior prom, he was outraged.

So Mr. Pearlman said we could have a junior dance at the end of the year, but it had to be before June. He didn't say why, but I know he's paranoid of anything that would distract us from studying for the Regents. As if a dance would even make a dent in the abundance of other distractions in our lives. It's like this: if a lot of kids pass the Regents Exams, the school gets a reputation for being good and the principal can go home happy at the end of the day thinking he had something to do with it. So the Last Blast dance is this Friday.

The whole scenario was supposed to teach us about compromise. But all I really learned is that money is powerful enough to bend the rules. Rhiannon: 0, Dad: 1.

"You better be treating," I say. "I have, like, four dollars."

Nicole picks up her half of the sandwich. Melted cheese oozes from her piece to mine. "Of course. That's the surprise!"

"Just so you know? I was about to get Steve back when you ran into me."

Nicole chokes on a huge bite of cheese. "How?"

"I have my ways. . . ."

"Ree." Nicole gets her serious look she always gets when she's trying to convince me to think like her. "I know you don't want to hear this, but . . . he might not want you back."

"So then what were the roses for? And I know he still loves me. Oh, and he smiled at me in lunch today. Why would he smile at me if it's really over?" I sprinkle pepper on my half of the fries. "He's just worried about us not being together next year is all. But we'll still have the whole summer."

"Are you sure it's only about next year?"

"Yeah. What else could it be?"

Nicole sips her lemonade through a purple straw. She doesn't say anything.

$$\mathfrak{D}$$

There's this project for Contemporary Design that's due next Monday. We have to pick a museum to do research at and go there sometime this week. I picked the MoMA because modern art rocks. We're allowed to work in pairs, but then the project has to be twice as long. And both people get the same grade, even if it's obvious that one person did all the work. Which I usually hate, because I'm always the one who ends up doing all the work. So I don't normally work in pairs if there's a choice, but Nicole's in my class so we're working together. We're doing our project on using recycled material in designs that enhance urban aesthetics.

After Chat 'n Chew, we argue about when we're going to the MoMA.

"Fridays are free from four to eight," Nicole advertises.

"But I don't want to wait that long. And there's the dance Friday."

"But we could go before."

"Can we please just go now? I seriously need something to distract me until I can see Steve tomorrow. I'm going *crazy*." I use my pity-me frownie face. It works.

"Okay," Nicole gives in.

"Let's go."

"Fine. But we need to hurry up. I've got stuff to do."

"What stuff?"

"Just stuff."

Lately it's like there's all this drama going on in Nicole's life she's not telling me about. And she hasn't even given me the remotest hint about what it is.

We go. We take notes on sculptures. I want to find this one Picasso sculpture called *She-Goat* that used all these recycled materials. Picasso totally put in a wicker garbage can and flower-pots and bottles and stuff when he was making it. That's hot.

But we can't find it. So I go up to a guard and say, "Excuse me. Where is Picasso's *She-Goat*?"

And he's all, in his snazzy French accent, "Zee goat is in zee garden." And he sweeps his hand in this grand gesture that's like, *After you, madam.*

The sculpture garden is awesome. I recognize *She-Goat* from some photos I saw online. I put my face really close to the surface. I don't know if you're allowed to touch the sculptures or not. There's no sign or anything saying not to touch them. I mean, I know you're not supposed to touch the paintings because the oil from your hands could damage the paint, but these sculptures are all outside. One of the photos even showed *She-Goat* almost buried in snow from that huge storm we had last winter. So it's probably okay.

But maybe not. I look closer.

"What are you doing?" Nicole says.

"Trying to find the garbage can."

"Huh?"

"You know how it's—"

"Oh, yeah. You told me."

I can't find the garbage can. Or the flowerpots. Or really anything.

We take notes for a while, not talking much. But I'm still wondering what's taking over Nicole's life these days. And why she hasn't told me about any of it. I'm trying to be okay with respecting her privacy, though. We had a big fight last year about how I felt like I was sharing a lot more of my life than she was. And she said how there were some things she just wasn't ready to talk about. But she promised to tell me about the important things. So whatever's going on, it's probably no big deal.

☽

The sound of the phone not ringing is the loudest sound there is.

It's distracting me from the poem I'm supposed to be reading for English. I can't concentrate on iambic pentameter. I can't think about anything but why Steve isn't calling me.

He gave me flowers. He should be calling me.

I get up from my desk and open my window some more. It's so nice out. I'm dying to walk to the pier and sketch the moon since it looked so incredible yesterday. But I don't want to go in case Steve calls. I can't have my cell on when I'm visiting the moon. That would be impolite.

I sit back down at my desk. I stare at the next page. My brain refuses to work.

The phone still doesn't ring.

I can't concentrate. But I have to do something.

Sitting still long enough to watch a movie is not an option. I need to move around, but I can't leave. Cleaning my room would be a perfect solution if it wasn't already perfect. I'm so anal about it. I don't know where it comes from, but I'm an organization freak. If even one thing is out of place, I have to put it back or else it totally distracts me. I guess that's why I want to be an interior designer. Or even a closet organizer. I think organizing people's stuff is super fun. The most fun is when someone is a total slob. You can organize their life for days. And inspire this calm feeling that permeates into all areas of their life. Since everything is connected.

Nicole is always saying my room is so cool. It has a puffy red couch against the wall with all the pillows I made that have satin trim and ribbons and sequins. And a stainless-steel mini fridge with a magnet that says, LEAP AND THE NET WILL APPEAR. Then there's my architect table with the special lamp that I love sitting at because it makes me feel all adult. Like I just came back from a hard day at work, figuring out how the skylights should look in a new green office building.

And then there's all my projects. Things I haven't felt like doing since The Incident. Like the decoupage jewelry boxes and bags I make for my friends.

There's just no inspiration anymore. The passion's gone.

The phone still doesn't ring.

At my computer, I click on my day-planner widget. I have this thing about writing down everything I have to do. I like the feeling I get when I finish something in my day planner and I can check it off. So maybe there's something pending I forgot about. But when I go through everything, there's only school-related stuff.

There's a pile of journals on my desk. Each one is for something different: fave quotes from books and movies, Top Five lists, and my general journal where I do my moon sketching. I'm not ready to take it to the blog level. Because how can you be totally honest about your feelings if you know someone's going to read all about them?

I decide to make a new list.

Top Five Reasons Why Steve Isn't Calling Me

5. He's cramming for a test.
4. He thinks I'm asleep.
3. He's asleep.

   2.   He'd rather talk to me in person tomorrow.

   1.   He hates me.

It feels like the walls of my room are closing in on me.

What if I organize my books by size and color instead of author? I saw that one time in *Real Simple* magazine and it looked sharp. And it's only ten thirty. Steve might still call for like another hour. . . .

By the time I'm done with Project Reconfiguring Bookshelves, it's after midnight. None of my homework is done.

And the phone never rang.

CHAPTER 4
Tuesday

"EAT YOUR EGGS," Mom says.

"They're too runny," I say.

"No, they're not."

"How do you know? You're only having coffee."

Mom gives me The Look. It's the look she gives me when I'm being persnickety.

"Someone woke up on the wrong side of the bed," she goes.

"That tends to happen when someone was up until three."

Mom sighs. "Do we need to take away your TV?"

That would be the royal we. She uses the royal we whenever she threatens, implying that Dad has input. But in reality, it's more like my dad is never here and Mom makes all the real decisions herself. He's not even here now. Dad leaves wicked early, because by the time we wake up in New York, people have had most of their day in Japan already. So all those finance guys have to be at work by seven—sometimes earlier. Apparently, no one is allowed to work on Wall Street plus have a life. And even when Dad's here, he's a severe CrackBerry addict, so it's not exactly like he's really with you when he's with you. Mom is a corporate lawyer, so she works long hours, too, but she doesn't OD like Dad.

"I was doing homework, Mom."

"Why so late?"

"I couldn't concentrate before."

"Why not?"

Here's what will happen if I tell Mom why not. She'll listen up to a point, with these strategically timed glances at the clock I'm not supposed to notice. So it's really just half listening, half thinking through her itinerary for the day. Then while she's giving me detailed advice, she'll pack files into her briefcase. And then her briefcase will click shut, along with my problem. Case closed.

It's not like she's a bad mom. I know she tries. It's just that when you're trying to balance so many things at the same time, it's inevitable that something's going to fall. And her job has changed her a lot. My parents didn't used to be this way. They were all into that seventies lifestyle, way more relaxed about life. They were just different people back then, wearing differ-ent clothes and even listening to different music. I basically grew up with our stereo (and, horrifyingly, our record player) exclusively playing all these songs about peace and love and a time when things were much easier for kids.

Question: What happens to people when they grow up?

It's like they forget who they originally were or something. But I guess some of it rubbed off on me, because I definitely have this seventies vibe/style thing going on.

I'm sure in another life, Mom would be one of those super involved soccer moms. But in this life, it's all about multitasking. Which means she's never completely here. And since I'm not really in the mood to race the clock, I'm not getting her started.

I poke my fork into my eggs. "Long story."

"I've got time."

"No," I say. "You don't."

☽

When Sheila and Brad show up way late to math, it's like I'm seeing her for the first time.

Sheila is the most put-together girl I know. Her makeup is always perfect, and she has this amazing style with clothes where it's like she has this different theme going every day. Like one day she'll come in all hard-core biker-chick and the next she'll be type peasant in lace and a flowy skirt. Plus, she's always in a good mood. Or at least that's how she presents herself.

But not today. Today she looks terrible. Actually, this isn't the first time I've seen her like this. Totally frazzled. It has to be Brad's influence. He's a mess and he's dragging her down with him.

I wish there was something I could do to make her realize. But how can she not already see it herself?

☽

We're doing a poetry unit in English. I usually don't like poetry, but we all got to pick a poet to do a project on. Mine is E. E.

Cummings. He totally rocks. All of his poetry is like this random, flowing thought process. He liked to use lowercase letters when they should have been capital. And unlike with other poetry, even when you don't get it, it's still interesting.

Today we're getting extra credit for presenting our original poems. It's optional because most of the stuff people are writing is way personal.

"Tatyana?" Ms. Portman says. "Would you like to present?"

Tatyana Dias is amazing. She has more self-confidence than everyone else in here put together. And she does all this eccentric stuff like paint her bags and write song lyrics all over her sneakers, and she wears this loud beaded jewelry her mom makes. I swear she has every color of Converse ever invented. Even the ones with polka-dots. And she's not afraid to say these weird, random things to stick up for herself, but it's like she's also being funny at the same time. Like if you press her, she'll be all, "You best back up before you get smacked up! And I put you on the bulletin board and you get tacked up!" Then she'll crack up for days. But the coolest thing about her is that she writes freestyle poetry that completely blows you away. Just hearing two lines of her poetry makes you feel really intense. She's already won two New York City poetry slams.

Tatyana strides to the front of the class like nervous is this foreign country she's never been to. She has this strong, clear voice. Totally unlike most kids who mumble so bad you can hardly hear them and the teacher always makes them repeat what they just said. And you still can't hear them.

Usually when someone goes to the front of the room, they're all jittery or they ramble or they say how they don't know what they're doing. And you feel bad for them because you can totally see their hands shaking the paper they're holding. But not Tatyana. She just reads.

Rebel

I have the might of separating the fight between
*   darkness and light.*
With ashes that surpasses my sight, crime in time
*   slashes, isolating my rights.*
I speak with my eyes, and visualize with my mind.
*   I'm on a quest that has left me*
possessed and stressed 'cause I envy the blessed
*   and pity the depressed.*
You can whip me, strip me, crucify me to a cross; my
*   imagination within my deepest*
destination will not fall!

The poem rocks me to my core. It's all about following your heart and never giving up until your beliefs have become reality. And how if you don't follow your heart, you'll never become the person you want to be.

Something just clicks for me. Like, hearing her words and feeling the power of her voice, I realize that I have to put myself out there to get what I want. Even if it means surviving a potentially humiliating experience. Because my life isn't going to wait around while I figure out how to make it work.

☽

I'm like, "This is it?"

No one else is here for tutoring. Not even Nicole.

"It would appear so," Mr. Farrell says. He's at his desk, grading papers. "Pull up a chair."

"What for?"

Mr. Farrell looks up at me.

"I mean . . . if nobody's here . . ." I can't wait to get to the library. Ever since my epiphany in English, I know how to get Steve back. But I have to do some research first.

"Are you implying that I'm nobody?" He smiles.

My pulse speeds up. It's remarkable that a man can look so incredible every single time you see him. Like, doesn't he ever have a bad hair day?

"You—no! I'm . . ."

Mr. Farrell waits.

I sit down at the desk in front of him.

"So," he says. "How's school going?"

Coming from anyone else, this question falls into the Extremely Annoying Small Talk category. But with Mr. Farrell, I actually care enough to answer. Maybe it has something to do with the fact that he could be a stand-in for Jude Law. All the girls have a colossal crush on him.

"Good." I clear my throat. "You know." I cross my legs. "Same old thing." I mash my lips together.

"Do you like school?"

"Sometimes."

"What do you like about it?"

"When we're on break."

He laughs. "There's that sense of humor we know and love."

No one is coming to tutoring today. It's obvious. I'm about to ask Mr. Farrell if I can go when he's like, "By the way."

"Yeah?"

"I want to tell you something."

"Okay." Here's the part where he tells me that I'm a sucky tutor and I'm not getting credit and I can't put it on my college applications because I suck so bad.

"Thanks for tutoring this year," Mr. Farrell says. "I know you've helped a lot of kids. You've really made a difference."

"Oh." I'm mad gassed. "Thanks."

"You're welcome."

"Is it okay if I go? I mean, since no one's here and all . . ."

"It's probably safe to say you've been stood up." Mr. Farrell picks up his pen. "Onward. Go be a teenager."

Yeah. I think I'm starting to get how to do that.

☽

Whenever I get this really strong feeling to do something, I know I have to do it. And right now I'm motivated to do something huge—like, way over-the-top huge—that I normally wouldn't do.

The thing that clicked while I was listening to Tatyana's poem has to do with something Steve said. It was two weeks before we broke up, and we were in my room listening to some new music I'd downloaded. Steve was lying on the couch with his legs in my lap, reading *The Outsiders*. I was trying to decoupage the front cover of a journal, but it was hard to balance everything on his legs.

One second I was bending over to pick up a tropical-fish sequin off the floor, and the next second Steve's saying, "Do you ever wish you were more spontaneous?"

"What do you mean?"

"Like . . . more . . . doing unexpected things."

I had absolutely no idea what he was talking about. "Where is this coming from?"

"Nowhere. Don't get mad. It's just a question."

"I'm not mad," I huffed. But of course I was. What was he trying to say? That I'm not exciting enough for him?

"Well?"

"Well what?"

"Do you?"

"I don't know. I've never really thought about it."

"Oh." Steve went back to reading.

"Wait!"

"What?"

"You can't just say something like that and not tell me why you're asking."

"There's no reason. It just came into my head."

"It just came into your head?"

"Yeah."

"From where?"

"Dude. You're being irrational."

"How is that being irrational?"

"You can't ask me where it came from. It's impossible to know."

I scrunched up my face like, *Do you even hear yourself when you talk?*

Steve closed the book. "You always say you want me to tell you what I'm thinking, right?"

I pressed the fish sequin over the journal.

"Right?"

"Yeah."

"So I'm telling you. You can't get mad at me." Steve sat up and rubbed my back. "I'm only doing what you wanted."

Which I guess in a way was true. But there was obviously more to it. And he just didn't want to tell me.

So now I know I have to be more spontaneous and exciting. Or that I already am, but I need to prove it.

☽

Question: Does it still count as spontaneous if you plan what you're going to do before you do it?

Steve is the only person I know who loves chemistry. So there's no way my plan won't get his attention.

I'm all about the pheromones when I'm going out with a boy. Like how Steve would sometimes let me borrow his shirt after he took it off. Then I would keep it under my pillow for a week. It would still smell like him that whole time. I loved breathing him in all night.

In the chem section of the library, I find a humungous college textbook called *Pheromone Biochemistry*. I lug it over to a table. I'm practically the only one in here, so I don't have to worry about anyone seeing.

I look up *moths* in the index. There's something about them on page 533.

There's this saying that goes something like, "I'm drawn to you like a moth to a flame." That's how I feel about Steve. There's always been this pull between us, like I couldn't turn away even if I wanted to. I happen to know that moths are all about the pheromones, too. I saw it on the Discovery Channel.

I open my journal for random things and take some notes.

"Mamestra configurata" — moth — phenethyl
alcohol $(C_6H_5CH_2CH_2OH)$ is the
pheromone
phenethyl — beta — glucoside precursor
pheromones are most extensively studied
semiochemical

It all means nothing now. But by tomorrow, it will mean everything.

☽

Nicole's like, "So . . . we're doing this?"

I think about it. After what Nicole just told me, this could be really embarrassing. Plus, I could get in so much trouble for doing this if anyone figures out it was me. But I want to do it anyway. I want to take that risk.

"Yeah," I decide. "We are."

"Are you sure?"

"Absolutely."

There's a courtyard area in front of our school that's not too close to the sidewalk, but far enough away from the front doors for people to notice. I take out the two packs of sidewalk chalk and rip them open.

"The flashlight's in here somewhere," Nicole promises. She's rummaging through her bag. "Could it *be* any darker?"

"Your bag is like the Bermuda Triangle."

"At least that explains why my history homework's missing." She finally digs the flashlight out of her bag. She glances around nervously.

"Don't worry." This block of West Tenth Street is pretty quiet at night. It's basically all residential except for our school.

"So how are we doing this?" she whispers.

"Okay." I take out the folded paper. "I think I should outline the letters first, and then you can color them in."

"Do you want patterns or solids?"

"Um . . ." If I were Steve and I was looking at a huge sidewalk-chalk message for me that took up the whole space in front of the school and everyone was going to see it, would I want the letters to have patterns or would I like it better if they were just colored in? "Maybe solid colors? That way after everyone walks on it, you'll still be able to see what it says."

"True. What colors do you want?"

"Whatever you think looks good." I survey the area. If we start over near the flowerbed and go all the way to right before the grass . . . and if we make each letter about two feet high . . .

I bend down with a pink chalk stick and start the first letter, which is tricky because it's an S. Those are always the hardest to draw in block letters.

Nicole holds the flashlight over me, because the streetlamps are too far away to see here. When she starts filling in his name, she puts the flashlight on the ground and angles it so we can both see. At first it's hard to keep the letters straight, but then I get the hang of it.

An old guy walking his minuscule dog stops to see what we're doing.

"We go here," Nicole tells him. "It's for a project."

"Oh," he gravels in his deep voice. "How nice."

I keep writing. Nicole keeps coloring.

A few minutes later, I look over my shoulder to make sure

he's gone. But he's still there. Watching. As if this is performance art or something.

I'm like, "But it's not done and . . . we're not allowed to have anyone see it yet."

"Oh," he says. "Well, I guess I'll have to wait till tomorrow, then."

"Pretty much," Nicole goes. "Sorry."

"Come on, Bear," he tells his dog. The dog's paws click away on the sidewalk, fading out.

I imagine what tomorrow morning will be like. The knots in my stomach tighten. What will everyone say? What will Steve tell everyone? Will he try to find out what it means before he comes to find me? Or will he come right up to me and say he's sorry for everything and he doesn't know what he was thinking and can I ever forgive him for being such an idiot?

When we're done, we look over our work. It says:

Steve—
My chemosensory organ occludes your phenethyl alcohol.
Love, Me

Not even Steve will know what it means at first. But he'll know who it's from. And it will be the perfect way to make him see that I can do unexpected things. Because there's no way that anyone would expect something like this.

Tomorrow will probably be the most humiliating day of my life. But when it's over, Steve and I will be back together. And that makes everything worth it.

NICOLE
CHAPTER 5
Saturday

SO HERE'S WHAT happened.

Danny was my boyfriend. He was sweet and funny and cute and he totally adored me. And that's why I had to break up with him.

I'm the kind of girl who gets noticed all the time. Which you'd realize is so ironic if you knew me, because I'd rather be the one watching than the one being watched. But the reason I get noticed is because supposedly I have this in-your-face wild-style thing going on, even though I don't think there's anything wild about it. Just your average graphic tanks and spiked belts and cropped vintage tees and funky jewelry and fishnets with combat boots, that sort of thing. Oh, and I have a nose ring, but technically it's just this small diamond stud that you can hardly see unless you get really close to me. Which I don't exactly invite a lot of people to do.

So most people assume I'm wild like my style, which isn't even that wild in the first place (like, *hello*, it's called the East Village, you might want to check it out sometime), but I'm really not. Just because a person chooses to express themselves in an extreme way doesn't mean they have an extreme personality. I'm just making a statement. It's not some rage against the machine, down with the man type deal. Plus, it's this whole new thing with me. I just put my wardrobe together last September and came back to school all different. I guess you could say I needed a change.

Anyway. Danny was my first real boyfriend. The thing with Jared doesn't count because he was only trying to score. So when Danny not only noticed me but also asked me out, I was like, "What's wrong with you?" Because normally people look at me but they don't exactly talk to me. They just kind of sneak looks like I can't tell they're gawking, or they get shocked into silence, depending on the person. But Danny was like, "Nothing." And I believed him because he was Danny.

He just came right up to me with his cute smile and customized Vans, which is the ultimate skater-boy sneaker that gets me every time, and his yellow rubber bracelet that says MOMENT OF ZEN and his radical attitude and picked me to be with out of everyone else. Maybe he thought my clothes matched his political fanaticism.

And it was great at first. But then there was that night. So I had to break up with him. I couldn't deal with it then and I still can't deal with it now and that's just the way it is.

Yeah. You know what? The whole thing is way too complicated to even get into here.

So I'm in my room listening to *X & Y* and ignoring Mom yelling how if I don't clean my closet I can't go out tonight and consulting the latest entries in my spy notebook. I've had one of these since fourth grade when I fell in love with *Harriet the Spy* and wanted to be her more than anyone else in the whole entire world. And I still have spy notebooks, because it's this thing I do to get plot ideas for the screenplay I'm writing. I spy on random strangers and kids at school all the time for ideas, and they don't even know it. No one knows about my notebook except for Rhiannon. Well yeah okay and I told Danny, but I'm sure he probably forgot by now. Who remembers everything about somebody?

My ultimate goal is to be a film director, but writing screenplays is an excellent way to get noticed in the indie world. I love being in control of everything that happens, like being the one to decide who gets a happy ending. It would be so kickass if I turned out to be like Todd Solondz (*Welcome to the Dollhouse, Happiness*) or Alexander Payne (*About Schmidt, Election*), who are, like, the ultimate mega gurus of film. And not to toot my own horn, but I have an amazing eye for detail, which is critical in this business. Like with Mike White? I totally noticed that he wrote *The Good Girl* (which is one of my all-time faves and if you haven't seen it, there is just no excuse for that kind of behavior) and that he was also a writer for season one of *Dawson's Creek*. But that's not the detail. The detail is that he had this almost identical line in both of them. Something about "going to the grave with unlived lives in your veins." I'm sure there was me and like two other people in the world who noticed that.

So I'm consulting my spy notebook and now Mom is yelling that dinner's ready and I *so* don't want to go down there I can't even.

But like I have a choice. So I slog down to the dining room. Or the part of the living room we call the dining room because we put a dining-room table there. It's from our old house and it doesn't even fit into this pocket-sized apartment, but somehow Mom crammed it in anyway. When we lived upstate in Water Mill, there was room for everything. Out in the country with a whole backyard and a stream. You could fit like ten of our apartments in that house, which was my grandparents' and where my mom grew up. Here it's a mega challenge to just get room to breathe.

❁

It's been three weeks. Let's just say Danny's still not over me. But I like him and I want to be friends with him and he said that's cool, but you can tell it's not. Because how can you be just friends with someone when what you really want is so much more? But he said he'd rather be friends with me than not know me at all. So now we're both at this party at Keith's place, and I heard that Danny might ask me to the Last Blast dance next Friday and I don't know what to say if he does.

I drink my 7-Up and watch Heather fake-sip her beer. I totally get that she's fake-sipping it because she knows Carl is watching and she has a major crush on him, but still. That's no excuse to act like someone you're not. It's like, if you don't want to drink then don't drink. It's so tragic. That's one thing I love about Rhiannon. She's straight-edge and doesn't care who knows, because she's proud of it.

Scanning the crowd for Rhiannon, I find her standing near the wall looking sad. I try to remember the last time she didn't look sad and I can't. And I can't believe Steve dumped her like that and didn't even tell her why. Who does that? But unfortunately for Ree, you can't argue your way into someone liking you again when they just announced that they don't anymore. It's over for them, so it has to be over for you, even though it's so not. I never used to get this, but after I broke up with Danny, everything was crystal.

I walk over to Ree and think about what I can say to make her feel better. Not to be shallow at a time like this, but her outfit rocks. She has the coolest sense of style anywhere. It's like she doesn't have "good clothes" and "bad clothes" categories, because all her clothes are hot. She has these retro orange-and-brown-striped pants and about three hundred jelly bracelets and an orange shirt that says CALIFORNIA DREAMIN'. Her bag has three pins—the fox from *The Little Prince*, John Lennon in his New York City tee, and one that says LOOK CLOSER. It's a whole different look from the party outfit I am currently working, which is my black knee-high biker boots (the ones with all the buckles and three-inch heels), shiny red vinyl micro-mini, and Hello Kitty tee. But you know. They both work for different reasons.

So I ask Ree where James is and he's getting a drink. And she looks so sad and lonely, and I hug her. And then she asks me if her eyes look red, and they're totally bloodshot but I tell her they're fine and that she looks gorgeous as always. Which is true.

She's like, "Can you believe this place? What do Keith's parents do again?"

And I'm like, "I think his dad works with Donald Trump."

Ree says how that's so typical. And then I'm preparing for another rant about Steve and how lacking he is, but Ree's not like that. Ree's like how she wants to get Steve back.

Danny passes by but doesn't come over, and I can feel him watching me from all the way over there.

Ree notices and goes, "How's the let's-just-be-friends thing going?"

I go, "Nowhere. It's impossible for a boy and a girl to just be friends." Ree smirks so I add, "Okay, except for you and James."

And she's all, "So it *is* possible." But I've never believed that Rhiannon and James are just friends. They have to like each other more than that. Even if they don't want to admit it.

So I say, "Are you seriously telling me that you've never . . ."

"What?"

"Didn't you ever want to get with him?"

And she's like, "James? No way! He's like my brother or something." And then she does this shudder thing, but I'm not entirely convinced. Plus James is her type—she goes for the smart boys with glasses.

So I go, "But he's mad cute."

And she's like, "Yeah, but . . . no. See? You can be friends with a boy as long as you're not attracted to him."

"But you just said he's cute."

"No, *you* said he's cute."

"But you agreed."

Rhiannon just stands there scratching her arm. Then she says how Keith just asked her out and I'm like, "You waited this whole time to tell me?"

And she's all, "Yeah because it's not like I'm ever going out with him."

And I'm like, "Are you crazy?" Because just look at this place. I have two words for you: rooftop pool. In downtown Manhattan. Some seriously sick stuff. Not that stuff is what's important in life. But I definitely wouldn't mind kickin' it with this caliber of stuff for a while, if you know what I mean.

Sheila comes over and goes, "I'm going up to see the pool. Want to come with?" And I'm about to say let's go but then I see Danny coming over. It would be mega rude to walk away when he's obviously coming over to talk to me and I've already seen him.

So Ree leaves with Sheila, and Danny comes over and he's trying to play the part of See Look How Fabulously We Can Just Be Friends, but it comes off more like I Really Really Miss You. And I'm trying to make him feel better by asking him how things are going and about the election and he's trying to act all casual and relaxed, but it's just not working and I should have gone up to the roof. So I say I'm going up and does he want to come? But he doesn't, so I go up alone.

The roof is amazing. You can see for miles up here, all the way to the end of Manhattan and across the water, and uptown to the Empire State Building, and it's beyond overwhelming.

I go over to where Ree and Sheila are sitting on lounge chairs at the other side of the pool. And Sheila's like, "Did you guys hear about Eliezer?"

We didn't. So she fills us in on the latest gossip, which is that Eliezer blew up a condom and put it under Jackson's chair in Web Design. Eliezer does things like this because he thinks they're hilarious. When in fact it's so sixth grade I can't even. So then Ms. Zigman pitched a fit and totally called Eliezer out on how when he took a practice SAT he thought *chicken coop* was some type of co-op housing deal for upscale chickens. Which is a really sad commentary on how the SAT is totally unfair and favors suburban kids, but whatever. Ms. Zigman will do something extreme like that if you act like a child in her class, especially if you try to embarrass someone else.

So after a while Ree decides she's leaving, which is totally disappointing but at least we got her out of the house for one night. So I hug her good-bye and tell her to call me if she needs anything.

It's just so nice, sitting up here on the roof all peaceful. But then Brad shows up and Sheila leaves with him and I notice that he's kind of demanding about it. But of course I don't say anything because it's none of my business. So I go back downstairs and notice Danny talking to James and Carl and Evan. There's something about the way they're talking, all conspiratorially and laughing. I don't even know why or what it is about the way Danny's talking and laughing with them, but it's kind of obvious they're all discussing some girl, and I want to know who she is and what he's saying.

I kind of sneak up behind Danny so he doesn't even know I'm there, and I position myself so it's like I'm standing there listening to this other group instead of totally spying on Danny. If I could get away with recording the deets in my spy notebook, I definitely would. But when I hear her name, I wish I had never come over.

They're not just talking about a girl. They're talking about *the* girl. Marion Cross. The school überbabe. I'll bet there's not one boy in our school who doesn't use her for nightly masturbation material. Naturally, she only dates college guys.

Anyway, I'm expecting to hear Danny laughing along with the others, like maybe one of them tried to ask Marion out or something equally ridiculous. But that's not what's going on. It sounds like they're encouraging *Danny* to ask her out. But it's hard to hear exactly.

Evan goes, "A score for you would be a score for the entire junior class."

And Carl's like, "Hell yeah!"

Danny's all, "Never say never, that's my motto."

It's like I can believe it but I can't believe it. Why is he even interested in her? I mean, okay, *duh*, I get it, but already? It's like he couldn't wait to get away from me so he could hit on her. And Ree keeps insisting how it's so obvious that he still wants to be with me, but I guess it's not so obvious after all.

I'm insanely jealous. Which is completely absurd since I'm the one who broke up with him. So I don't exactly have a right to feel this way. But that's the thing about feelings. They're totally illogical, especially when it's not fun for them to be.

So it's totally illogical that I do this next thing, which is walk right into Danny's group.

He looks completely guilty, like I just caught him talking about something he didn't want me to hear. He's all like, "Hey, Nicole! I didn't see you."

So I'm like, "What's up?"

And Carl's like, "Nothing yet." Then he nudges Evan and they do that snorting/laughing thing you do when there's an inside joke.

Evan goes, "Yeah. I'm not as lucky as some people," and he looks right at Danny when he says this.

Danny laughs uncomfortably, and it's so obvious he's dying right now because he's afraid they're going to say something about Marion in front of me and blow up his spot, and I hate the way this is making me feel. I don't want to know but at the same time I want to know everything.

But then Danny says later to the guys and asks if the roof is cool and I say it is, and he asks if I want to check it out again. I just stare at the window wall.

And he's like, "What's wrong?"

So of course I say, "Nothing." When really it's everything.

He goes, "Sure you don't want to go up?"

I say I'm sure. So he leaves and I immediately start having those thoughts. They're the same thoughts I've been having for months anytime I'm alone and unoccupied. Or even when I'm occupied, like with doing homework or shaving my legs or trying to decide if I want cereal or waffles for breakfast.

But the thoughts are interrupted by Joni barging over and going, "It's *so* terrible about Rhiannon and Steve. I heard her talking about it with Sheila before? Yeah. I thought they were a serious item, but I guess I was wrong. Is she still devastated?"

She can't seriously be asking this question. Is she really that dense?

But apparently she is, because she's still waiting for a response. So I say, "Yeah, she's still . . . devastated."

And then she starts in on this whole thing about how there's this trend at our school of boys dumping their girlfriends out of nowhere and getting away with it like it's not even wrong and did I hear about Brad and Sheila?

I didn't.

So then I have to stand there for like twenty minutes while Joni tells me every last detail of Brad and Sheila's lives and how tragic it was that he threatened to break up just because she had to take care of her little brother after school and didn't have time to see him as much. And how it traumatized her so bad that she failed a French test and it wasn't even that hard. But they ended up staying together because Sheila told her mother that she can't babysit every day because it was affecting her grades. And how can any remotely involved parent argue when you play the grade card?

And then Joni goes, "I just can't get over it about Steve, though. And to go out with Gloria? I really thought he was above all that."

I'm like, *"What?"*

So Joni explains how Gloria's been after Steve since he was still with Rhiannon. Ever since Joni's party where she totally watched Steve string Gloria along like he might actually break up with Rhiannon (not that Joni could believe it, but she does have eyes and they don't lie). And how Steve is out with Gloria right now, which is why they didn't come to the party because Steve didn't want to cause a scene because he knew Rhiannon was going to be here and he's trying to keep it on the DL. Of course Gloria wanted to come and rub it in Rhiannon's face, but Steve said no.

I'm like, "How do you know all this?"

So Joni gives me this complicated story about someone who heard from someone who heard from someone else, and it all sounds like a big fat rumor, obviously, but I just tell her that I have to go. Because there's no way that load of bull is even remotely true. Which is why I'm not even going to dignify this freak show of a rumor by bothering Ree with it. She's depressed enough already.

All I want to do is be in my room listening to music and clearing everything out of my head until it's all about him. He's the only thing I want to think about. And he doesn't even know it. But it's hopeless, because Mom is in one of her chatty moods and I can't get rid of her.

When she gets all *let's sit around and share about our lives because we have such a good relationship* about it, the whole thing comes off as kind of desperate. We're supposed to talk for fifteen minutes every day as part of our family-therapy homework, and if we don't our shrink can totally tell. There's no way to avoid it. I guess it's good for when I'm actually in the mood to talk about my problems, but that's hardly ever. Especially now.

So it's partly what we have to do for therapy. But it's also partly Mom being suspicious about where I just was and who was there and what I did. Not that she would actually come out and ask all this. She's just checking in her own sneaky way that I'm not drunk or doing drugs or pregnant and it's totally annoying that she doesn't trust me, and I don't want her in my room. I've told her a thousand times that I'm not going to mess up my life, but she doesn't believe me. So every time I come home from a party, she attacks me to make sure I haven't suddenly decided to throw my life away. It's infuriating.

She's like, "How was the party?"

And I'm all, "Fine."

And she goes, "Who was there?"

So annoying.

I'm like, "Mom. You know who was there. I told you who was going before I left."

Then she just stands in my doorway leaning against the wall while I try to find my iPod. This could take a while. It's not that I'm morally opposed to cleaning my room or anything. I just don't see the point. Like, you clean it but then it gets messed up again, so why bother with something that's just going to disintegrate anyway?

Mom offers up the brilliant idea to check the closet. So then I have to explain to her that my iPod wouldn't *be* in the closet because I would never put it there.

And she's like, "How do you know?"

Here's the thing. Questions like that? Irritate me. Because she's basically saying that I have no clue about where I put things. So I ignore her and keep searching around, and why does she have to keep standing there if she's not even talking?

According to my shrink, my need for lots of alone time has to do with being an only child. It's supposed to be normal, but sometimes I feel like a freak when I'd rather be alone than hang out with my friends. I don't know how people deal with brothers and sisters. It must be so weird to live with another person your age like that, someone sharing the bathroom and listening to their music all loud so you can't hear yours and all of the drama that comes with having another kid in the house. I just can't imagine having someone in your face all the time like that. I can never relax completely when I'm with someone else, even if it's just one person hanging out in the same room. It's like I can't be myself unless I'm by myself.

I know. I have issues.

CHAPTER 6
Sunday

IT TOTALLY ROCKS when you wake up from a really intense dream and you still have that really intense dream feeling going on. Love that. And I'm way into the whole dream-interpretation thing. I used to have this dream notebook where I'd write down all the details of my dreams. I kept it right by my bed, and the first thing I'd do when I woke up was write down everything I could remember from my dreams that night.

But then it was like the more I got into it, the more dreams I'd have. Which made everything really complicated, because then I'd have to record what happened for like three different parts of just one dream. Or I'd be writing for over an hour and show up late for first period and dreams were kind of taking over my life. I also noticed that once I started recording all my dream details, I started having dreams with way more details, and every night was like this crazy complex movie screening. So I had to stop it with the notebook.

But whenever this happens with the really intense dream feeling, I try to remember everything about the dream for the whole rest of the day so it can be like it's all still happening. And like it happened with him for real. Instead of only in my dreams.

❀

So I'm digging through my tees and figuring out what to wear today, and I can't decide if I feel more like vintage rainbow or edgy statement. Which are on two extreme ends of the spectrum, so it should be easy to pick, but I'm all kerfuffled. That's what really intense dreams do to you.

I decide on edgy statement. So I'm going through the pile, and I pick out one that's folded up all the way at the bottom. And it turns out to be the black one that has BAD KITTY in sparkly silver with the spastic cat that looks like he's being electrocuted. It's the shirt I was wearing when Danny started talking to me.

He'd never said anything before that day. But it was like all of a sudden, something triggered him and I noticed him notice my shirt from the next table over in the caf. And when it was time to go, he came up to me and he was like, "Nice kitty." And I was so caught off guard all I could say was, "Thanks." Because the truth is, I had been crushing him for months. But that's the thing about me. Everyone thinks I'm super confident and like I could go up to anyone and say anything I want, but actually no.

So the next day I dressed even more extreme. I had my choker with the spikes and my skirt with the severe slit up the side with my ripped spiderweb fishnets and stiletto boots. And at lunch I had zero appetite—which is like a serious event in my world—and I could feel Danny watching me the whole time. And when it was time to go,

Danny came up to me again the same way he did the day before and he said, "Nice boots."

I was stoked. But then later I got called into the assistant principal's office and he chewed me out for violating the dress code. And I was like, "*What* dress code?" Because as if it's even *enforced*. As if Leanne doesn't come in every day with her shirt cut so low you can see every freaking thing and nobody says anything to her. But now all of a sudden *I'm* a problem? I mean, yeah okay, today I'm on the subversive side, but most days I tone it down for school so I can get away with floating just under the radar.

It's such a joke because when the AP tries to talk to some girl about the dress code, you can tell there's this whole huge struggle going on for him over trying not to look at her breasts. I guess that's why he avoids Leanne. So all that happens is you go in, he yells about how what you're wearing is inappropriate and threatens to take away your activities or whatever, and then two days later he forgets all about it because he's completely scattered and overworked so you can go back to wearing whatever.

Like this one time? He conferenced or whatnot with Joni, and then she shows up two days later with her jeans cut so low that she had major butt cleavage hanging out all tacky. It was so extreme that boys kept getting up to sharpen their pencils just to get a look at it. And she totally got away with it.

So when I'm expecting the meathead AP to just yell at me for a while and make some of his infamous empty threats but instead he makes a big deal out of it and writes me up, I can't believe it's actually happening. He never does this. Maybe he got in trouble for not doing his job.

Anyway, the next day I toned down my outfit just to be safe. Danny didn't even wait until the end of lunch to come up to me this time. He just came over and pulled up a chair, and the girls I sit with at lunch immediately stopped talking and snuck looks at him.

Danny was either oblivious to all the swooning or was excellent at acting oblivious. He was like, "How's it going?"

And I was like, "Oh. It's *definitely* going."

Then Danny went, "I heard you got reamed yesterday."

"Where'd you hear that?"

"From Heather."

"How did she know?"

And he said how she answers the phones when the AP's secretary goes to lunch so she knew. And then she was talking about it eighth period.

So I told him what happened and, being Danny, he got all agitated and lecturing how that's selective discrimination and everyone knows the dress code is a joke.

He was all, "Dude. They never even enforce the dress code!"

"I know!" I yelled.

"Do you even know what it says?"

"No!"

"Me neither! So how are we supposed to follow something that wasn't even given to us?"

"I think they assume we all have the same concept about what's appropriate. Which obviously doesn't work for me."

But then Danny was like, "It works for me." And he leaned in a little. And the tone of everything changed.

And the whole time we were talking, my friends kept sneaking looks. Danny has that effect on girls. He mesmerizes them with his opinions and theories and ideas. But it's not just about how smart he is or how hot he looks when he's all wound up about some issue. It's like he's a natural leader. He's got this irresistible quality.

The next day, Danny whisked right into the AP's office and defended me. I didn't even know what he was doing until he told me at lunch. He did all this research and found out that our school doesn't even have a clearly defined dress code. There's all this neb-ulous language in the Department of Ed guidebook, like how attire should be "appropriate for a classroom setting." But it's up to each individual school to create a specific dress code, like how skirts can't be more than two inches above the knee or whatever, and our school never did. Or there was some committee a few years ago that was supposed to do it, but then there was this whole scandal and nothing was ever resolved. So the meathead AP was forced to remove the report he wrote from my file and that was it.

Danny called me that night and asked me out.

❁

"Next guest step down!"

It was a total miracle that I snagged a table at this Starbucks on a Sunday afternoon. But instead of getting homework done, I'm lis-tening to the fight the couple at the next table is having and writing in my spy notebook and getting distracted by what everyone's ordering. I have this theory that the drinks people order say a lot about their personality.

Like this Mr. So Busy and Important Guy who's ordering his freaky drink all, "Venti macchiato no whip half caf French Blend caramel swirl."

And the Starbucks dude goes, "Did you want foam or—?" but Mr. I Can't Just Order a Coffee Because It's Not Original Enough interrupts with, "I said, no *whip*."

I finish my apple fritter and pack up my stuff. Trying to concentrate here is useless. And on my way out, I hear Mr. Annoying Complicated Drink Guy bitching about how this wasn't what he ordered. I'm not entirely convinced that he even knows what he ordered. Or that he's ever going to get what he wants, with such complicated demands. He's in some serious need of yoga. Or at least a hot-stone massage.

Walking is the only thing that helps my brain calm down. And this is an awesome walking neighborhood. It's so weird how in different parts of the city, some places have this incredible energy, like even the sunlight looks cleaner there. And it's all about light and space and streets that seems to extend forever. And then you go to other places and it's like some random sketchy neighborhood where no one wants to live.

This lady with big sunglasses and even bigger hair bumps into me as she passes by and doesn't even say she's sorry. That's the thing about saying "sorry" or "excuse me" in this city. No one ever does. Or when we do apologize, we don't actually say it clearly. We just whisper the outline of *excuse me* or form the word *sorry* with our mouth, as if we expect people to lip-read. It's one of my frequent observations that I've listed under Quirky New Yorker Behavior in my spy notebook.

Not that I'm dissing on my people. New Yorkers are the most fabulous people anywhere. Especially if someone needs directions. I actually watched two people argue on a street corner for like five minutes over the best way to direct this tourist to Little Italy.

These three college girls are walking ahead of me. Probably going back to their NYU dorm. I can't wait until I live in the dorms, with my own life and own rules and own way of living, without anyone constantly bothering me to clean my room.

The girls are so into their conversation that they don't even realize I'm totally spying on them, walking way too close on the sidewalk.

They're like:

"So then what'd you say?"

"I was just like, 'Why are you being like this?'"

"What'd he say?"

"He said he didn't know."

"And then what'd you say?"

I don't want to stay too close to them, but I have to be close enough to listen. It's walking a fine line, the whole invading-personal-space thing.

"You can tell a lot from a person's body language," one of the girls is explaining. "Did he have his arms crossed?"

"I don't think so."

"Then how was he standing?"

"Can we go back to the last thing about him saying he's not emotionally available?"

They're obviously trying to decode some boy behavior, like what he meant by what he said and whether he's ever going to like her as much as she likes him. That's what it's like when you're in it. When you're in it so deep you can't see anything else and all you want to do is analyze everything he said and did until you're exhausted. I'd be doing the same thing now with Ree, if I could. But there's no way I can tell her about this.

Mom busts into my room like she was invited or something and goes, "I thought you were going to clean your room."

And I'm like, "That was just my closet. Remember?" And I'm

digging through piles of dirty laundry because I can't find my iPod recharger cord, and Mom is inspecting the laundry piles with this disapproving look.

She's like, "How hard is it to put your clothes in the hamper?"

I can't believe she's in here again. I really can't even. Was she not just in here last night, ragging on me for being a slob?

But apparently that wasn't a rhetorical question. So I'm like, "Um, well, let's see. I have to pick them up, walk down the hall to the bathroom, lift up the lid to—" but she interrupts and goes, "These piles can't continue." As if they're some mysterious random problem that keeps mutating and no one can control them. As if they're bad behavior.

So I inform her that piles are a method of categorizing. And she's like, "Categorizing what? A tremendous mess?"

Then I explain that just because my room doesn't look like hers doesn't mean I'm any less organized than she is, and didn't she just lose her keys last week? But of course there's nothing she can say to that because it's true. She doesn't even have anything on her walls except for this one artsy-looking black-and-white print of some courtyard in Paris. My walls are so covered with posters and photos and pictures I ripped out of magazines that you can barely see the dark red walls. And there's like a million different flowers, because flowers are my thing. Flowers are everywhere: prints, pictures, my own artwork, postcards, even ones pressed in clear contact paper. And I have these sweet gel flowers on my window, and when sunshine filters through them it makes bright flower patterns on the walls. I can't imagine having walls with nothing on them.

I'm tossing aside stuffed animals and sneakers and CDs and I go, "There's a method to my madness. Just because you don't see what I'm doing here doesn't mean it's not organized."

And she's all, "Oh, really?"

And I can tell by her tone she's just playing, but I'm not in the mood for games. So I'm like, "Yeah. Everything's—I can find anything. I know where everything is." Okay, maybe except my iPod recharger cord, but that's just one thing. That happens to everybody.

I guess Mom decides that we've connected enough for today, because she drifts off down the hall. My stress level begins its descent to normal.

But it's not like I want to be organized like Rhiannon or anything. Because this one time when she was packing for sleepaway camp? She made a list of everything she needed to bring and stuff she still had to get. But it wasn't just your average list. That list was on the way other end of the spectrum. She developed this whole color-coded system with all these complex classifications and footnotes, and even when Rhiannon makes a simple list it turns into a PhD thesis. And then she actually said how there was a reference guide for the color-coding, and even though it might have been a joke I was still scared.

My cell makes cricket-chirp sounds, and I go to my bag to take it out but it's not there. But it sounds like it's definitely in the area. So I start tearing through another laundry pile and papers and books, and I find it buried in my bag under my makeup case and this cardigan I have to keep in my bag because the computer lab at school is always freezing while the rest of the rooms are like a sauna. There's a text message from Joni. It says:

Does she know?

Which confirms that the sad rumor about Steve and Gloria is a lie. It's so obvious that Joni's trying to instigate this whole big thing where I tell Ree what I heard, so that Ree ends up mad at me for not telling her when I first heard or for being the one to tell her or whatever other twisted plan Joni is cooking up. There's some reason Joni wants me to be the one to tell Ree, and I'm not falling for it. If it's true, and Joni wants Ree to know so badly, why hasn't she told her by now? And why would she care if Ree knows or not?

Or it's probably that Gloria's doing this to get back at Ree and Joni is one of the few girls who are actually friends with Gloria (out of fear, I'm sure) so if I tell Ree, it'll be exactly what Gloria wants me to do all according to her evil plan. And I'm nobody's puppet.

I'm not going to let her get to me. And I'm not texting her back. I have better things to do with my time, thank you very much.

I grab my laptop and take it over to my bed. There's something I want to check. Because I still feel jealous about last night and Danny strategizing to ask Marion out. So I get into Gmail and click on my Danny archive and look through all the subjects until I find it.

I love you
Danny Trager to me
Beautiful Nicole.
I was going to write you an e-mail explaining all the reasons why I love you, but that would take forever. So I just want you to know that I will never stop loving you.
—Your D

I remember when he sent me this back in January and how it was the best e-mail ever. Because around everyone else, he's always all fired up about something and joking around and no one ever gets to see the sensitive side of Danny. Not the way I did.

But if what he wrote is true, which I totally think it is, then that means he still loves me. And if he still loves me . . . then how can he want someone else?

❀

I'm in the backyard on this really hot August night, watching the fireflies. It's so hot that my tank top is sticking to me, and the back of my neck is all sweaty. I listen to the stream, water moving around stones.

He comes outside, letting the porch screen door slap shut behind him. Maybe he's just checking that I'm out here. Or maybe he came out to smoke. But then I hear him walking toward me, across the dark grass.

He sits down next to me. "Hot, huh?" he says.

I agree that it is hot.

For a while we sit like that, watching the fireflies.

But then he touches my leg, slides his finger under the fringe of my cutoffs. And I know it's only the beginning, right when I am so desperately wishing for the end.

CHAPTER 7

Monday

THERE'S SOME CHALK dust on his left sock and I can't stop staring at it. That chalk dust is so cute. All I want to do is go over and wipe that chalk dust off and be like, "You had some chalk dust on your sock."

But of course I can't do that. Then everyone would know.

Mr. Farrell is asking if anyone wants to put number thirty-two on the board. I look down at my homework to avoid eye contact so he won't call on me, but I know he's going to call on me. I can *feel* it.

And then he goes, "Nicole? Thanks." As if I had volunteered or something.

So I take my homework pages up to the board and when I pass by Mr. Farrell sitting on top of his desk (which I think is so cute, by the way) my heart flutters around and it gets hard to breathe. Which is the same reaction I have every single time I get within ten feet of him.

I pick up the chalk and write *"32.)"* on the board and look at what I did for it on my homework and I have no idea how to do this problem. Over on the other side of the board, Jackson already has half his problem done. I wonder why his brain works differently from mine. Like, what is it about his brain that lets him get math?

I scratch the chalk over the board to create what I really hope even remotely resembles what this is supposed to look like.

He's staring at me. I can feel it. But if I turn around to check, then he'll know that I know. So I do a few more lines of the problem. But there's no way I can fake my way through it, so I give up the charade that I'll ever get this and put the chalk down.

And Mr. Farrell's like, "Not so fast, Nicole." And I love it when he says my name, because every time I hear it my heart does this little flip-flopping thing. I wish I were mad smart and he'd be all impressed and I could get the highest grade in the class and he'd fall in love with me and have to marry me, but I'm not that girl. You're either smart or average or some early childhood trauma prevented you from developing necessary brain cells and I think we all know who we are by now. Not like I don't have other talents he can easily discover.

So I tell him that I didn't get this one and there's no way I can finish it, and he says I need to at least try. Which I think is really interesting, because isn't that what I've been doing this whole time? So I say that I *did* try and that's why half the problem is on the board.

But he's like, "You need to try harder." Which is pretty much the biggest insult ever, because if he only knew how late I stay up doing his stupid homework every night and how many weekend hours I dedicate to these problems in some coffeehouse instead of doing something fun like spying on people's conversations.

But apparently there's something even more humiliating than that. Because right when the room's all quiet and everyone is staring at me, waiting to see what I'll do, Gloria goes, "Like she's ever gonna get it."

I cannot describe the degree of embarrassment I'm feeling at this second in time. It's like every cell in my body is completely mortified.

There's no way she just said that. Because if she just said that, then everyone heard it. Including Mr. Farrell. And now he's giving her this harsh look and I can't turn around and face everybody and I can't do the problem but I can't sit down. All I want to do is run out of the room. But I can't do that either.

So I pick up the chalk again and stare at the board, and I wish we were in the country somewhere sitting on a back porch drinking lemonade and watching clouds wisp across the sky instead of being here in complete and total agony. Just the two of us, where we could finally be together for real.

Mr. Farrell comes over to see how it's going, which is of course nowhere. I'm all nervous and sweaty with him standing so close. I get the same way when he leans over my desk to look at something on my paper and I feel his breath on my cheek.

Jackson is all impatient and wants to explain his problem even though everybody knows you can't explain yours until everyone else at the board is done. Mr. Farrell tells him to chill.

So I'm standing here like a big fat dork while everyone watches me being humiliated and there's no way I can even come close to finishing this problem and I want to cry. And I guess Mr. Farrell finally gets a clue, because suddenly he says he'll help me with the problem.

He'll help me with the problem? He never helps *anyone* with their problems.

I swear, he's so obvious.

So I'm floating to my locker and playing my favorite fantasy through my head again for the millionth time. In this one, Mr. Farrell and I live together and everyone knows it and all the girls are jealous because everyone says how he looks so much like Jude Law except younger. So we walk into school together in the morning and I don't have to use my locker because I get to keep all my stuff in his room behind his desk next to his bag and jacket, and we're walking down the hall holding hands and I'm laughing at something he told me and everyone's looking at us and—

I stop thinking. I stop walking. There's no way what I'm seeing is real.

Down the hall, right in front of Steve's locker for the whole world to see, Steve and Gloria are kissing.

Right in front of his locker.

Next to Rhiannon's locker.

Where she's going to be any second.

I jump the stairs two at a time and bolt to her eighth-period class. I look in but she already left and I hope she's not there yet please *god*. I run down the hall to the stairs Ree always takes but she's not there either. And there's only one other way she could have gone, and she has to be there she has to be there please let her be there, because she so cannot see this. So I run like a maniac the other way and cut down the side stairs and fly around a corner and I smack right into Rhiannon.

She's like, "What's wrong?"

And I didn't really have time to think about what to say during all the running, so I blurt out the first lie I can think of, which is that I have a surprise for her. And Ree smiles because she loves surprises. So of course she wants to know what the surprise is and I really wish I knew. Then there's this whole complicated thing about books and lockers and finally I get her out of there.

So I zip down the hall and try to give off a convincing vibe as I run-walk to our lockers. But now I have to actually go to our lockers which means I have to go to her locker which means there's no way I can avoid Steve. Kissing Gloria.

I slow down and approach the lockers and they're still there, majorly sucking face. In fact they're so into it, there's a possibility that they won't even notice me. So I sneak up to Ree's locker and turn the dial on her lock.

Please don't look over at me please don't look don't look.

So of course Steve looks and I have to look back and now Steve knows that I know. But the whole rest of the school will know by first period tomorrow, so I guess he doesn't consider this to be a problem. Especially because all he does is look away like I'm not even here. Like it doesn't even matter to him that I'm going to tell Rhiannon.

❀

There's no way I can tell Rhiannon.

I mean, yeah, okay. I know I have to tell her. Even though there's a chance she'll hate me for being the one to tell her. But she's my best friend and I have to take that chance and hope that if she does end up being mad at me, she'll eventually get over it. Plus if I was her and she saw what I saw, I'd definitely want to know. I'd probably be mad at her for *not* telling me. So I risk her being mad either way.

But I'm too nervous and dreading it so I go, "So what's up with the roses?"

And Ree lifts them out of her bag and sniffs them and she's like, "They're from Steve."

And I swear I almost spit lemonade all over the table.

I'm all, "Wait. They're from *Steve*?"

"Yeah."

"He gave them to you?"

"Yeah."

"What did you say?"

"No, he left them in my locker. I didn't get a chance to talk to him yet."

Okay, this is like . . . I can't with this. Why would he give her flowers and then be all hooking up with another girl? Who *does* that?

When our food comes, I try to force myself to tell her. Especially since Ree's talking about getting Steve back. But here's the thing. She actually looks happy for the first time since forever and she's laughing at some of my jokes, and there's no way I can tell her but I have to tell her.

I'm like, "Hey, Ree?"

And poor Ree who has no idea what's coming, who never did anything to hurt anybody, goes, "Yeah?"

"Um." I pick up a fry and then put it back down, because if I eat anything now I'm going to hurl. "I have to tell you something."

And Ree's just like, "What?"

I'm mentally fast-forwarding to visions of what this conversation will look like five minutes from now, with Ree's face all smeared from crying and her nose running in front of the whole diner and people sneaking looks over at her and wondering what's wrong. It's just not right. It's not the kind of thing you do in public.

But Ree's waiting for me to tell her, so I go, "It's just . . . I really think you should know that . . ."

She sniffs her roses again.

". . . they have cupcake cake."

❀

I try not to have a complete and total meltdown on the subway ride home. Because not only do I have to deal with when and how to tell Rhiannon, but the Mr. Farrell situation is seriously out of control. I wanted so badly to go up to him after class, but when class ended he was surrounded by a crowd of girls and I can't stand that so I left.

The subway stops at Times Square, and I have to restrain myself from bursting through the doors and running to the downtown train and going back to school and finding him in his room because I know he's staying late today and saying, "You have chalk on your sock," and finally rubbing it off for him. But of course I can't do any of that.

So I get out at my stop and this impulse to walk really far takes over my entire body. There's all this energy clanging through me, and I know it'll be impossible to concentrate on anything else if I go home. Whenever I get all worked up about him, walking is the only thing that saves me. So I walk and walk until I hit water. If the Hudson River wasn't right here, I swear I'd keep walking straight into New Jersey.

❀

I take this film elective, and every Monday afternoon there's a seminar that goes with it at NYU. But instead of having the last class today, we're having a party tonight. Which is sweet, since our professor got us pizza from my fave place and we can just chill and talk with people we didn't really get to know during the semester. And there are some really interesting people in here.

Like this one guy? Is so super quiet I'm dying to know what his story is. Like, is he just shy? Is it an antisocial thing and he's always been like this? Or does he just think we're all pretentious posers so he doesn't have time for us? For some reason, I really want to know.

So when everybody's eating their pizza and sitting in pairs or threes except for him, I go over and put my plate down on the desk next to him and say, "Is this seat taken?"

He gives me this exasperated look like, *Clearly it's not, hence the empty area hovering above the chair.*

He goes, "No."

I'm like, "Mind if I sit?" He doesn't know this yet, but I'm sitting here no matter what he says. I'm not fooled by the prickly-exterior thing. I know all about that stuff from personal experience.

He goes, "No."

So I sit. I can see this is going to be a challenge, but I knew that before I came over here so it's all good.

I decide to start with, "I'm Nicole."

He's like, "I know. We introduced ourselves the first day."

"Yeah, um, I remember that? But see, lots of people forget names and then they're too afraid to ask. And then like all of a sudden it's the last class and people still don't know everyone's name and they're still too afraid to ask. And by that time it's way embarrassing, because then you're admitting you didn't know their name this whole time, you know?"

Quiet Guy just chews his crust.

"Yeah, so . . . hi, and I'm Nicole, and I'm not embarrassed to admit that I don't remember your name."

"Max."

"Hey, Max."

And then he chews more crust.

I'm all, "I can't believe this class is over already. It's *so* weird. It went really fast, right?"

But Max just grunts noncommittally. I have no idea why I feel the need to talk to him. I just have this really intuitive feeling that something's there. So I keep trying. I ramble about what my favorite parts of the class were and stuff about the screenplay I'm writing, and then my favorite directors come up. So then I ramble about movies I love, and that actually gets Max talking. It turns out we have the same taste in film. So I tell him how I passed Todd Solondz on the street a few months ago.

Max goes, "You saw Todd Solondz?" All fixated.

And I'm like, "Yeah. He walked right by me." All nonchalant.

Max says, "Dude. He's one of my favorite directors."

So I'm like, "I know! And I touched his sweater."

Max goes, "What?"

"Yeah. He was wearing this ratty old sweater with a hole in the shoulder? And so I asked him if I could touch his hole."

"Are you making this up?"

"No!"

"So he just . . . let you touch it?"

"Yeah. He was like, 'If it pleases you.' So I put my finger through it."

"Whoa."

"Totally."

"Where?"

"I told you. On his shoulder."

"No, where was this?"

"Oh. Near my school, up on West Tenth."

"You go to Eames Academy?"

"Yeah. You know it?"

"My brother goes there."

"Who's your brother?"

"Brad Tropper."

"No *way*!" That's so weird! This whole time I've been in class with this guy and I didn't even know he was Brad's brother.

"You know him?"

"Totally! I mean, I'm not exactly friends with him, but I'm good friends with Sheila."

And right after I say that, Max shuts down with the barricaded attitude again. It's like he's all storm clouds and despair.

He's like, "You should tell her not to go home with Brad anymore."

So I ask why, but Max doesn't say anything. He just starts crumpling up our paper plates and cups.

I touch his arm and he stops crumpling and gives me this strong look. And I go, "Please tell me why you said that."

And Max says, "I think you know."

Obviously, he knows that I know what's happening to Sheila because anyone can see it. But he means something else. Because that look on his face looks like fear.

Max leans closer to me and says, "Look. There's more to this than you probably know. Just . . . warn Sheila, okay? She could get hurt worse if she keeps going over there. But don't tell her you talked to me."

And then he gets up to go, so I grab him and I'm like, "Wait!" But he walks right out the door. I could run after him and find out what he means, but if he wanted to tell me more he would have.

Anyway, there's something about that scared look he had that's familiar. It's probably the same look I get when people try and force me to talk about things I wish I could just forget.

❀

I get my iPod and turn the light off. This is my favorite part of the day, either just before I fall asleep or just lying here like this, listening to songs that remind me the most of him and replaying my favorite fantasies a zillion times. Like the one where we're at school together and everyone knows and it's okay. Instead of it being against the rules that someone who had obviously never been in love made up.

CHAPTER 8

Tuesday

HIS APARTMENT IS dark except for a lamp in the corner.

I tug nervously on my skirt.

I say, "I'm not that young."

He looks up from the papers he's grading at his desk. He drops his pen. He stands up. He stands there for a while, considering.

But then he walks over. Slowly. Making me wait.

My breath is raspy. I'm breathing like I'm running, instead of just hanging here in his living room. Could this mean he wants me, too?

And then he's right in front of me. I want this so badly I'm shaking.

He reaches out and puts his hand on the back of my head. He slides his fingers through my hair. He couldn't be any closer to me.

I see what's going to happen before it happens. His eyes give everything away.

I stare at his lips. And then he's kissing me.

And that's when my alarm clock goes off, shattering the dream.

❀

Half an hour later, I'm out of the shower and exhausted but also wired like I've been chugging the Jolt. I'm excited and nervous and I don't want to lose that intense dream feeling. But I don't really have much of a choice, because it's called Welcome to Reality.

I picked up the phone like ten times last night to call Ree, but I couldn't do it. It's just not the kind of thing you do over the phone. Or in public or . . . yeah, I know, I'm making excuses, but I *so* don't want to do this.

But I have to do it. So if Ree gets to school before first period, I'll take her into the bathroom or somewhere away from everyone, and I'll tell her. Only, she usually sleeps late, so that's probably not happening. But sometimes she's online in the morning, so I could try IMing her and tell her to meet me before first. So I turn on my laptop and get into my e-mail, and there's a new message from Ree.

> **who i am**
> **rhiannon ferrara to me**
> **hey, nic.**
> **the good news is, we know he's waiting for me to**
> **do something** ☺
> **the bad news is, i have no idea what to do** ☹
> **and no, i don't just want to talk to him. that's exactly**
> **the type of boring thing someone who's totally not**
> **exciting or spontaneous would do.**
> **so i'm trying to figure out the most amazing way to**
> **prove who i am.**
> **xo—**
> **ree**
> **p.s. the roses are gorgeous.**

Okay. Don't panic. She doesn't even know what she wants to do yet. And if she comes up with something and it sucks and you know it won't work, just tell her that it's not a good idea and then tell about Gloria so she doesn't do it anyway. But if it sounds like it might work . . . then don't tell her about Gloria—and hope she doesn't find out by the time she does whatever it is—and let her try it? Because if it's good, it might work?

I forget what I decided before. Everything's all confused. The last thing I want to be is the person who stands in the way of them getting back together, if that's even possible. But I also don't want to be the best friend who knew this whole time and didn't tell her.

Anyway, she's not online, so I'm about to shut down my computer when a new e-mail from Danny pops up.

> **cruller and thinking**
> **Danny Trager to me**
> **Nicole—**
> **I'm leaving for school in a minute. Will pass by**
> **Krispy Kreme and grab a cruller, your favorite.**
> **I'll be eating my cruller and thinking of you.**
> **—Danny**

❁

When I see Sheila come in gangsta late to math, I know she's on the road of no return.

Here's the thing. Sheila was my good friend up until a couple months ago. Not that she's not my friend anymore, but now it's all about Brad. So our friendship isn't what it used to be.

I get that he's hot and all, but what I don't get is why she's doing this to herself. Like, how can they have anything in common? I mean, I know love makes you do crazy things, but this is ridiculous. Sheila is the one person who's totally put-together every day and super cheerful even early in the morning and always has her projects done like two days before they're due, and now she just walked in looking like a truck ran her over.

Mr. Farrell is going in for the kill. He's all types of heated when you're late like that. It's pretty much the only thing I don't like about him.

He's all, "Ah, if it isn't Mr. and Mrs. Punctuality."

Sheila totally looks like she's about to burst into tears, and I know it's because she's never been late in her life and she's mortified and she knows that Mr. Farrell isn't going to leave it alone until he's sure they're both embarrassed to the max.

Sometimes I don't get him. It's like he's two different people. Like right now he's talking about Sheila as if she's not even here, saying things about her to Brad like how she's his questionable companion of impeccable taste, which is just a nasty way of completely dissing both of them simultaneously. And the whole time Sheila is just sitting there, dying. But what else can she do?

So after class I grab Sheila and drag her into the bathroom and I'm like, "What's going on with you?"

And she just starts crying and saying how she never thought it would get this bad and she had no idea and how did her life get this messed up? And even though mascara's running down her face and she's obviously been sleeping over at Brad's because she's wearing one of his ratty old Cult T-shirts that's all wrinkled, she still looks pretty.

So I say, "Why are you letting him ruin your life like this?"

And she says, "He's not."

And I'm like, "Um, not to be rude? But I think he sort of is."

So Sheila goes, "No, I mean . . . it's all my fault."

I go, "Are you serious?" Because Brad is a pothead and a burnout and he's totally failing everything and he'll probably be a super senior, one of those lowlife kids who never gets it and is still sitting in a desk that's way too small for him when he's like twenty-five, and why is she wasting her time with such a loser?

Sheila looks at herself in the mirror and rinses her face off and there aren't any paper towels. So she stands there with her face dripping all over the ratty Cult T-shirt and tells me how Brad is totally not her type but she loves him anyway.

She says, "But a few weeks ago he started smoking more pot. I don't even know why. It's like . . . I knew he smoked, but before it was just to spark up at a party or whatever, nothing heavy. And now he's wasted all the time. Like he can't even get through a day without smoking." She wipes her cheek. "And plus he's drinking hard-core and . . . his temper keeps getting worse. One minute he's fine, and the next he's furious over the most minor thing. I don't even know who he is anymore."

So I'm about to ask if there's anything I can do, but Sheila keeps talking and she says how her mother doesn't approve of Brad and how she's neglecting her family and that they never see her anymore. And they got into a horrible fight two days ago and Sheila just packed her stuff and left, and she's been staying with Brad ever since. Which is a disaster, because he never lets her have time to do homework, and she's so depressed it's like she doesn't even care anymore. She's too tired to fight it. And he stays up way late, so just getting to first period is like this major challenge.

"And then there's this thing with my pills," she says.

So now I'm thinking she's about to tell me that she's on Zoloft or something, but she goes, "I'm on the pill now." Which is news to me. I wonder how else she's changed since we were close.

Sheila's like, "I forgot to pack them when I left home, and I just remembered about them today. So I snuck home to get them, but by the time I took one I'd already missed taking the one for yesterday. And even with the one today . . . it wasn't at seven o'clock when I usually take them."

I go, "I'm sure you're fine," even though I really have no idea about being on the pill. She's just so upset.

Sheila goes, "But when I started taking them, the doctor at Planned Parenthood told me I have to take them at the same time every day or they won't work. And there's no way you can skip any or they *definitely* won't work." So now on top of everything else, she has to worry about being pregnant.

And I'm watching Sheila tell me all of this, and I can barely remember the girl who used to have it all together. Not that it was that long ago. And I remember what Max said about warning Sheila to not go home with Brad anymore or she could get hurt. But I'm also not supposed to tell her I talked to him, so I say, "Maybe you shouldn't go over to Brad's anymore."

And Sheila's like, "I know. I know I have to stop. But that fight with my mom was so bad, Nicole. And I can sleep over at Brad's anytime."

I'm like, "Doesn't his dad care?"

She goes, "Not really. It's not like his dad's even there at night anyway. He's a security guard for Con Edison, and he works the night shift."

I have to think of another way to convince her. So I go, "I know you love him, but why are you still with him if things are like this?"

And she's like, "It's not that simple. Everything's different now. At first it was just about acting out this bad-boy fantasy thing, you know?"

I nod because I can totally relate. How cool would that be? Like the fantasy where you're swept away by this hot road-trip-motorcycle guy who's all rugged and living on the edge. But something like that would only be fun for a little while. Then I'd want to go home and sleep in my own bed.

Sheila explains how at first everything was exciting and adventurous and she's always wanted to experience something like that for real, and now it was finally happening to her and she fell for him so hard. And then she wipes her hands on her jeans and goes, "But now it's too much. I know I need to go back home, but I can't face my mom. But I can't keep doing this either. I'm—" And she starts crying again.

So I'm like, "Is there anything I can do?" And I'm wondering if my mom would let her stay at our place.

And Sheila says, "Thanks, but I'll be okay."

But I wonder if that can ever be true when you're in love with a boy who hates himself so much. Because anyone who treats their body like it's garbage the way he does isn't exactly in the best place to love someone else.

❀

Danny's doing another one of his Random Hallway Polls. He's taken over the area next to the water fountain and the bathrooms, and he has poster boards on the wall and a whole bunch of pencils I know for a fact he "borrowed" from the main office because they're all labeled PROPERTY OF DEPT. OF ED. But that's Danny. He did service credit in the main office in ninth grade and so he knows all the secretaries and school aides, and of course they all love him because he's smart and charming and it doesn't matter that they're old. Or maybe it works on them especially because they're old. So the secretaries totally trust him, and if he wanted to he could manipulate files or print things out or find teachers' private info or whatever.

Kids crowd around Danny, reading the posters and filling out ballots. I watch Danny laugh and joke with everyone. Which is so easy for him since he's one of those people who can get along with anyone. I've always admired that about him.

The poll has to do with the lacking administration in this school. There's been a whole bunch of issues lately that everyone's unhappy about, from minor to major. Like how we don't have enough books, so Ms. Portman has to copy book pages and no one wants the copied versions because the copy machine is always broken and the papers come out all smudged. Or how one kid threatened a teacher and he wasn't even suspended. And Tatyana told me how she was supposed to meet with the principal about this peer-mediation thing she wanted to set up, and when she got to the office for the meeting his secretary said he had to reschedule because he was meeting with parents at the moment. But Mr. Pearlman didn't close the blinds all the way on his office window, and Tatyana could see in and he was sitting at his desk reading the paper.

Because of incompetent people who are supposedly in charge around here, things aren't the way they're supposed to be. We're pissed because we deserve a better school.

So on the top poster it says: IS THIS SCHOOL'S ADMINISTRATION EARNING ITS SALARY? And below that are the average salaries for principal,

assistant principal, and teacher in the New York City public school system. It's absolutely appalling that to get paid as much as a new principal, a teacher would have to work for like fifteen years. When everyone knows it's the teachers who do all the work.

I watch Danny some more. It's addictive, in a way. My mom says he has charisma and that's why everyone wants to be around him.

Okay, the truth? Is that Danny has these soulful eyes and he gives me these soulful looks across the hall or street or wherever and they get me every time. Every time. So when he catches me staring at him now, and his eyes lock into mine with one of those looks, I can't break away from him. And I remember what it felt like to be with him. And the reason we're not together isn't clear anymore.

When I see Steve at the vending machine, it doesn't matter about Ree wanting him back. All that matters is how he treated her and how wrong it was.

I go right up to him and say, "How can you do this to Ree?"

And Steve's like, "I'm not trying to hurt her."

So I'm like, "But you *are* hurting her."

And he's all, "That's not my fault."

And I'm like, "Well then whose fault is it?"

Then he says how it's no one's fault, it just happened, and I swear that it-just-happened line is the flimsiest line in the Book of Excuses for Lame Boys.

"Nothing," I tell him, "just *happens*. You either make it happen or you don't. There's a reason it happens in the first place."

He's like, "Look. It's not like I hurt her intentionally or anything. Things weren't really working out with us anyway."

And I go, "Since when?"

He's all, "We're just . . . different people."

I'm like, "What are you even *talking* about? You're not even giving a real reason." Because this is news to me. I know for a fact they had a lot in common. And right now? It sounds like he's just throwing out any excuse for breaking up with Ree and he doesn't even know why.

I can't believe this is the same boy.

I'm like, "And what about the roses?"

He goes, "Huh?"

Oh. So now he's going to act like he didn't give Ree those roses yesterday? He'll probably deny smiling at her in lunch, too.

That's it. I just can't with him.

❁

I'm the only person in the whole school who actually looks forward to tutoring.

But unfortunately I'm running late because I just spent fifteen minutes in the bathroom dealing with my hair. It's funny how my hair always looks great when it's totally unnecessary or like when I'm hanging out at home all Saturday afternoon and no one's going to see me anyway, but when it actually matters, I can't do even the simplest thing with it.

When I get to Mr. Farrell's hall, Rhiannon's walking away from his room. So I'm like, "Where are you going?"

And she says, "I'm leaving. No one showed up."

"Um, excuse me, but who am I?"

"I'm going to the library to—oh! I need your help tonight."

"What for?"

She glances around to see if anyone's listening and whispers, "Operation Steve."

I go, "Oh, um. What's that?" And I'm thinking that maybe I should just tell her now and get it over with. But then she says she can't talk about it anywhere in school because the walls have ears and she'll call me later. And then she's running down the hall, and for some reason, I don't run after her. I still think it's better not to tell her here.

I get to his room and stand in the doorway and look in with my heart beating so hard I can hear it in my ears. Mr. Farrell is bending over a stack of papers on his desk and doesn't even see me. But then I guess he feels my eyes on him, because he suddenly looks up and says, "Come on in."

So I go in and put my bag down on a desk and I'm like, "Hey," and I try to act all casual and he's like, "Hey," and I'm pretending that it's just another typical Tuesday, when in reality this is the first day all year that I've been alone in here with him. Like this.

So he says how my tutor left and no one else showed up, but I'm welcome to stay and go over some Regents problems, and I can't believe he's going to tutor me individually! He always has kids tutor other kids because he thinks that's the best way for everyone to learn, and that since he already explained everything in class, it's better to have other people explain to get a different perspective going on. So of course I feel totally special and I'm so jacked up on nerves and adrenaline that I'm shaking and I have no idea how I'm going to make my hand write with my pencil in any way that results in even remotely legible numbers.

I've only wanted to be alone with him like this all year. There were tons of times when I walked by his room after school and I wanted to go in, but then I was like, what if he's solving some really important equation or something and I'm all walking in with a personal matter? How unprofessional is that? But finally it's just the two of us. And this time, I'm not dreaming.

He's like, "Hot?"

And I'm like, "Huh?" And I'm all freaked out because two seconds ago I was thinking how I'm totally sweating and I must look disgusting and I can feel the sweat pooling on my upper lip and how attractive is that? Not very. And I was thinking how I should go to the bathroom and make sure I look okay, but I *so* don't want to leave this room, and then all of a sudden he asked if I was hot like he could totally read my mind. Which just proves how connected we are.

So he says, "Are you hot?" And I'm starting to suspect that maybe he doesn't just think about math all day.

I go, "I guess I am. A little."

And he goes to turn on the fan and I laugh at the absurdity of it all, and he's like, "What's so funny?"

And I'm like, "Nothing."

But he's all, "Oh, come on. I could use a good laugh. Do you know how boring derivatives are?"

So of course I have to say, "Well, actually, yes. I do." And I pick up my pencil and say how it's really nice of him to tutor me, because no one else is here so he could have canceled altogether, and I really appreciate the extra help, and I'm just babbling like one of those crackheads talking to themselves on the subway.

And he's like how I can come in anytime, and it doesn't have to be only on Tuesdays since he stays late most days anyway. So I tell him how I was going to come in the other day but I was afraid that he might be busy so I didn't but I wanted to.

He goes, "What did you want to talk about?"

I'm like, "Um . . . I don't remember." Because of course all of this is just an excuse to be in the same room with him as often as possible.

He's like, "Well, you know where to find me."

And then he winks at me!

He goes on about how hard it was for him junior and senior years, all stressed about college, even after he got in.

I'm like, "Where'd you go?"

He says, "NYU."

And I'm like, "Oh my god! That's where I want to go! I mean, I'd rather go to Columbia, but I don't exactly have a four-point-oh."

Then he laughs and says, "Yeah, that was my case, too. But only the cool people go to NYU, so . . ."

I go, "Totally. We're way too cool for Columbia." And I swear it feels like I'm talking to a friend instead of a teacher. He's just so easy to talk to and super nice and he's young . . . like probably twenty-four or twenty-five. And if he's twenty-five, then by the time I'm his age he'll be thirty-three, which is totally not scandalous at all. I really want to ask him how old he is, but you don't do that.

And then he's like, "You've never thought about going out of state?"

And I'm like, "I just love it here so much. It's like . . . the energy is so amazing, you know?"

Then he nods and I say, "Well, I can't wait to move out, of course," and he laughs, and I'm just having the best time. I can't remember ever having this much fun with Danny, just sitting around talking and laughing like there's no one else you'd rather be with. With Danny it was always about having fun for a while, but then it usually turned into him ranting about how so many people in the States can't afford health insurance or how all these people are starving around the world while we have hot-dog-eating contests on Coney Island.

Mr. Farrell says how he loves the energy here in the Village. So I'm like, "Yeah, same here. Rhiannon lives down the street, so I hang out here a lot."

And he's like, "I'm surprised I've never seen you around, then. I'm here a lot, too. New York is like the smallest town on the planet with"—and I have to interrupt him and go—"running into people! I know!" Because it's totally freaky how like eight million people live here, but you could be walking down some random street at a time when you're never out and you turn a corner and all of a sudden you run into some kid you went to elementary school with a lifetime ago. It's so weird how that happens. I used to think it only happened to me, like I have some kind of special power to make those kinds of things work. But maybe it happens to a lot of people. Or maybe it's just us and we both have the special power.

I look down at my textbook and wonder if we're ever getting back to tutoring. Not that I want to, but it's interesting how Mr. Farrell is just talking like this as if we're sitting in some café or something. Like he wants to know me just as much as I want to know him. But then I get scared that he's noticing me looking at the book, and I don't want him to think that I want to get back to doing problems or anything.

So then we compare places we like to hang out and it feels totally comfortable and like we could be really good friends in another life. And I ask where he lives and he says Upper West Side so I say, "Me, too! I'm on West Seventy-third Street, near the park."

And I say how I love to hang out in the park when it's all nice out like this. Then he says how he chills in the park a lot. So I tell him about going to Strawberry Fields to work on my screenplay sometimes or to listen to the guys with guitars play old Beatles songs. Or to Café Lalo for Heath Bar Cheesecake, and just to Barnes & Noble and coffeehouses and stuff.

And he gets all excited again and says how he loves Café Lalo and have I ever been to Crumbs and I'm like, "I *live* at Crumbs!" So we debate about which cupcakes are the best there and he says how he has a major sweet tooth and I'm like, "No one has a bigger sweet tooth than me!" And we argue about who has a bigger sweet tooth for a while, but he keeps insisting that he does. I can't believe we have so much in common, but of course we do. This would kind of feel like we were on our first date if it wasn't in school.

But then I get paranoid, like what if he thinks I'm only talking to him for some grade enhancement? And the custodian comes in to empty the garbage can, and I look up at the clock and it's 4:45. Which is so weird, because I came in here right after school at 3:10 and it feels like we've only been talking for five minutes.

Mr. Farrell's like, "Wow. Time flies when you're having fun."

And I'm thinking, *You're having fun? Sweet!* And then I swallow way too loudly.

Out in the hall I hear someone say hi to James and then James walks in and wants to know where Rhiannon is. And I can't even answer him because I'm wondering how long he's been standing there. But then I'm like, *Why am I being so paranoid? He obviously stopped by just now to pick her up.*

So Mr. Farrell tells him that tutoring was canceled and Rhiannon went to the library, and James gives me this look like, *If tutoring was canceled, what are you doing here?* But you know. Maybe I'm just imagining things.

❀

He puts his hand on my thigh and squeezes. I feel his other hand brushing my hair off my back. He blows against the back of my neck, not really cooling it off.

His lips brush my cheek. I grit my teeth. I hate when he gets like this. And he always gets like this when he drinks too much.

When he pushes me down, the grass feels wet against my back. Grass pokes into my arms. I feel his fingers sliding under my shirt, rubbing over my stomach. His breath smells like beer.

I want to scream. But that only makes it worse.

❀

The only thing I was allowed to know about what we're doing tonight is that I was supposed to bring a flashlight. But now Rhiannon's explaining about Operation Steve and it's obvious that I have to tell her now, and I'm kicking myself for not telling her sooner.

She goes, "It's not like I'm signing it or anything, so I should be okay, right? And Steve's really the only one who's going to know what it means, because who else is into chem like that?" And she's all using big Italian hand gestures the way she gets when she's excited, and I can't believe how daring it sounds. I love Ree forever, but this is the last thing I'd expect her to think up.

I'm like, "Ree."

She quits with the gesturing.

I go, "There's something I have to tell you. And I'm really sorry I didn't tell you before."

So she's like, "What's going on?"

And then I tell her everything. About hearing the rumor from Joni but thinking it was bogus. About seeing them kissing in the hall. About going up to Steve and what an ass he was.

Ree stands there, staring at the sidewalk. She doesn't say anything for a few minutes.

Then she goes, "I guess we should just go home then."

I don't know what to tell her. I mean, I obviously don't want her to do something that will probably be totally humiliating tomorrow, but I don't think it's that simple. True, Steve was a total jerk when I talked to him, but there's obviously more to it than what we know for him to give Ree those roses. And then deny it like that. I just get the feeling there's more going on, especially since he was acting all weird with me.

But it's totally up to her. So I say, "If you want."

Ree's like, "What's the point of doing this? He's with Gloria now."

But she's not walking away or anything, so I just wait with her. I can tell she's still thinking about it.

She goes, "Or maybe not."

I'm like, "True."

And Ree's all, "Maybe he denied about the roses because he was mad at me for not saying thanks. Or maybe he thought I got you to go up to him because I was avoiding him. Like I didn't want to talk to him or something."

I go, "Yeah maybe," because I'm liking this exciting new Ree. I'm really passionate about expressing yourself, and Ree was majorly psyched about doing this. And I just think that if you believe in something and you want it so much and you're not hurting anyone else, you have to go for it. Which sometimes means taking a risk, even if it's scary. But the thing you want most to happen doesn't stand a chance unless you give it one.

She says, "So then he probably thought I didn't want him back, so he denied about the roses to save face."

I'm like, "And one kiss in the hall doesn't mean anything. Especially with a skank like Gloria who, P.S., is probably just trying to get you back and doesn't even *like* Steve. She just took advantage of the situation to make it look like Steve broke up with you for her."

"Isn't that what he did?"

"No. We have no idea what Steve's problem is right now. When I talked to him before? It was like . . . he was a different person. I swear you would *not* have recognized him."

"At first I wanted to do this so I could prove to Steve that I could be more exciting. But now it's like . . . I just want to do it for me. To prove it to myself, you know?"

"Totally."

"And if whatever it is with Gloria is nothing now but it might turn into something, then this could be my only chance to get him back."

I don't want to see her get hurt even more, but if she doesn't do this, she'll always regret it and wonder What If. And the What Ifs are the worst.

Ree takes out two packs of sidewalk chalk from her bag. She's like, "Remember that episode of *Sex and the City* when Carrie says how anything is possible in New York? This is what she's talking about! Right now!"

I go, "Rock on! So . . . we're doing this?"

Ree rips open the sidewalk chalk. She looks around the court-yard.

Then she goes, "Yeah. We are."

I'm stoked. If she didn't do this now, she'd regret it forever. And if Steve doesn't come back to her, then she'll get the closure she needs to move on. She's not going to move on just because James and I are telling her to. She's not going to let go until she sees for herself that there's nothing left to hold on to.

JAMES
CHAPTER 9
Saturday

IT'S ABSURD TO walk by a thirteen-million-dollar brownstone with some homeless guy sleeping on the sidewalk right outside. Something like that really makes you think about how the world works.

I live in this really upscale neighborhood. Which is a joke, because if you saw my crappy rent-stabilized apartment, you would never assume this. Especially with the roaches in the kitchen we can never seem to get rid of and the noise that never ends.

Incessant noise.

Like right now. I'm trying to get this Industrial Design report done, but the beeping is driving me crazy. And it's not going to stop until I make it stop. Our insane neighbor who blasts the TV at three in the morning doesn't help things, either.

It's not like our apartment has other features to make up for the constant noise. Highlights of our "living room," which is techni- cally a converted space where Ma strategically placed screens to create a separate living room and dining room, include a pool of candle wax on the ancient radiator, a lamp from 1964 with a broken shade, and a dusty philodendron hanging in the window. The window, of course, overlooks an alley, in which the classier guys pee when they get too drunk at the bar next door. And that would be why we keep the window closed.

Whenever the smoke detector goes off like this, it's the same story. Ma wildly smacks at it and swings a towel around in a frenzied fit, knowing the whole time that both methods are entirely ineffective. The smoke detector goes off when it's having a bad day and/or the oven's been on for at least twenty minutes. And since Ma is currently baking bread, the alarm naturally decides to go off.

I pull on some jeans and yank a T-shirt over my head, pulling it down as I walk to the kitchen. The alarm sounds like an air-raid alert.

"Sheesh!" Ma's towel frantically jabs at the air. "James! Can you—?"

"I'm on it." I drag a chair across the floor so it's under the smoke detector. Then I stand on it and snag the detector's cover so hard I crack the plastic. I guess you could say I have some repressed anger. Or maybe not so repressed. I grab the batteries and throw them on the floor.

Silence. Finally.

"Thanks, hon," Ma says.

"Anytime."

Except, really, it's more like all the time. I don't know how much longer I can take it. Sharing a room with my little brother. Never more than three consecutive seconds of quiet. The neighbors with the music playing all night. The other neighbors with the loud sex.

In fact, the only redeeming neighbor around here is Mrs. Schaffer.

My parents mean well. Ma nags because she cares about me. I get it. But that doesn't make it any easier to live here. It's just too suffocating when all I want is some time to myself, to do what I want without everyone on top of me all the time.

I'm sick of never being able to do homework without being interrupted. Or work on my computer projects. Or even think clearly.

This is why I'm going to be a software designer. So I can do something I love, and make tons of money at the same time. So I can get the fuck out of here. Buy a huge house with so much space I can't even use it all. And then I can send money home. My parents have had a hard life. It's not easy when you do what you love but it doesn't pay. And you have four kids. My two older sisters moved out, but it's not like my parents can afford to help them much with college. So I'll send my parents money, and maybe they can get a bigger place, too. They can relax when they're older, the way they deserve to. Without having to worry about how they're going to survive.

But for now, I'm the one who has to survive. Which sounds a lot easier than it actually is.

I have to walk way over to the East Side to get the 6 train. And then I have to go uptown to the Citicorp Building. It's my favorite skyscraper, with that cool slanted top. It's Rhiannon's favorite, too, but we like it for different reasons. She just has a thing for buildings with slanted tops.

I like what it symbolizes. You can smell the money all the way down the street. And I know how obnoxious that sounds, but to me it means freedom.

When I was thirteen, I wanted to be a finance guy like Rhiannon's dad. I used to ask him tons of questions about his job. And I found out that going into finance is a guaranteed way to get rich. The only problem is that I'm not a shark. You have to be ruthless to be an extremely successful stockbroker. I'm too much of a nice guy to make that possible.

I also got the impression that having a lot of money can turn a decent person into an asshole. So when I'm successful, I'll have to make sure that doesn't happen to me.

Schlepping it to the East Side isn't exactly my idea of fun times. But I have to do it. Rhiannon is bumming hard-core. We have this thing where we help each other out. I already have a girlfriend—it's not like that, we just go way back is all. We're solid.

When I get to her place, Brooke answers the door.

"Hey!" She immediately zeroes in on the Cinnabon box. "Aww! For me? You shouldn't have."

"Yeah, I guess that's why I didn't." The biting sarcasm is our thing. It's this game we play where we pretend to hate each other. It never gets old.

"Oh, well. There are worse things."

"Speaking of . . ."

"She's not up yet. I'm afraid she's never getting out of bed again. But!" Brooke snatches the box from me. "This will most definitely help."

"So . . . can you just . . . ?"

"No prob. Isn't there that party tonight?"

"Yeah."

"Because I don't think she's going."

"Don't worry," I say. "She's going."

Although the prospect of returning to my decrepit apartment is highly appealing, I decide to go over to Thompson Street for a game of chess with the NYU geeks. I'm not doing Mrs. Schaffer's thing until four, anyway.

Max is already sitting in the window seat. He's working out strategies. He's waiting for a decent opponent. And then I walk in.

He's like, "Dude. You're late."

"Sorry," I go. "Emergency intervention."

"Shit happens."

"Big-time."

Max and I have been playing chess all year. He was asking about his brother Brad last week. Which was weird because we don't hang out or anything, we just go to school together. So there wasn't much to tell.

Twenty minutes later, he's got me.

"Checkmate."

"Fuck." I study the board. I go over my last five moves. "How did that happen?"

"Um . . . maybe because I'm a genius and you suck?"

"Maybe not." I'm off my game. All unfocused. Story of my life.

I'm too stressed all the time. Not sleeping enough. There's always too much work that never seems to get done. And when it does, there's tons more. I'm pressurized, ready to explode any second.

Something has to change. I don't know what. But something.

It's righteous that I convinced Rhiannon to go to the party. But now I have to call the one person I'm dreading the most. Because I already know how she's going to react.

"Hello?"

"Hey. It's—"

"Hi, James! I know your voice by now."

"Oh. Well . . . how's it going?"

"Great! What about you?"

"Great. Except . . . there's something I have to ask you."

Nothing from Jessica's end.

"You still there?" I say.

"Yeah. But I'm not sure I want to hear this."

"I know we're supposed to go to the party as a date, but—"

"What are you telling me?"

She does this every time. I don't get why she goes ballistic if I even mention Rhiannon's name. It's like I'm not allowed to have friends who are girls or something. Which is absurd, considering all the straight guy friends Jessica has.

"Just that . . . would you mind if Rhiannon came with us?"

"Would I *mind*?"

"Yeah."

"What do you think?"

"That you might."

"Ya think?"

See? I knew this would happen. This is exactly what I wanted to avoid. Why can't there be an easy way to do this? It's not like I'm saying I don't want to go with her at all.

"You know what I think?" Jessica has this bitchy, sarcastic tone. Which I've never heard from her before.

"Um . . . not really."

"I think you'd rather be with her."

"With who? Rhiannon?"

"Duh."

"Come on, Jess, that's crazy."

"Oh, really?"

"You know it is."

"No, what I *know* is how it makes me feel when you never talk to me about your problems but you always talk to her!"

"When did I do that?"

"Oh my god! Like, I don't know, *all the time?*"

"I talk to you."

"Not like you talk to her."

"How would you know?"

"Let's just say I've overheard some of your conversations."

"Like what?"

"Please. The *point*. Is that I always ask you what's wrong and if everything's okay, and you never tell me anything. And I want you to come to me, but no. You always have to go running to her."

"I don't—"

"And those walks you guys take? What's that about?"

"They're just walks."

"Well, did it ever occur to you that *I* might want to go?"

"We've walked before."

"Oh, yeah, like what, twice? And we never go to the pier. Like that's your secret place or something. Did you ever think that maybe I'd want to go, too?"

This blows. Big-time. I was only calling to see if Rhiannon could

come with us, and now I have to deal with this crap. Jessica seriously needs to get her jealousy issues under control.

"Look, Jess. I'm sorry I asked about the party. Just forget it,
okay?"

"No! I can't forget it! You obviously want to go with her instead,
so why don't you just admit it?"

"Because it's not true."

"Whatever."

"It's not!"

"Do you even realize how much time you spend with her compared to me?"

"Why are you acting like she's my girlfriend? We never even
went out!"

"Why would I be acting like that? *I'm* your girlfriend, remember?"

I don't know how to get out of this. It's like no matter what I say,
she's determined to think what she wants.

"I guess not," Jessica decides.

"Yeah, I remember, but . . ."

"But what?"

"Why are you getting so crazy about this?"

"Oh, so now I'm crazy?"

"Come on, Jess. You know what I mean."

"You know what? It's funny. Because I thought you were different."

I have no idea what to say to that. Different from what?

"But," she says, "I guess I was wrong."

I check the time. "Look, let me just call her and—"

"Go be with her then! She's the one you want!"

"I was—"

"Forget it. I really don't care anymore."

And then she hangs up.

I'm pretty sure I've just been dumped.

I should feel all tragic right now. But I don't. I feel . . . empty.

And I don't even know why.

"Is that you, James?"

"It's me, Mrs. Schaffer."

Three locks click open. The chain lock rattles. Mrs. Schaffer peeks out. She examines the bags of groceries I'm holding.

"An angel, this one." She opens the door all the way. "Come in, come in."

I go over to her kitchen counter and put the bags down. Then I start unpacking.

Mrs. Schaffer shuffles over in her slippers. "Now, you leave those, James."

"That's okay." I pull out a gallon of water. "I don't mind."

It's this thing we do. I start unpacking. She protests. I keep unpacking. She orders me to sit down at the kitchen table, where she has a plate of cookies out for me. They're really good cookies. She always has these green and pink ones shaped like leaves with chocolate in the middle.

And then later, after we've talked for a while and I've eaten all the cookies, I unpack the rest while she's dusting in the living room. She pretends she doesn't know what's going down, and I pretend the same thing doesn't go down every week. This way I can help her out and she doesn't have to be embarrassed. Which she would be if she ever admitted that her arthritis makes it really hard for her to unpack the heavy stuff.

"I'm an old lady. Haven't you ever heard of respecting your elders? Get over to that table and sit."

"Yes, ma'am."

"I put your cookies out nice, the way you like."

"Thank you."

We sit. I eat.

She watches me eat.

"So and?"

"Yes?"

"What's happening with the girl?"

"Nothing so far."

"How can this be?" Mrs. Schaffer gets up to pour me a glass of milk. "How can it still be like this?"

"I told you. She has a boyfriend. Well, *had*."

"Oh? So, a new development?"

This would be referring to the potential development Mrs. Schaffer keeps hoping for. She met Rhiannon once outside my apartment and hasn't stopped talking about her. Old people tend to get treated like crud in this city by teens, like almost getting knocked down by kids running past them on the sidewalk and stuff. So she couldn't get over how sweet Rhiannon was to her. And now she thinks we should be together. At first I tried to explain that we're just friends, but Mrs. Schaffer wasn't hearing that. She only wants to hear that we're together. So now I go along with her. To keep her happy and all.

"Sort of. I mean, yeah. Her boyfriend just broke up with her."

"And why was this?"

"We don't know."

"What?"

"He didn't really explain it."

"What? Who does such things?"

"That's what I'm saying."

"These kids nowadays. Such frivolity."

I eat another cookie.

"Well? This is good news for you, yes?"

"Uh . . . maybe . . ."

"Why the uncertainty?"

I smile at her. I don't want her thinking I'm a total loser. "I'll let you know if anything changes."

"Good, good." She gets up. "Now, what am I doing up?" She presses her hand against her forehead.

"Mrs. Schaffer?"

"What did I get up for?" She stands there, holding on to the back of the chair.

"Are you okay?"

"Fine, fine. Just some old *mishegoss* running around in my head."

I eat another cookie.

Mrs. Schaffer looks at me adoringly. "You and those cookies."

"I love these cookies."

"I don't know this?"

"Where do you get them from?"

"From the nice Jewish bakery around the corner. You know the one."

"They all come from there?" Sometimes she'll mix it up. Like sometimes there's these rainbow sponge cake ones with choco-late on the outside. Or these flaky thin ones that are round with chocolate along the rim. Somehow, chocolate is always involved with these cookies. Rhiannon would think that's cool.

"All of them from there. Nice man, that baker."

I've been shopping for Mrs. Schaffer since fifth grade. I wasn't so into it at first, but Ma made me do it. Now I do her grocery shopping every week and I like it.

We have this thing. She gives me money and a grocery list and coupons every week. Then I bring over her groceries and we check in with each other. Not that there's a lot to check in with on her end. I feel bad for her. Mr. Schaffer died of cancer six years ago. She has like no other family, because she never had any kids. A couple of Bingo friends stop by now and then, but for the most part it's just Mrs. Schaffer, here in her apartment all alone.

I'm probably the only teenager who's worried about dying the scary New York City death. The one where you die old and alone with no one to even notice that you're gone. Until someone smells your dead rotting body three days later from all the way out in the hall. Or just this fear of being eighty and alone, crying at the bottom of the stairs because no one's there to help you up.

"Is that you, James?"

"Yeah, Ma."

I try to escape to my room without her coming out of the kitchen. I need a shower and a nap. And maybe I can finally get that report done.

She comes out of the kitchen.

"James, do you think you can give me a hand?" She's got the tall broom. That means she wants me to sweep the muck out from behind the refrigerator and in between the stove and the counter because she can't reach.

"Where's Dad?"

"Out interviewing someone important."

Dad's a journalist for *The New York Star*, which is like a bootleg version of *The New York Times*. But it's supposedly gaining more of an audience.

"Who?"

"Don't know. It's top secret."

I take my glasses off and rub my eyes. It feels like I haven't slept in about a year. "All right." I reach for the broom.

"Were you next door?"

"Yeah."

"How is she?"

I shrug.

"What's that mean?"

I'm all bent over, trying to stretch the broom handle to the corner where the nastiest gunk is. For added fun, it feels like I'm in the process of pulling a key muscle. Or an entire muscle group.

"James?"

"*What?*"

"What's with the tone?"

"I just . . . Look, can you give me a minute here, Ma? I'm trying to get this."

"So what, you can't do that and answer a question at the same time?"

It's like this constantly. *Constantly.*

She comes over and stares at my face.

"*What?*"

"Are you eating?"

"Yes, Ma, I'm eating."

"Enough?"

It never ends. She's always bugging me to eat more. As if I can help being skinny. It's like, dude. If eating more actually worked, I wouldn't be such a joke. I'm like one of those walking stick insects all the time. Highly appealing. But at least they don't call me Noodle Arms anymore when we play basketball.

Finally in my room, I take inventory of my clothes situation. Not to be a girl about it, but I have nothing to wear. And it would be nice to appear at least remotely attractive. Now that I'm officially single again.

"Can we read now?" Brian says from his area.

One of the myriad amenities of these refined living conditions is the need to share a room with my little brother. I call it his area, but really it's two inches away from my area. Ma's brilliant solution was to put up a screen between our beds. Which is supposed to look like a wall and provide the illusion that we have some privacy. Which of course we don't.

"Not now," I tell him.

"Why?"

"Because I have to do something."

"What?"

"Just something."

"Can I help?"

"No."

"Why?"

"Because you just can't."

"Why?"

I sigh this really big sigh. The sigh is like, *I have to pick out a shirt that's not entirely repulsive and then endure dinner with its endless questions and nagging and try to get some work done on this new computer program and it never ever ends.*

Even if everyone just left me alone, it's too loud to work anyway. Trying to block out the noise with my iPod only works if I blast it, which totally prevents me from concentrating.

What I would give for an hour of peace and quiet. Or even five minutes.

It was even worse when my sisters lived here. When it was us and my parents, with my sisters sharing the room Brian and I share now, and me scrunched into a walk-in closet that posed as a room, it was bad. My sisters would fight constantly. I tried to keep out of it by being quiet, but that only works for so long.

It's amazing how you can be surrounded by so many people every day who care about you and still feel alone.

Keith did not just ask Rhiannon out.

I don't like the way he's looking at her. And I definitely don't like the way he said, "If you ever feel like hanging out . . ."

Whatever. It's her life. She can do what she wants. But Keith? He bothers me, man. He shouldn't be anywhere near her. I don't know why, but it's like I go into this hyper-protective-bodyguard mode whenever some dude tries to hit on Rhiannon. Especially when I think he's not worth her time.

"Oh," Keith goes. "Are you two . . . ?"

"No!" Rhiannon yells. "We're just friends."

Dude. Why'd she have to yell like that? Is the thought of us together so horrendous? I mean, it's not like I want to be with her, but jeez.

Keith's clearly not leaving until Rhiannon agrees to have his children.

"Can I get back to you?" she asks him.

"Sure," Keith says. "Take your time." Then he looks me over. "I don't doubt your answer will be yes." He laughs.

"Egomaniac," I mumble.

"What?" Rhiannon says.

"Nothing." I hope she's not seriously interested in that moron. "I'm getting a Coke."

Danny's over by the window. Well, over by the entire wall that's one huge window looking out over the city would be more accurate. There's a telescope over there. So of course a pack of guys are shoving each other, trying to be next. Seeing if there's anyone having sex in the other buildings. Danny's maneuvering the lens, trying to find some action. Apparently, he's been hogging the telescope. He's getting called out for it.

"Dog! You've been on that for, like, ever."

"Type rude to bogart the view, yo!"

"Get off the fucking scope, Trager!"

Danny reluctantly pries himself away. He sees me and comes over.

"That thing is sick! There's some chick taking a bath in the next building."

One of the most excellent things about Manhattan is that no one has curtains. Or they do, but hardly anyone uses them.

"Nice," I say.

"So," he goes. "What's good?"

"Same old."

Evan and Carl come over. They're mainly Danny's friends. Radical leftist types. Carl's dad owns a printing shop and gave Danny a discount on his election posters. I roll with them sometimes.

We pound fists.

Evan goes, "You guys hear about Marion?" Which immediately gets Danny's attention. He's been sweating her since the thing with Nicole ended. I'll admit that Marion Cross is gorgeous and easily the best-looking girl in our class, probably in the whole school, but she's not my type. Too shallow.

"What?" Danny says.

"Son." Evan pauses for dramatic effect. "Word on the street is that Marion might actually like . . . *Carl.*"

Carl looks like he just won the lottery. And not the cheap discount game where you have to split it with a thousand other people. We're talking Mega Millions. Exclusively.

"Word?" Danny goes.

"Word up, yo."

"How do we know this?"

Evan clarifies. "Well . . . allegedly."

I'm like, "Allegedly?"

"Yeah," Carl says. "Supposedly."

"And where did this information come from?" Danny presses.

"Jared says she was asking him about me," Carl insists.

"She never does that," Evan adds.

"This is true," I confirm. I heard that Marion only dates college guys. I've never heard that she was asking about one of us. The news would have been legendary.

Danny goes, "Sweet!"

"Oh, man," Carl says. "If she wants me . . . *fuck*. The things I'd do to her."

"He's only been choreographing them for two years," Evan informs us.

"Way before that, dude. Maybe I didn't know she existed, but she was still the ultimate babe."

"A score for you would be a score for the entire junior class."

"Hell, yeah!"

"Never say never," Danny says. "That's my motto."

And then Nicole walks over. Danny's smile immediately dissolves.

He's like, "Hey, Nicole! I didn't see you." Using his Girlfriend Voice.

I recognize the voice. It's the same strained voice I use when a girl I like catches me saying something stupid. Danny has to do some serious damage control right now, so he says later to us and breaks out with Nicole.

I look around for Rhiannon. I don't see her anywhere, so I hang with Carl and Evan some more. And then someone touches my arm, and I'm expecting it to be Rhiannon. But it's Nicole.

"Hey," she says. "Ree wanted me to tell you that she left."

"What? Why?"

"She was tired and just . . . she just wanted to leave. But she knew if she told you, you'd go with her, and she wanted you to stay and have a good time."

"She should have told me."

"But then you would have left."

"Yeah, but . . ."

"So, yeah."

I smile at her. "Thanks for telling me."

I watch this kid Tony do his professional Mr. Pearlman imitation. It distracts me from thinking about why Keith is getting on my nerves.

CHAPTER 10

Sunday

"I THOUGHT SHE felt it, too. You know?"

"Yeah."

"Aren't girls supposed to be way more sensitive about stuff like that?"

"That's what they say."

We're waiting for *Thank You for Smoking* to start. Danny's all into political issues. His goal is to become some upper-level politico type without getting corrupted by the system. He's always fired up about how people in charge make stupid things happen, like pointless wars and trashing the environment. He pretty much worships Jon Stewart in a godlike way. He has to watch *The Daily Show* every night it's on and check in with like two dozen different Web sites.

What blows my mind about Danny is that he's got this huge speech coming up Friday and it doesn't make him nervous. He hasn't even mentioned it yet. He's been obsessing about Nicole.

"Freaks me out," Danny admits. "It wasn't like it was just *her* first time."

"That's messed up."

"How's she gonna act all weird the next day? Like she didn't even know me or something?"

I just shake my head. I didn't get it then, and I don't get it now. The day after Nicole and Danny slept together, she totally iced him. Which is not like her at all. And then she breaks up with him for no reason. Usually I can't figure girls out to save my life, but this? This was out there. And Danny's still not over her.

He's completely uninterested in any other girls. Except Marion. But that's just his testosterone talking. I keep telling him that once he wins the election, he can have any girl he wants.

The guy in back of us keeps pushing. I give him a warning look. He pretends not to notice. The Magnolia line on weekends is usually halfway down the block, but that's no excuse for rudeness. This would be the perfect opportunity for a Mr. Inappropriate Alert Guy intervention.

Mr. Inappropriate Alert Guy is this character Danny and I made up freshman year. It's a concept that never gets old because it's so perfect. Here's how he operates. If anyone does something rude, harsh, or obnoxious, he taps them on the shoulder. And then they turn around and he says, "Excuse me. But do you know how inappropriate you're being right now?" And then he goes on to explain how what the person did is wrong and what they should be doing instead.

And the thing is, he's not some huge bouncer-type guy. He doesn't come off all scary and threatening. He's just an average height. But he wears a tux. He seems more legit that way. So it's not that he's physically intimidating. He's smarter than the person being offensive, so he's intellectually intimidating. Wins every time.

Rhiannon stands on tiptoes to try and get a look in the window. She wants pink icing. She wants particular sprinkles.

"So," I say.

"Yeah?"

"Keith was so random last night." Not to stress about this. But that guy's a dumbass. She deserves someone better.

Rhiannon tries to look in the window again. "He called me before."

"He did?"

"Yeah."

"What did you say?"

"I told him no."

"Why?"

"Please."

All this tension drains away. That's one less thing I have to worry about.

"As if I'd ever go out with him," she says.

If the guy wasn't such an egomaniac, I'd almost feel sorry for him. "What's so bad about Keith?"

"Like he's anywhere *near* my type."

"And what's your type?"

Rhiannon's bouncing up and down. Now she can see in the window. And my question splats on the sidewalk like a water balloon.

I could ask it again. But whatever.

One of the many reasons Rhiannon is a cool girl is because she understands that I don't want to talk all the time. Other girls expect you to act like them with the nonstop talking. But she gives me room to be myself.

So we're sitting on the pier and I'm thinking about Jessica. Not because I miss her or I regret what happened. Which is what you'd expect me to be thinking. But because it's not the first time I've been dumped with Rhiannon indirectly involved.

I've only had two girlfriends. Three if you count the thing with Jessica. I broke up with my last girlfriend because I felt like it was getting too serious. She was always talking about stuff she wanted us to do like three months down the line, and when did I want to come over for dinner, and I just wasn't feeling it. Don't get me wrong. She was great and all. Curvy, killer smile, laughed at all my jokes. Maybe it could have worked out. It's just that she rushed things before they had a chance to go anywhere on their own.

So that was all me. But the one before her blew me off after I called her "Rhiannon" by mistake. Which totally didn't mean anything. That's the kind of thing that happens when you spend a lot of time with someone. It happens to everyone. And it wasn't even at some crucial time, like when we were making out. Obviously, there was more to the story than she was telling me. We'd have these weird conversations. Ones that made me think there was some cryptic subtext I wasn't getting.

A typical conversation would go like this:

Me: So when do you want to hang out next?

Her: Hang out?

Me: Yeah.

Her: Um . . . I'm not sure.

Me: How about Saturday?

Her: Saturday night or afternoon?

Me: What difference does it make?

Her: *[looking at me like I'm the biggest bonehead ever]* There's a difference.

Me: Oh. Well . . . what about Saturday afternoon? We could go to the planetarium for that new show.

Her: I might be busy.

After conversations like these, I always felt like I was missing something. Like I did something wrong. Even though I had no idea what it was. Or this other thing she'd do was ask me questions like, "Do you like Rhiannon more than me?"

Dude. How was I even supposed to respond to that? They're two completely different concepts.

When a girl asks you a question like that, there's no way you can be honest. They say they want you to be honest, but then they get all upset when you are. You can't win. There's no way to win. There are questions you just can't answer without manipulating the truth. Like, "Does this make me look fat?" Or, "Do you think she's prettier than me?" Or, "Do you ever think about other girls?" Because the truth, in any of these cases, could potentially crush a girl.

For some reason, I haven't had a serious girlfriend yet. No big. Maybe it's the kind of thing you don't find until you're looking for it.

Brian is sitting with Rhiannon on the couch, all curled up in her lap. She's reading to him. And I'm just standing in the kitchen doorway, watching them. All mellowed out for once.

But then after we finish Parcheesi and move on to Chinese checkers, I'm all wound up again. I'm only half-thinking about my moves. The other half is thinking about this huge Science League tournament coming up that I haven't even started getting ready for and my Industrial Design report that's still not done and this new computer program I need to finish so I can enter this competition and—

"Why'd you move there?" she says.

"Why not?"

"You missed this whole jump." Rhiannon points to the space I should have moved to. Then I could have jumped three of her guys in a row.

"Oh," I say. "I didn't even see that."

"Are you okay?"

"Yeah."

No. I'm totally out of it. All this stress has put me off my Chinese checkers game. I never miss a jump like that. Ever.

So after Rhiannon leaves and Brian is asleep, I'm relieved that I can still work on my software design. This thing will be bigger than anything Apple has invented. My ideas will make iTunes look old-school. I'll revolutionize the computer world, as Danny would say. He's always talking about starting a revolution.

The neighbors are fighting again. Which is only slightly more desirable than listening to them having sex. Sometimes the fighting turns into sex, though, so I'm hoping they stay mad at each other. And the other neighbors are blasting that techno-house crap again, so everything in here's shaking like *boom boom boom*.

I bang on the wall along with the beat like *boom boom boom*. As if they can even hear me.

Of course I can't concentrate. One minute I'm writing code, and the next I'm lost in a haze of my future life.

House: Some three-million-dollar job near the river. Badass amount of space.

Car: Mazda Ryuga. Black.

Job: Software designer for Apple. Sick bankroll.

Girl: Victoria's Secret model. Also smart and into gaming.

"James!" Ma yells.

"What?!"

"Did you do your homework?"

"I'm doing it, Ma!"

I always do my homework. I've never *not* done my homework. Shouldn't she know this by now?

When she comes in ten minutes later to see that I'm doing it, I almost blow a gasket.

"Why are you checking up on me?"

"For your information, I was coming in to see if you wanted your blue shirt ironed."

"No, that's okay."

She lingers in the doorway.

"Anything else?"

Ma comes in and sits down on my bed. "You seem kind of edgy lately."

"That would be because I'm edgy."

"And you're taking it out on me because . . . ?"

I stop typing. I turn around to look at her. "I'm sorry, okay? I just have a lot on my mind."

"Anything I can help you with?"

"No. It's just . . . life."

"Are you sleeping better?"

"Not so much."

"Do you—"

"I'm going for a walk."

"I thought you had homework."

"I always have homework. I need a break."

Ma looks worried.

"Don't worry," I tell her. "I'll be okay."

Walks are never as good during the day. At night, when everyone's apartments are lit up and you can see inside, that's where the action is.

Everything about this fascinates me. Windows, lampposts, building facades. Looking into other people's lives. The way it all comes together, this entity greater than the sum of its parts. I feel inspired. I'm excited about my future life.

Then I pass a twenty-four-hour deli and there are all these flowers outside. For some reason, I notice them. And that's when I see those flowers Rhiannon likes.

I don't think about what it means when I get them. I just know that I want to give them to her.

CHAPTER 11
Monday

IF MY NEIGHBORS weren't having the loudest sex ever last night, then maybe I would have gotten more than three minutes of sleep. But the sad reality is that they were. And that's why I'm dragging my tired ass into physics like it's a remake of *Night of the Living Dead* and I'm the most exhausted zombie ever.

I need coffee. Big-time.

I collapse into my chair and lean back. I take my glasses off and rub my hands over my face. I have no idea how I'm going to make it through the day. But whatever. It's not like I haven't been up all night because of them before. It's especially embarrassing when I see them the next day. Because then I have to pretend like I've never heard them having sex. Like this one time after a night of particularly loud screaming from her, I saw the guy in the basement dumping his recycling. I tried to ignore him completely, but I couldn't help staring. And he's not even all that. He's like some schlub you see eating alone at Noodle Bar, all slurping down his soup and reading the paper.

The bell rings. Everyone's opening notebooks and yelling conversations across the room and turning off their Sidekicks and copying homework problems from other people. I'm lusting a double espresso. It's a problem. The orange Mudtruck where I always get my coffee wasn't in its usual spot. Their coffee rocks something extreme. And Joe isn't on my way to school, so I decided to have no coffee instead of some weak deli schlock.

Danny slides into his desk, next to mine. Danny's a vegetarian, with his weird tofu bacon and egg substitute sandwiches he gets for breakfast at this special vegan deli. He wolfs down the last part of his sandwich.

"Can you do it by Friday?" he wants to know.

"Definitely."

He's strategizing for his big speech Friday. Danny has mad public-speaking skills. Some people are just naturally talented in that area. I, however, am not some people. I practically pass out when I have to talk in front of people. But Danny is the only one who can keep us awake when we have to do oral reports. He can make even the most boring things seem interesting. Like politics.

"I can't believe turning out the lights is considered a fire hazard," I complain. "What about for movies and stuff?"

"That would be why we never see movies in there."

"But isn't an auditorium supposed to be for everything?"

"Ideally. And then there's realistically."

Danny has this righteous idea for his speech. But to make it work, the lights need to be off for a minute. The principal wouldn't even let him do that. It's so bogus. They're always telling us to be creative and think outside the box, but every time we do, we get shot down. So I'm helping him out.

"I'll take the heat if you get caught," Danny says.

"Don't sweat it," I tell him. I mean, really. If I get caught, what's the worst they can do?

I raise my hand in calculus and ask to go to the bathroom. But that's not where I'm going.

When I open my locker, I'm psyched to see that the flowers still look decent. And there's a history with them. One time I was walking with Rhiannon down Charles Street, and someone had these flowers planted in their front yard. She said how they were so pretty. She stood there for a long time, staring at them.

Yeah, so I got her flowers. Maybe they'll make her feel better. It's the kind of thing we do for each other. Except I've never given her flowers before. But it was just one of those impulsive-type things.

I take the flowers out of my locker and make sure the little water containers on the bottoms of the stems are still on. Then I turn her lock combination, which I know because we tell each other our new ones every year. I'm leaving the flowers in there without a card. Since girls remember everything, she has to know they're from me.

Girls are always complaining about how much stuff guys forget. I can't wait to see how impressed she is that I remembered.

The decent thing about lunch is that Rhiannon's been sitting with me since the thing with Steve ended. The crappy thing about lunch is that even though she's sitting with me, she's staring at him.

It's annoying. He rips her heart out and stomps all over it, and she's still hoping he'll look at her.

She sat with me a couple times when they were in a fight. And it was great and everything, but in a way it felt like I was just good old James, always there, like some comfortable sofa. Which gets irritating.

"So I'm doing this computer program for Danny's speech," I ramble. "It's what's up. Really cool lighting effects and original fonts and . . ."

When did I start babbling? As soon as she sat down? And since when do I say things like *It's what's up*?

Rhiannon hasn't said anything about the flowers yet. She probably didn't go to her locker.

I should just get to the point here. Something I was thinking about last period. Just this idea that showed up out of nowhere. No big or anything.

"And then the dance is that night."

Rhiannon goes, "Um-hmm." Still staring at Steve.

"So, like . . . are you going?"

She finally looks at me. "Where?"

"To the dance."

"Oh. Um . . . yeah. I think so."

"So, like . . . with Nicole or . . . ?"

"Well . . . maybe with Steve."

The Hot Pocket sticks in my throat. Obviously, my hearing's on the fritz. "Huh?"

Rhiannon blushes. "No, I mean . . . I don't know for sure, but . . ."

"Yeah . . . didn't he break up with you, though?"

She gives me a harsh look. "Technically maybe. But things change."

I'm shocked. Why would she still want to be with that dumbass after everything he put her through?

Rhiannon looks at Steve again. And this time, he looks back at her.

And he smiles.

And she practically melts all over the table.

Screw this. I get up to leave.

"Where are you going?" Rhiannon says.

"I'm done."

"But . . . don't you want to sit with me?"

I'm tired of being taken for granted. Does she even appreciate me at all?

I don't want to fight with her. I really don't. But if I stay here and watch this, I'm going to blow.

"I gotta go," I say.

And I'm out.

I can see Mrs. Schaffer on our stoop from half a block away. She's just standing there, holding on to the railing. I run up to our building.

"Hey, Mrs. Schaffer!" I climb the stairs up to her.

"Oh good. Would you . . . ?"

"Of course."

I help Mrs. Schaffer inside and up the rest of the stairs. It's so weird how a lot of older people live in walk-up buildings without an elevator. How do they get around when they live alone and there's no one to help them? Living in a third-floor walk-up is nothing for me, but it's a serious deal for her. It takes her like ten minutes just to get up to her place. And lately it seems like she's struggling more.

We stop on the second-floor landing for a breather. The hallway smells like mothballs. Mothballs and cabbage. I hate it when people cook stuff that takes over the entire building.

"And so?" Mrs. Schaffer prods. "What's new with the girl?"

Man. This is the last thing I want to talk about. I just want to go to my room, get my homework done, and work on programming for Danny's speech. Keep busy until it's time for 24. Then go to bed. And forget how warped Rhiannon's being.

"Nothing to report yet."

"Oh? And why is this?"

What am I supposed to say here? I hate stringing her along like this, but she always gets so excited about the prospect of me having a serious girlfriend. Someone I can take over to her place for visits. And so she can feed us cookies. I just can't let her down. Especially since she has such high expectations of me.

"I'm waiting for the right opportunity to arise," I explain.

"In my day, a boy liked a girl, she was the first to know. None of this scheming."

Mrs. Schaffer is like a grandma to me. My grandparents on Ma's side live in Germany, where she's from. But I haven't seen them since I was small. I hardly remember them. Just fragments. Pieces of another life. And on Dad's side, my grampa died and my grandma lives in a nursing home.

So I'm really protective of Mrs. Schaffer. Over the years, I've felt like it's my responsibility to take care of her more and more. She's family now.

When I get to Danny's, I can't believe how tricked-out his roof is. There's a huge cooler with subs and a bucket packed with ice and soda. Four chairs are set up around a TV. Which is plugged into what has to be the longest extension cord in the world.

"James, my man!" he yells. "Come on up!"

Tonight's the season finale of *24*, so Danny's having a farewell screening on his roof. Evan and Carl are also coming. We're all hard-core *24* fanatics. Danny and I have been watching since it came on when we were in seventh grade. I remember being scared because it premiered right after September 11 and it's all about terrorism, but I was riveted at the same time. I haven't missed an episode yet. It's the one show I have viewing rights for at home, but I usually try to watch it at Rhiannon's. It's so much cooler on the big screen.

We eat and drink and bullshit about nothing in particular. I watch the sun set over the Manhattan skyline. Which is so cool since these two final episodes tonight take place between five and seven in the morning, so we'll be watching the sun rise right after the sun sets. Metaphysical, yo.

And then suddenly there's yelling from the stairs. We turn to watch.

"Secure the perimeter!"

"Copy that!"

"Send the coordinates to my PDA!"

"Call for backup! We need a chopper!"

Carl kicks open the door. Evan runs onto the roof, pointing his imaginary gun toward us.

"CTU! Do not move!"

Carl comes running over. He's all, "Drop your weapons!"

"I already used them on your mom," Danny says. He takes another swig of soda.

"Yeah," I go. "But just the handcuffs."

Evan goes, "Tick *boom!* Tick *boom!*"

By the third commercial break, we're all running around acting like Jack Bauer and reenacting the scenes with cell phones pressed to our ears. And the endless lit-up windows and the street noise and planes flying overhead all blend into the background.

CHAPTER 12
Tuesday

SHEILA AND BRAD are fighting again. Mr. Inappropriate Alert Guy should really let them know how tacky public fighting is.

And they don't even care that people can hear. They're right in the middle of the hall, yelling at each other.

Not that I'm watching or anything. I'm digging a book out of the back of my locker.

Here's the fight:

Sheila: Just forget it.

Brad: Why are you freaking out about this?

Sheila: I'm not!

Brad: Then why aren't you coming later?

Sheila: I have to go home.

Brad: But you left!

Sheila: Yeah, but now I'm going back!

Brad: Why?

Sheila: Because I have to!

Brad: What for?

But Sheila doesn't answer. So Brad grabs her arm and pulls her over to the lockers. Sheila yelps like she just got burned.

Brad says, "Let me see?" Now he's all quiet.

Sheila pulls up her sleeve. She's facing away from me, so I can't see anything.

"I said I was sorry."

"That's not good enough, Brad."

"I told you I didn't mean to."

"Too late."

Brad looks around. I already found my book. But I pretend that I'm still digging for it.

"Did you tell Nicole?" Brad asks.

"No."

"But you told her something."

"We were just talking."

"About what?"

"None of your business!"

"Why won't you tell me?"

"Can you just leave me alone?" Sheila says. She walks away from him.

"Sheila!" Brad yells after her.

But she doesn't come back.

I couldn't do the whole sitting with Rhiannon while she drools over the dumbass during lunch thing again. So I camped out in the computer lab instead. I wanted to get this English paper out of the way so I could focus on the program for Danny tonight.

But I didn't really make much progress, due to a persistent combination of exhaustion and distraction. Which is why I'm back here
in the lab after school.

Mr. Clements wants us to learn how to do Internet research
without plagiarizing everything we find. Which is what everyone
always does. Because everyone knows there's no way teachers
read everything we hand in. Especially long reports. Carl once
wrote "I sucked your mom's ass last night" in the middle of his
Kierkegaard report just to prove that the teacher never reads anything. He got an A.

So for Mr. Clements's philosophy class, we're supposed to
Google a few practice concepts and record any sites that look
suspicious. This is to prove that not all information on the Web is
valid. Just in case we didn't already know this.

I Google the first entry. It's Alain de Botton. He's this contemporary philosopher dude who talks about how relationships are never
what we think they are.

Everything looks legit. Even this site called Bookslut belongs to a
book reviewer who's legit.

What's up with all these sites? Okay, I'm a computer geek. It's
not exactly a secret. But there's no way I'd spend all my free time
creating these unnecessary sites. I'd rather put my energy into
something that can change the world.

Suddenly this surge of exhaustion hits me. Almost knocks me off
my chair. I stayed up way too late again.

It's hard to focus on this.

A couple teachers are in the corner of the lab, using the
faculty computers. Of course I figured out the faculty password,
but I haven't had the need to use it yet. There's a bulletin board

on the wall above them with all the teachers' names and their classroom numbers. Teachers' first names are always so weird. It's like, someone calls Mr. Clements "Richard" in real life? Far out.

I type *Richard Clements* in the Google box. I find out that he's a master glassblower, an oncologist, an Australian journalist, and likes to fly planes with wild paint jobs. And the list goes on. It's draining to even think about searching ahead enough to find the one who teaches here.

After I'm done, I'm passing by Mr. Farrell's room when I hear someone talking. For some reason, I stop. And listen.

". . . especially around here."

Today's Rhiannon's tutoring day. Is he talking to her?

"Yeah, same here. Rhiannon lives down the street, so I hang out here a lot."

That's Nicole. Except it doesn't sound like her exactly. Something about her voice sounds different.

"I'm surprised I've never seen you around, then. I'm here a lot, too. New York is, like, the smallest town on the planet with—"

"—running into people! I know!"

Now I've got it. What's wrong with her voice. It's got that high-pitched, bordering on hysterical tone girls get when they're in hyper mode.

Because they like some guy.

This can't be real. She can't seriously like Mr. Farrell.

I lean against the wall, stuck. Do I listen more? Or do I go in and get her out of there? And where's everyone else? I don't hear anyone else talking. Maybe the rest of them left early. But then why would Nicole . . . right.

Nicole goes, "Where do you hang out around here?" And he actually tells her.

This can't be real. Teachers don't have these kinds of conversations with their students, about their personal lives and where they hang out. Right? That's just way too much information.

Now he's actually telling her that he lives in her neighborhood. Which I'm sure breaks one of the top ten rules listed under What Not to Do If You're a Teacher. And she's talking to him like . . . like they're going out or something.

I'm so skeeved with the whole thing that I don't notice Evan walking toward me until he's halfway down the hall. I put my hand up like, *Don't say anything!* but it's too late.

He goes, "'Sup, James."

I nod to him. He walks by the room. So now I have to go in.

I stick my head in the doorway. "Hey." I make up a quick excuse to be there. "Did Rhiannon leave?"

And Mr. Farrell's like, "Oh. Tutoring was canceled." Like I need math tutoring.

Slick. The guy is slick. He's playing it off like he wasn't just flirting with some underage girl with a crush so huge you can hear it from the hall. And it's obvious when you see her. Nicole's all flushed. Her eyes are big and glassy. I've never seen her look like this. Even with Danny.

"So, uh . . ." I look at Nicole. "You ready?"

"Huh? Oh! No, yeah, I'm . . . yeah." Her math book falls on the floor with a loud splat.

"Here." I walk over and pick it up.

"Thanks," Nicole says. She takes her book back. She avoids eye contact.

I stand there. Waiting. Trying not to look at Mr. Farrell.

I rub my left temple. I tap my pen against my notebook. It's infuriating. There's this whole jumbled mess of stuff I'm feeling, and I don't know why.

"Whatcha doing?" Brian wants to know.

"Working on a computer program for someone."

"For who?"

I tap my pen.

Brian hangs over my shoulder. "For *who*?"

"Danny."

"Is Rhiannon coming over?" Brian loves it when she comes over. Especially when she sits with him on the beanbag chair and reads to him.

"No."

"Why not?"

"She's busy."

"With what?"

"Okay, Brian? I'm busy right now. I can't really talk."

"Everybody's busy! No one wants to talk to me!"

One of his temper tantrums is definitely brewing. If I don't intercept this now, it's going to get ugly. Fast.

"Weren't you guys reading *Lafcadio* last time?"

His lips are all pouty. "Yeah."

"Do you want to finish it?"

"I thought you were *busy*."

I put my pen down. "Not anymore, little man. Let's move."

We squish together in the beanbag chair in the corner. I'm too tall for this, but I kind of dig it when Brian presses his cheek against my shoulder, looking at the pictures while I read.

Right when Lafcadio is getting a marshmallow coat, Ma yells, "James! Phone!"

It's Danny. He wants to meet at Cozy Soup 'n' Burger, and he's buying.

When I have so much money I don't even know what to do with myself, I'm getting a personal chef. And every day she's going to cook these exotic, elaborate dinners, exactly how I describe them. And I'll invite over whoever I want. Friends who won't ask annoying questions. Or a girlfriend who just wants to relax and watch a movie while we eat.

Or maybe I'll just order in every night. And eat alone.

"So, how's the speech?"

Danny takes a swig of his egg cream. "Almost done."

"Nice."

"How's the program coming?"

"Almost done," I tell him. Even though I have a ton more work to do on it. But it shouldn't take that long.

"Thanks again, man."

"No sweat."

"Yeah, so." Danny picks up his veggie burger. "I'm thinking of asking Nicole to the dance."

I never know what to say when he brings up Nicole. Neutral is the best approach.

"Yeah?" I go.

He nods and chews. "What do you think?"

"Well, yeah. I mean . . . if you think she'll go."

"Why wouldn't she?"

Now's probably not the best time to remind Danny that she was the one who dumped him. Since he's apparently developed a severe case of selective amnesia. And me trying to cure him will only piss him off.

"No . . . you should. Go for it."

"You gotta put it out there to get it back. It's all about the karma."

"Exactly."

"So. What about you?"

"Meaning?"

"Who are you asking?"

"Oh." The thing is, I don't really want to ask Rhiannon anymore. "I don't know."

"Now that Jessica's out of the picture, you're free, bro."

"And?"

"And . . . what are you waiting for?" Danny's looking at something behind me. It's the third time he's looked.

"What's up?"

He leans over the table. "Those girls over there? Have been checking us out since they got here."

"Word?"

"Dead ass."

I turn halfway around. He's right. They do that thing where they snap their heads back so fast you know they were just looking at you.

"Nice," I say. I take an onion ring from the pile between us.

"That's it?"

"What?"

"That's all you're gonna say?"

"About what?"

"Man." Danny chews his veggie burger. "You're hopeless."

"If you're talking about those girls, they're not my type."

"Not your *type*?"

"No."

"What's that supposed to mean?"

"What does it sound like it means?"

"It sounds like an excuse to be miserable. What happened with Jessica anyway?"

"I told you."

"Well, I wasn't convinced."

"She was . . ." I pick up another onion ring. "She was jealous of Rhiannon."

Danny watches me.

I give him an exasperated look. "She didn't get how we're just friends."

"So why didn't you explain it?"

"I tried."

"Right."

"Whatever. I wasn't that into her anyway."

Danny glances over at the girls. There's a burst of giggling from their booth. "Let's see. Jessica is gorgeous. And smart. And funny. And interesting."

"And your point is?"

"She's all those things, but you weren't that into her."

"Exactly."

"Unbelievable, man."

Danny is the smartest person I know. So I really don't get why he consistently evades grasping this simple concept. Just because some girl is girlfriend material to him shouldn't imply that I have to agree. I mean, the guy derives equations to predict future climate change due to global warming for fun, and he can't get *this*?

"I'm setting you up with someone for the dance," Danny mentions.

"Who?"

"Just someone from Millennium."

I really don't want to start something up with another girl right now. And I'm sure this fix-up will be a disaster.

The girls from the other table get up to leave. They stare at us as they walk by our table. Slowly. Staring.

Danny and I attack the pile of onion rings.

PART TWO
May 24–26

☽ ✿ ⊞

*Have the courage to follow
your heart and intuition.
They somehow already know
what you truly want to become.*
—Steve Jobs

RHIANNON
CHAPTER 13
Wednesday

THE WHOLE THING looks awesome the next morning. Huge and exciting and scary. Like something that would only happen in a movie.

Kids crowd around it, trying to figure out what it means.

Someone says it's a bomb threat.

Someone says school was canceled.

Someone else says the police were already here and it's not.

This other girl says how it's the terrorists.

So now I'm nervous about getting in some serious trouble. I've never been in any kind of trouble, so possibly getting suspended is really scaring me. But I don't think I'll get caught. There's another Steve in this school who's a sophomore, so there's the possibility that people will think it's for him instead. And as far as the school is concerned, Steve and I are ancient history that people can hardly remember. So much drama has happened with other people since we broke up that our relationship is like something from way back in the Cretaceous Period. Plus, it's not like I signed it or anything.

I walk right over the message and push open the door like it doesn't even interest me. Like I didn't even notice it. I'm too nervous to stop by Steve's locker. I keep walking to Earth Science. Did he see it by now? He must have seen it by now. Unless he's late. I wish I knew what he was thinking right this second.

By second period, a lot of people are talking about it. I'm pretending to stretch in my squad on the gym floor, but I'm listening to Joni and Maria talking behind me.

"It's pathetic," Maria seethes.

"How desperate can a girl be?" Joni adds.

"Which Steve do you think it is?"

"The sophomore. Mamusu totally likes him."

"Totally."

"I bet she did it."

"He's not even that cute, though."

"Well, it can't be Steve Cannavale," Joni says. "Unless . . ."

Silence.

I stretch my leg out to the side and grab my sneaker. I peek at them from between my leg and my arm.

It's obvious that they're not only talking about me but they're talking about me behind my back. Literally.

I twist around. "What?"

Maria is inspecting her nails. Joni gives me this look like she feels sorry for me.

"What?"

"Don't you know?" Joni says.

"About what?"

"Did you write it?" Maria digs.

I lean over to stretch again. "I don't even know what you're talking about," I insist.

I try to look unaffected, but my heart is pounding so hard. Don't I know about *what*? It can't be the whole Gloria thing, because there's nothing to know. It was just a kiss. Which means absolutely nothing. Steve and I have a history together and what do they have? Some sleazy groping in the hall? Big whoop.

But then why was Joni looking at me like that? I could ask her, but I'm too afraid of what she might tell me. Maybe it's just that she doesn't think the message is going to work. But that's only because she doesn't know how it was with us.

I stretch out my other leg. A group of three girls is whispering, all of them looking over at me. I know the look they have. It's the look where you know something about someone but you don't want to be the one to tell them what it is.

So people *are* assuming it's me.

It's official. I'm mortified.

I just hope I'm mortified with a really sweet payoff.

☽

Question: Why can't I just stay in bed, where it's safe?

☽

We're supposed to be working with our neighbor on this math worksheet. But I'm not paying attention to any of the problems.

Because I'm trying to hear if anyone else is talking about what I wrote.

"... You're supposed to minus point A from point B."

"Let me see your calculator?"

"You don't need a calculator for twelve minus five."

"What is it then? ..."

"... Clements gave homework?"

"Not in my world."

"Nice. ..."

"... Do it like how he did on the board."

"That *is* how he did it."

"Oh snap. ..."

It all sounds like normal conversation. But I keep listening just in case.

Today Mr. Farrell is wearing his light blue shirt with the dark purple tie and navy pants. Someone needs to sit the man down and have a serious conversation about color coordination.

I glance back at Nicole's desk. I want to give her a look like, *Get me out of here. Now.* But she's weaving through the desks up to the front. Then I hear her tell Mr. Farrell that her pencil ran out.

"So you'd like to borrow another one?" he says.

Okay. This is weird. Nicole knows I always have a whole row of mechanical pencils, plus sharpened ones, all lined up in my bag. And a pencil sharpener in my pencil case, which also has erasers and mini glitter pens. So why is she even up there? She always asks me for a pencil or my sharpener or whatever else she needs. Since when does she go to someone else? Especially a teacher? Plus, a few minutes ago she was totally zoning out, which she never does in math.

I swear, between this and everything in gym and Steve avoiding me all day, I'm seriously angsting. At least, I think he's avoiding me. I didn't see him at any of our usual places. Even though it's only third period. But whatever. We have lunch next. There's no way he won't want to make up by then.

And maybe I'm just being paranoid about the people-talking-about-me thing, because I still don't hear anything. All I hear is a group arguing about the answer to number four.

"OD! Why you beastin', son?"

"That's it. No more answers for Lemarr."

"You're fired!"

"Except you can't be fired from school, genius."

That would be so cool. If the same rules applied to school as they do to jobs. I could really use a personal day. You can take personal days at work. Which would only be fair, since we're forced to do all this work and we don't even get paid for it.

Thunder rumbles. Everyone looks out the window. The sky is all dark. Great. I just had to wear my new sparkly flip-flops today. And I didn't bring my umbrella. The sidewalk chalk is going to be washed away soon. I hope Steve saw it. But like duh. Of course he saw it. Everyone's probably been interrogating him about it all day. And as much as I want to pretend the queer looks I've been getting from people are just a figment of my imagination, I should probably admit that they're real.

Nicole passes my desk on the way back to hers. She's been talking to Mr. Farrell this whole time, but I couldn't hear what they were saying because everyone else was talking too loud. She glances at me and then looks away quickly. I get that bad feeling again. Maybe she's heard stuff about me.

I look over at Mr. Farrell. He's staring out the window.

☽

When I get to the cafeteria and see Steve, I don't even look for James or put my stuff down. I just go over to his table.

But right before I get there, Gloria slinks over. And all of a sudden I get it. Everything that's been happening comes rushing in at me. I know before I know. I know she's going to sit down next to him.

And I know it wasn't just a kiss.

Oh my god. This is why.

Gloria sits down next to Steve. She pulls her chair all the way over so it's touching his. She puts her hand on his shoulder. You can see her perfectly done nails from all the way over here. She has this clingy black shirt with bold-colored stripes, and jeans that fit all her curves perfectly. And her perfect hair has that glossy thing going on that boys love.

That's the thing with Gloria. She's beyond gorgeous. So it's obviously a physical thing. I just can't believe that Steve would be such a *guy*. But there it is.

Gloria leans toward Steve and says something.

And that's when he finally looks up and sees me staring at them.

My stomach churns. I have no idea what to say. Her hand is still on his shoulder. He's avoiding eye contact with me.

Maybe I'll say something like, "So . . . did you get my message?" all facetiously, the way we like to joke around. The way we used to.

Some boys at the table look up at me. Then they look over at Steve and crack up. They make noises. They snort into their cheeseburgers.

It's official. I'm pathetic. I'm a pathetic, groveling, desperate ex-girlfriend.

I wish I had never come over here. I wish I could erase everything that's happened since last night. But it's already out there.

So I say, "Hey, Steve."

When he looks up at me, he's not Steve anymore. He's someone I don't know. My Steve would never look at me like that. Like I don't belong here. Like he doesn't even know me.

Gloria examines me through perfectly mascaraed lashes. She goes, "Hey, Rhiannon."

Question: Why is she answering for him?

"We've been going out for two weeks," Gloria informs me. "Which is why he dumped your ass. Or didn't he tell you?"

I stare at her.

Gloria glares at Steve. "You didn't tell her?"

"No—I . . ." Steve rips a piece of his napkin off.

"You did or you didn't?" Gloria demands.

"Um . . . I was . . ."

But Gloria looks back at me. "Haven't you been scary stalker chick enough for one day? Or are you a masochist, too?"

The whole table cracks up.

Steve doesn't defend me. He just keeps ripping his napkin apart.

I turn around and look at the table I usually sit at with James. But he's not there. He's not anywhere. I'm all alone.

I can't escape fast enough.

That did not just happen. There is no way that just happened.

I keep walking down the hall. Blocking out the hall monitor who asks for my pass. Blocking out the sound of everyone laughing at me. Blocking out everything. I have four more classes today. I won't be in any of them.

The front doors double-dare me to push them open and ditch this disaster area. It's not just raining. This is technically a torrential downpour. Rivers of water flood down the street. I stand in the hall, looking out at the world. The sky is so dark it's like night out. Lightning flashes. Thunder booms so loudly the floor vibrates.

Normally in a situation like this, I would wait it out. Well, no, normally I wouldn't cut class in the first place, but drastic times call for drastic actions. Or I would walk with James. I know he has an umbrella, because he listens to the weather forecast every morning. But James can't save me this time. No one can save me except myself.

I push the door open. I step outside. I am immediately saturated. My message is a smeary swirl of purple and pink and blue, written for someone here who was already gone.

I don't make a run for it. I'm walking all the way home.

I walk slowly in the rain. It feels like buckets of water are being dumped over my head, one after the other. My jeans are soaked. My white T-shirt is totally see-through now. Two crusty guys standing under a deli awning whistle as I go by. My flip-flops are drenched, squishing over puddles.

I need this rain to wash it all away.

It's not until I get home and put my bag down that I realize my shirt is destroyed. My bag is from the Strand, this bookstore that sells dyed canvas bags. I guess I never thought about what would happen to a red bag against a white shirt in a downpour. I peel my shirt off. It was my favorite white shirt. Now it's all streaked with red blotches.

Everyone has a breaking point. I've just reached mine.

The crying starts. And it doesn't stop.

☽

My phone's ringing for like the tenth time. I let my machine pick up again. My cell is off. I don't even care who it is. Probably James or Nicole. But I don't feel like talking to anybody.

I open my lists journal and make a new one.

Top Five Reasons to Avoid Killing Myself

5. Won't ever get to meet Topher Grace.
4. Would miss out on the whole career/travel/family thing.
3. Snickers would be lonely.
2. No more cupcakes at Magnolia.
1. Being dead probably sucks.

Snick-Snick purrs like a motor. He's in this fluffy sleeping ball next to me on my bed. I wish I could be like that. All oblivious to how disgusting life can be.

I'm listening to "My Immortal" on repeat. Because apparently I haven't felt enough pain for one day. Bring it. Maybe next I'll even read over all of Steve's old love letters.

The pain.

There's a knock on my door. I look at the clock radio. 6:42. Mom's home early.

So real.

She opens my door. "I've been calling you for dinner. I got Chinese."

Too much.

"You okay?"

I turn over. Mom lingers in the doorway.

But then she sees how damaged I look, so she comes in. "I got your favorite. Pot stickers."

Even that doesn't make me smile.

"Do you want to talk about something?" she says.

Maybe. But talking to her feels like work. And I'm just too exhausted.

"No."

"Are you sure you're okay?"

I crawl over Snick-Snick and slide out of bed. I feel like I've been run over by a cement truck and then pounded by a wrecking ball. "Yeah," I croak. I'm all groggy. "I'm going to the bathroom first."

But I'm not okay. I can't imagine ever feeling okay again.

Question: Is it possible to die of a broken heart?

☽

When I check my messages I can't believe it. James only left one message. Then there's a bunch from Nicole.

Normally he'd leave more than that. Normally he'd be crazy worried about me.

It's like he doesn't care as much as he used to.

I call his house. His mom answers.

"Hi, Mrs. Worther," I go. "Is James there?"

"Hello, Rhiannon! He's not here right now."

I hear Brian in the background, asking if he can talk to me. But I don't have the energy right now.

"Oh. Well . . . do you know where he is?"

"It's laundry day." Which means he's at Wash World. "I'm sure he's having a marvelous time over there. Maybe you could keep him company?"

"I think I might. Thanks."

The second I walk into Wash World, I feel a little better. It's an automatic response. I've sat here with James so many times while he did laundry. He hates being here by himself. So we sit on the couch and talk, and whatever's bothering me usually gets worked out by the time we leave. Kind of like an eighties sitcom.

I find him sitting on the couch, reading a book.

I'm like, "Hey."

James looks surprised to see me. He says, "Hey."

The dryer dings. James gets up.

"I, um. Are you mad at me or something?"

"No."

"Are you sure?"

"Yeah."

I'm all shy for some reason. Which is really weird. Because James and Nicole are the only people I feel totally myself around.

James takes a load of clothes out of the dryer and starts folding them.

I just stand there. Watching him fold.

"Why would I be mad at you?" he finally says.

"I don't know." I can't exactly tell him. Like, how would that go? *Hey, yeah, so I noticed you only left me one message instead of five. What's that about?*

"I got your message."

"I'm sorry about—"

"Yeah." The whole thing is beyond words. That's the cool thing about having a best friend. They know what your pain feels like already, so you don't have to explain it.

I want to ask him why he wasn't there. I want to tell him how hard it was for me. How alone I felt. But I have this feeling that I shouldn't talk about Steve anymore. With Nicole, yeah. Just not with James.

He has to wait for another load of laundry to get done. So I wait with him. I lean back against the couch, sitting really low the way I like. I scrunch over and put my head on his shoulder.

We sit like that for a long time. Watching other people's laundry dry.

CHAPTER 14

Thursday

MIGUEL'S RIPPING APART his notebook, frantically searching for the extra-credit assignment. "I had it right here," he gripes to no one in particular. "It was *right here*."

The thing about extra credit for Earth Science is that Ms. Parker hardly ever gives any. And when she does, the only way to get it is if you're the first one to hand it in. Thus, Miguel's present state of conniption.

I feel bad for him, all frantic and scrabbling through his harassed folder like he misplaced the cure for sleep or something. He's super smart, but I've told him a thousand times how his life would run a lot smoother if he'd just organize his binder.

Question: What's so hard about understanding that?

Miguel wildly flips through more papers. "Where the—?" A wave of papers crashes to the floor.

He's on the floor picking everything up when Eliezer creeps

in, still half asleep as usual. He saunters by Ms. Parker's desk with this bored expression that makes you tired just looking at him. Then he takes a folded piece of paper out of his pocket and drops in on her desk and goes, "Here's the extra credit," just as Miguel triumphantly whisks the paper he's been looking for out of the mess on the floor and yells, "I found it!"

Life is so not fair. Kids like Miguel who work crazy hard and do all these activities like being in charge of lighting for plays and community service in the South Bronx are constantly disappointed. While burnouts like Eliezer think they can do one extra-credit assignment and it'll make up for an entire marking period of failing tests and not doing homework. It's some kind of twisted slacker logic.

We're doing a rock-identification activity. Ms. Parker tells us to get into think tanks, which I hate. It's her idea of working together and helping each other to make sure everyone understands everything. When really it's just a smart kid paired up with a slow kid, and the smart kid ends up doing all the work and the slow kid just copies because it's easier than the smart kid trying to explain a bunch of stuff the slow kid will never get.

So I'm paired up with this girl Heather who never talks. I guess Ms. Parker ran out of smart kids when she matched us up, because we're both lost when it comes to science. All I know about her is that she's into designing water fountains.

We use the Reference Tables to figure out the name of a weird rock that looks like sheets of paper all stuck together. Since we've been on this one for like five minutes and Heather's not exactly an abundance of assistance, I listen to another team to see if I can hear what they got for it.

"You're so retarded."

"That's not metamorphic."

"It's schist."

"My stomach hurts."

"Try eating sometime."

"Is it shale?"

"Dog. I told you. It's *schist*."

"This isn't rocket science, people."

Alrighty then.

I was expecting to wake up today even more depressed than I was the day Steve broke up with me. But it's not like that. I'm wicked angry. Angry at Steve, angry at Gloria, angry that this is my new reality. Basically, I'm angry at the whole world.

But I don't want it to be like I'm angry and I just have to get over it. I want to do something about it. Because how can Gloria do this to me again? And get away with it like it's nothing?

I want karmic retribution.

Heather's looking at me funny. I try to pay attention.

But it's like, when will Gloria learn that you can't go around hurting people this way? That if you do, karma will never allow you to achieve true happiness? And yeah, I'm seriously mad at Steve, but she obviously has him under some spell. It's her fault he's treating me like this.

The anger bubbles up so harshly I feel sick. I shift in my chair. Heather's completely given up on trying to figure out any of this stuff. She's doodling a water fountain in the margin of her paper.

Tony starts making his sound effects. He especially likes to imitate the way Marion laughs. Or this one kid with asthma who coughs like a truck horn.

Eliezer laughs his har-*huh!* laugh.

Tony imitates Eliezer, all like har-*huh!*

We all think Tony's imitations are hilarious because he sounds just like whoever he's imitating. Sometimes I'll be on the subway or sitting in a different class and I'll think of him going har-*huh!* and I'll crack up. But then I feel bad that I'm laughing at him, because how he makes fun of everyone is just too wrong.

Ms. Parker is getting angry. Tony is always interrupting her with the sound effects, and it drives her crazy. Or he'll ask some really hard question she doesn't know the answer to, but he only does it to bother her because she's not even a real Earth Science teacher. We just have her because there's a serious shortage of science teachers who actually know what they're doing.

As she's ranting, I'm thinking that there has to be some way to expose Gloria. But in a fair way, or else I'd be just as bad as her. Some way where Gloria would be forced to realize how wrong she is.

I want revenge, but I don't want to screw up my karma. I have no idea how to do this. I just know it's something I have to do.

☽

The election is tomorrow, so Danny's in the hall doing an impromptu crowd razz. He's running for next year's senior-class president and has already done two crowd razzes this week. They're kind of these random speeches in the hall that are always hysterical. He also does spontaneous TGIM rallies on Mondays and Random Hallway Polls, where the results get printed in the school paper. Which comes out like never because Ms. Portman resigned as faculty advisor when she got mad about kids on her staff not doing anything. The Random Hallway Poll he did Tuesday was hilarious. But apparently it was all controversial, and he got called to the principal's office. Nothing happened, though. Nothing ever happens when you push the rules. You have to totally break them to get in any kind of serious trouble.

Out of everyone running for student council, Danny has the best posters. He took images from the Jon Stewart *America* book and superimposed them over photos of himself trying to look like he's on *The Daily Show*. Not that anyone watches that show besides Danny. But that's what makes the posters weird enough to work. And the tag lines are completely irreverent. They're all like, DANNY TRAGER. PRESIDENTIAL. A FAN OF NACHOS. Or, VOTE FOR DANNY. FRIEND OF TREES. Everyone thinks he's totally going to win. I definitely think he should. Politics is his life. As long as I've known him, he's talked about revolutionizing the world one day. His ultimate goal is to make everyone realize that world peace is possible.

Danny's standing on a plastic milk crate in the middle of the main hallway, waving around a head of lettuce.

"I summon the energy of the lettuce to stimulate world peace!" Danny yells. "No more war! No more massacre!" He waves the lettuce over his head. "Praise to the lettuce!" Kids stand around him in a circle and cheer. Brad sticks out his arms in front of him and makes worshiping motions at the lettuce. Another kid yells, "It's the apocalypse!"

Mr. Pearlman comes running down the hall. Kids are crowded three deep around Danny, so he can't get through. He gets shoved into someone so it looks like he just pushed a kid.

"You best step *back*, son!" this boy goes. Because he knows he can get away with it now.

"Hey!" the kid yells. "Yo, lettuce god! Mr. Pearlman just pushed me! That's physical abuse!"

A surge of booing engulfs the hall. Some hard-core stoner guys yell at Mr. Pearlman to lay off. In the rare event that a teacher breaks the rules, you can shout them out as loud as you want and nothing can happen to you. They could totally lose their job for even touching you. And if an administrator does it, it's ten times worse.

Mr. Pearlman looks nervous. He looks like he's scared we're all about to stomp over him in an angry stampede. He backs away and motors down the hall. He's probably going to get the AP to break it up.

But in the meantime, Danny still has the floor. And everyone's attention.

"A vote for Danny! Is a vote to end the senseless physical violence perpetrated at Eames Academy! We're taking back the academy, people! Let me hear you say, *Oh, yeah!*"

And the crowd goes wild.

☽

It's only five minutes into the math test and Brad is already trying to cheat.

I mean, it's subtle. Brad's an expert at subversive activities. But I can see it. I can tell.

Brad sits next to Jackson, and I can see him sneaking looks at Jackson's paper while Mr. Farrell reads a book at his desk, oblivious. Brad's technique is so good that Jackson doesn't even know what's going on. It's so unfair. I hate when burnouts get away with doing nothing, plus use people like me who actually do their work. It's like, *Yeah buddy. I'd like to sit in front of the TV for six hours every day, too. There's a reason I don't.*

Maybe there's a way to let Jackson know what's happening without Brad finding out. Ratting him out to Mr. Farrell isn't an option. Unless I want to coincidentally find everything in my locker totally destroyed or someone lurking outside my house. There has to be another way.

Someone has a bad cough. I hate how that's all embarrassing, when you're taking a test and you're sick and you have that dry-throat thing and you're coughing but trying not to so you start making those retching noises and everyone gives you evil looks. Or when your stomach is growling all loud and you cough to cover up the noise.

Coughing. Hmm.

I try coughing all ragged to see if that will make Jackson look up. Four people whip their heads around, but not Jackson. He's completely into those inverse functions. A nuclear bomb detonating in the hall wouldn't stop him. The boy is a machine.

Direct contact is the only way to do this.

I put down my mechanical pencil and reach into my bag for an old-school one. I do the legal looking reach where you unzip your bag all slowly to be quiet and watch the teacher while you're feeling around inside for what you want so he doesn't think you're scamming on some cheat sheet. But Mr. Farrell doesn't even look up from his book.

So then I get up to sharpen my pencil, but I time it so it's in between Brad's peeks. I already figured out he has this rhythmic pattern to his peeks going on. I sharpen my pencil and do a sideways glance at Brad. Then I start walking back to my desk. I decide to walk by Brad's desk, on the other side of Jackson.

The timing is perfect. Right when Brad is looking at Jackson's paper, I cough in this loud, spastic way. It works. Jackson snaps out of his test haze and glares at me. And he totally catches Brad looking right at his paper.

But Jackson's not stupid, either. He knows what will happen if he tells Mr. Farrell. So he slides his paper to the other side of his desk and tilts his desk away so Brad has no chance of seeing.

I sit down and sneak a look over at Brad to see if he knew I had anything to do with it. He's clueless.

A few minutes later, I look over again. Jackson snaps his head around to see if Brad is still trying to cheat off him. Then Brad mouths something to Jackson that makes my arms break out in goose bumps.

He goes, *You're dead.*

☾

We just had ten minutes to discuss who we picked for our poetry projects. Which basically means Tatyana and I spent nine and a half minutes gossiping about what happened with Mr. Pearlman and the lettuce thing and thirty seconds on what we were supposed to be talking about.

When it was Tatyana's turn to explain about her project, she pushed over a poem by Allen Ginsberg, copied onto gorgeous stationery in her arty script. The poem was about a llama with a bamboo backscratcher.

Enough said.

Then she asked me about the sidewalk thing and I admitted it. Which I'm not worried about. She knows how to keep a secret. Anyway, she was in the middle of telling me something about it, but we had to break up.

Now we're supposed to be writing a description of our project ideas. We have to justify why we picked who we picked. So far I have three sentences.

Rhiannon Ferrara   English Lit
Period 5   Ms. Portman

The most compelling characteristic of E. E. Cummings is that he refused to be confined by society's expectations of what poetry should be. During the process of shaping artistic expression in a way that changed how the world perceives the realm of poetry, he dissolved predetermined creative restrictions. Thus, he exemplified the importance of taking risks.

I tap my pen on my notebook. I lean over to Tatyana.

"How long does this have to be?" I whisper.

"One page," she whispers back.

Hmm. Maybe I should put in part of my favorite poem. That'll take up like four more lines. And I don't write huge or use ridiculous margins like some wingnuts around here.

I flip back in my English section for my favorite E. E. Cummings poem. I pick out the best parts and write them down.

> *i fear*
> *no fate (for you are my fate, my sweet)*
> *and it's you are whatever a moon has always meant*
> *and whatever a sun will always sing is you*
> *i carry your heart (i carry it in my heart)*

I'm trying to think of what to write next when a note flies over my desk. The note was apparently supposed to land on my desk, but Tatyana spazzed and now it's on Jackson's desk.

Fabulous.

Tatyana is trying not to laugh, but it isn't exactly working for her. She's hysterical, smooshing her hands over her face and hoping Ms. Portman won't see. Meanwhile, I'm giving her a look like, *How hard is it to aim a note at the right desk?*

I glance over at Jackson, waiting for him to toss me back the note. But that's not what happens. What happens is that Jackson unfolds the note.

What a dick!

He sees Tatyana having a conniption. I can imagine what's going through his head. He's thinking she's laughing at him and, therefore, the note is all about him. Jackson has been picked on for being a geek for as long as I can remember. He's used to this kind of treatment by now. I don't even know what the note says. But I'm pretty sure it's about the sidewalk-chalk thing, since Tatyana got interrupted when she was trying to say something else about it. Which means that in about three seconds, Jackson will know I did it.

Not that people didn't figure it out. But as long as it's just a rumor, I can't get in trouble for graffiti. If the note's about that, it means there's hard evidence on paper that I did it and Jackson could get me in trouble.

"Here," I whisper to him. I hold out my hand.

No chance. He's reading it.

Tatyana notices what's going on. That shuts her up. Her eyes get huge.

Jackson shoves the note into his binder and goes back to work.

I hiss, "Give it back!"

But he totally ignores me.

I rip off a corner of the next page in my notebook and write:

What did you write?

I pass the note to Tatyana. Then I try to get Jackson's attention. He ignores me.

Tatyana passes the note back. Now it says:

It was about the sidewalk-chalk thing. Just that I'm really proud of you and I respect how you did that. You GO, sista gurl!!! Woo!!! Oh, and how Steve is a butt munch.

I write:

This sucks! Now he can totally turn me in.

She writes:

Why would he, though?

I write:

I don't know. But then why isn't he giving it back???

My nerves are twanging to the extreme. I jump when the bell rings.

"Hand in your papers on the way out!" Ms. Portman yells over the noise of everyone suddenly talking. Mine is, naturally, still incomplete.

☽

"But why would Jackson do that?" Nicole says.

"I wish I knew."

"God." She slams her locker shut. "What is his *damage?*"

We just can't figure out why Jackson kept that note. Why would he want to get me in trouble? I try to think if I've ever been mean to him. I can't think of anything.

"Anyway," Nicole says. "I'm sure he's just being his usual weird self. No worries."

"I hope so." I really wish this were the only crisis I had to worry about. Because the humiliation from yesterday has seeped into my skin so deep I can barely feel anything else.

Nicole knows. She's like, "Forget Steve. He's so beneath you I can't even with it."

"Yeah."

"He's going to be kicking himself that he let you go. Seriously. He'll be walking down the hall one day and see you go by, and he'll have to take his big stupid head and bang it into the wall, he'll be hating himself so much."

Everybody's been telling me to forget Steve. How he's totally lacking and a bonehead and not worth my time. And how it's not me, it's him. But, clearly, it was me. Because he dumped me. And he picked *her*. The spontaneous and exciting girl. The gorgeous and perfect girl.

I can't believe I was such an idiot. Here I was thinking it was all about Steve going away next year, when the whole time he just didn't love me the way I thought he did.

My brain won't stop playing a continuous loop over and over of 1.) Steve and Gloria making out in his room with John Mayer playing and 2.) the whole school laughing at me for writing that sidewalk-chalk message and 3.) every single sweet thing Steve ever did for me, all condensed into one humungous lie.

"Do you think my nose is too big?" I ask.

"What?"

"My nose? Would you get a nose job if you were me?"

"Where is this coming from?"

"Maybe I'm not pretty enough."

"Oh, yeah! I'm sure he broke up with you because of your nose. Which, by the way, is perfect."

"Maybe if I—"

"Look," Nicole interrupts. "You could be Marion and he wouldn't care. No one is good enough for him right now."

"Except Gloria."

"No, she's just some skanky ho-bag who he's gonna be over yesterday." She switches her bag from one shoulder to the other. "I am so over these boys. Who do they think they are? It's ridiculous what they get away with."

"Seriously." I can't wait to get home and take a nap. "Let's go."

"We're not leaving yet."

"Why?"

"We have a surprise for you."

"Really?"

"Um-hmm."

"Hey," James says, walking up to us. Danny's with him.

It must be really hard for Nicole, knowing Danny still likes her. Or maybe he even still loves her. I could never be just friends with someone I loved. We'd be hanging out and I'd want to kiss him and then what? But I guess Danny thought having part of something was better than having nothing at all.

"Hey, Nicole," Danny says.

"Hey, Danny," Nicole says.

Then there's this look between them. Nicole smiles a little at Danny. He smiles back.

"You guys ready?" James asks us.

Danny's cell rings. He flips it open and goes, "Talk to me."

"Okay," I say. "Can someone please tell me what's going on?"

"Not here," James says. "Let's go to Westville."

The four of us only go to Westville when something big is about to transpire. This is because Westville has the best hot dogs and fries anywhere. Which is the all-time best combination of comfort food to reduce stress. They even have these awesome veggie dogs for Danny.

"Wait," I say after they tell me about this note they found and their plan for how to use it. "We're supposed to meet back at school for this tonight?"

"Yeah," Nicole goes.

"How are we supposed to get in?"

"Aha!" Danny pulls his keys out and jangles them around. "Remember when the secretary gave me a key to come in on Saturdays? When I was doing that yearbook stuff?"

"Yeah?"

"Guess who still has the key?"

"She never asked for it back?" Nicole says. "That's so classic."

It really is. All the secretaries love Danny. To the point of giving him a key to the school and trusting him so much they forgot he even has it.

"So we're in," Danny reports.

"I don't know if this is such a good idea, you guys," I say.

"What are you talking about?" Nicole says. "It's totally brill."

"No, it is. And I appreciate it and everything, but—"

"If you're worried about getting caught, don't," James goes. "Because we won't."

"How do you know?"

"We thought of everything. There's a volleyball game tonight, but by seven everyone will be out of there. If we show up at seven thirty, no one will be around."

"Even the teachers with no lives who stay late," Danny adds.

"It's not just that," I go. "Isn't this unfair to Jackson?" The plan is all about Gloria getting back the same kind of energy she's been putting out, which is cool. Especially since I couldn't think of anything good and here it is, all planned out for me. But it also involves Jackson. And not in a good way.

"He might see it differently," Nicole says.

"Like how?"

"Well . . . it's not like he was the one who wrote the note."

"Yeah, but he doesn't deserve this. And wouldn't it just make him mad? Then he'll totally want to get me in trouble."

"But he wouldn't know you had anything to do with this," James explains. "If he's going to turn you in, it'll happen regardless."

"He doesn't have anything on you anyway," Danny says. "It's not like that note had your name on it. Anyone could have written it, right?"

I think.

"Right?"

"I don't know. I didn't see if it had my name. Or if it was signed."

"Even with names, anyone could have written it," Nicole says. "Like a setup. It doesn't prove anything."

This is definitely the type of thing that is huge enough to get Gloria's attention. This would really make her think about the way she treats people.

"Oh!" Danny yells. "And it's so karma! How Jackson took your note and then he dropped this one? *Yes!*"

I'm still not completely convinced, though. Wouldn't I get blamed for it? Half the school saw what happened with Gloria and Steve in the cafeteria. "Okay, but—"

"We've got it covered," James says. "No worries."

They all look so determined. I know they have their own reasons for doing this, too.

I guess that's it, then. I wanted to find a way, and here it is. My best friends found it for me.

☽

When I go back to school because I forgot my dirty gym clothes, I see them outside the locker room. Steve has Gloria pressed up against the wall. And they're kissing. He's kissing her the same way he used to kiss me.

That's it. Now I'm way beyond angry.

Because maybe the breakup was all about Steve instead of me being lacking in some way. It's like Brooke was saying about the whole manwhore phenomenon. Maybe there's nothing wrong with me. I'm probably fine the way I am. In fact, I *know* I am. Wasn't I a confident person before The Incident? How could I let him change me like that?

☽

Brooke's leaving for Europe tomorrow. You'd think Dad would take us all out for dinner tonight to say good-bye. But no. He's still grumbling about how Brooke dissed the whole internship opportunity. So he's at work, same with Mom, and Brooke and I are celebrating with Chinese food for the second night in a row in front of the TV. Since *Sex and the City* is Brooke's favorite show, we're watching a DVD from season four.

Brooke sticks her chopsticks into my box of chow fun. She goes, "So I finally met a real man."

I choke on a noodle. That's, like, the last thing I ever thought I'd hear from her.

She holds up my glass. "Water?"

I grab my glass and glug the water. "You *what*?" I gasp.

"You heard me."

"Is this for real?"

"It seems real."

Um-hmm. I've been there.

"Proceed with caution," I warn.

"Will you just let me tell you?"

So of course it's this eternal story about how she went out last night with a bunch of friends. They were in this random bar she didn't even want to go to, and there he was. He came up to her and they talked for a really long time and when he asked for her number, she gave it to him. Which she never does. She always takes the guy's number instead, for safety reasons.

But she was just so swept away that she gave it to him. And things were going great and they walked outside to leave, and that's when she freaked out. Because what if he never called her? What if he was asking for her number just to get it?

So he was saying bye, and she was so freaked out that she started walking the wrong way. To go *home*. And there was something about a bus almost running her over, but I'm not really clear on that part. So now she's all paranoid that he'll never call her because she acted like such a goober.

She's like, "And naturally this has to happen right when I'm leaving for six weeks."

"Don't worry. If he likes you that much, he'll call you when you get back."

"Yeah, right. Him and his new girlfriend. Arrggg!" Brooke slams her box of fried wontons down on the coffee table. "This is so *frustrating*!"

"Relax. He'll call."

She calms down a little. She looks over at me. "You think?"

"Definitely. It sounds like he likes you for sure."

"Really?"

"Totally."

We start a new episode since we pretty much talked through the last one.

"Oh, and thanks for the Cinnabon last weekend," I say. "Sorry I was so out of it. . . . Did I even say thanks?"

"No. But you're thanking the wrong person."

"What?"

"It wasn't me. I was just getting out of the shower, remember?"

"Then who—?"

"James! James brought it." Brooke gives me a look like, *How dense can you get?* "I thought you knew."

We start watching again. This is the one where Aidan moves in with Carrie and they keep fighting about stupid stuff. I mean, to them, in the moment, it all seems important. But by the end of the episode they realize that those things don't matter. What really matters isn't where someone puts their stuff or how much closet space someone is taking up. What really matters is who a person is. And how you feel when you're with them.

☽

Danny lets us in the back door.

"So what's the game plan?" James says.

James and Danny went to Kinko's after school and made one thousand copies of the note. They used five different paper colors. There's enough for everyone to get a copy on their locker, plus we can put them up around the entire school. We're naturally at risk for getting in serious trouble, but it's so worth it.

"Why don't we split up by area," I suggest. "Like, someone can put one on each locker, someone can do the halls, someone can do the stairways, and then someone can do the bathrooms and locker rooms."

"That's cool," Nicole says.

"Did you get the ladder?" James asks Danny. He had this epiphany at Westville that we should hang a bunch of copies really high up so teachers won't be able to rip them down. I said how no one would be able to read them that high up, but Danny said it would make a statement. He's all fired up about how this whole thing's making a major statement. That and the karma thing. Because Danny knows what Gloria said when Nicole was trying to do that problem in math. And how she humiliated me in front of everyone at lunch. So those fiascos plus skanking around with Steve equals Danny's unwavering determination to expose the truth.

"No," Danny tells him. "The janitors were already gone."

"What about doing classrooms?" James says.

"Bad idea. The teachers will be pissed."

"Like they're not gonna be pissed anyway?"

"Yeah, but that'll make it worse. I like Rhiannon's idea."

Nicole gives everyone two rolls of tape. Then we each take a pile of copies.

"Wait!" Danny yells. "Group huddle!"

We scrunch together in a circle. Danny puts his hand out. We take turns slapping our hands, one on top of the other. Then Danny goes, "One, two, three—*break!*" And we're off.

I'm in charge of lockers. I tape one copy to every locker, mixing the colors randomly. I was going to alternate the colors in order, but I've decided to live a little.

☽

When I get back to my room, I take down every single picture of Steve from around my mirror. I don't cry. I don't think about the good times we had when each picture was taken. I just take them down, rip them up, and throw them away.

CHAPTER 15

Friday

FURIOUS **IS NOT** the word to describe Gloria.

Rabid dog foaming at mouth seeking death as vengeance is a slightly more accurate description.

We all knew she would come after me. And probably turn me in. So when the main office secretary comes on the PA and announces that I have to report to the principal's office, I'm not exactly the most surprised person in the room.

"Sit down, Rhiannon," Mr. Pearlman orders. He's into the dictatorial approach to being a principal. Because, you know. Being friendly just wouldn't be more effective.

He indicates a chair.

I sit.

"Now, as you're probably aware, we seem to have a problem today."

I wait.

"It seems that someone hung copies of a note Gloria wrote . . ."
He rustles through some papers. "Two years ago? All around the building."

He stares at me for a response. So I say, "I've noticed."

"It also seems that this someone had access to the building after school was officially closed for the night."

He stares again. What, does he expect me to crack just because he's staring? Is he trying to make me nervous with his beady eyes and spooky moustache?

"It's come to my attention," he continues, "that you might have had a hand in this. Is that true?"

Okay. The plan was that if they came after me, I would deny everything. There's no way they can prove I did it. It could have been any one of Gloria's enemies. But what if he knows something else and he's not telling? And if I say I didn't do it and he busts out with evidence, I'll be screwed worse than if I admitted it right away. And if I lie and he finds out, he'll be wicked pissed and might suspend me. And if anything gets in the way of me eventually getting into Parsons School of Design, I won't be a happy unit.

"Is that true, Rhiannon?"

I open my mouth to say it. And that's when James comes bursting through the door.

And he says, "I did it."

☽

Normally the ivy outside my window is just a bunch of dead branches in a twisty pattern. But now the leaves are thriving.

It's like the ivy has finally come back to life. Just like me.

Nicole flops onto my beanbag chair and says, "I love me some Friday."

"I feel you," I say. This week could not have been longer. I'm looking forward to the dance tonight. But I'm not looking forward to seeing Steve and Gloria there. Just because I'm moving on doesn't mean I don't still feel hurt.

"Wasn't Danny awesome?" Danny's speech is, like, the only thing Nicole's been talking about for the past hour. And yeah, it was amazing. He's totally winning the election. But I'm getting over it already. Especially since James was even more awesome.

I swear, the National Honor Society kids get away with everything. Just because James is this physics/calculus/engineering genius and like second in our class and all the teachers love him, he got away with it. It's amazing. If anyone else even looked at the principal wrong, they'd get detention for a week (citation: inappropriate facial expression). But James barges right into the principal's office and admits he did it, and they don't do anything to him. Incredible. But it was still amazing for him to do that. No one told me that was how I wouldn't get in trouble.

"Yes. Danny was awesome. Now can we change the subject?" I sit down at my desk and open my lists journal. I read over the list I made last Saturday. The one called "Top Five Things I Miss About Steve." It feels like I wrote this a million years ago. As I read it, I realize that all these things aren't about who he is, they're about what we did together. Things that I could do with someone else who will actually feel lucky to be with me.

Nicole's like, "Can I just say how proud I am, and go you?"

"And add it to the five million times you already told me?" Nicole has not stopped raving about how awesome the sidewalk-chalk thing was. Even though it didn't work out. That's not what matters. What matters is that I did it. And in its own way, it rocked. "Okay!"

"So was that the first thing you ever did that wasn't scheduled in your day planner like a week in advance?"

"No!" I huff. But of course it was. I'm proud of me, too. Proud and mortified.

Snickers walks onto Nicole's stomach and purrs like an airplane engine. He starts digging his claws into her shirt.

"Ow ow *ow*!" Nicole tries to pry his claws out. "Get him off!"

"Snick!" I pick him up, his claws still sticking into her shirt. She yanks her shirt back down.

"Can you believe it about Gloria?"

"Only because you were there." Nicole ran into Gloria in the bathroom and she was actually *crying*. Like a real person or something. "I almost feel bad for her."

"Please. That girl is getting everything she deserves."

"I know but . . . maybe we shouldn't have done it. It's just, everything was happening so fast yesterday. I didn't have time to think."

"Yeah, that's the point. You were being impulsive! Isn't that how you said you wanted to be?"

"Maybe but . . . if being impulsive means ruining other people's lives, then maybe I should just stay the same."

"Or maybe you should be who you want to be and stop making excuses."

I don't want to get in a fight. I know she's right, anyway. Which is annoying. So I go over to my iBook and click on my day-planner widget. I have to get my life back on track. Order as an antidote to chaos. Calm after the storm.

"Ree," I hear from the beanbag.

"Yeah."

"It's Friday night. There's a dance. Can you chill with the anal-retentive tendencies for one night, please?"

Of course she's right. I've been an organization freak my whole life, and where did it get me? I thought I had control over something that went crazy. I thought following a straight road would lead me right to my destination. Like the road would just take me there because I was following all the rules. And if the road curved, I couldn't be sure about where I was going. But look where it got me.

Maybe it's time for a detour.

☽

Everybody's at the dance. Some dances turn out to be lame, but half the school is here. They're playing some dead house music, though, so not a lot of people are dancing. But then the Gorillaz come on and "Dare" is playing and everyone pours onto the dance floor. All the boys are grinding against all the girls. The chaperones don't even try to break it up, because how do you break up an entire gym of horny, grinding kids? So they look anywhere but at the dance floor, pretending it's not happening.

And then Tony starts doing this crazy dance he invented in ninth grade that he busts out at every dance and party. Random people are yelling at him.

"Aw, *hell* no!"

"Tony! You've been with that dance for like three years!"

"He wildin'!"

"Dude! Get a new dance!"

"Try some Chicken Noodle! It just came out in Harlem!"

I like watching everyone going crazy. All free and uninhibited and not caring how they look. Just having fun.

And then I see Jackson over by the snack table. I didn't get a chance to tell him how sorry I am that he got caught up in the middle of all this. We had a test in English and he bolted after. I feel so bad. Worse than bad. I should go over to him and apologize for being such a loser.

But then he walks toward me and my stomach does this nervous, fluttery thing. Will he give me back my note, or tell me he turned me in?

"If you do this, then we'll call it even," Jackson says.

"What is it?"

"Well, um . . ." He looks over toward the bleachers where some kids are sitting. "You know Heather, right?"

"Yeah. She's my partner in Earth Science."

"Yeah. I know."

"Then why'd you ask?"

"No, I was . . . just checking."

I wait for him to tell me. He looks miserable.

"Do you like her or something?"

He scuffs his shoe on the floor. It squeaks against the polish. He doesn't answer me.

"So . . . what do you want me to do?"

"Could you just . . . like . . . go over and say I want to talk to her?"

"That's it?"

"Yeah. And then tell me what she says."

"And if I do it, you won't tell on me."

"Right."

202 TAKE ME THERE

"And I can have my note back?"

"Yeah."

"Okay. Deal."

Jackson puts his hand out and we shake on it.

"I didn't mean to keep your note," he says. "I just did it because I wasn't sure if you'd help me with Heather without a reason, you know?"

"Oh. That's okay."

"Anyway . . ."

"So . . . I'll go over now?"

"Okay. I'll be over by the water fountain."

"Okay. And hey . . . Jackson?"

"Yeah?"

"I'm really sorry about what happened. I never meant to... I didn't mean for it to be anything bad against you."

"I know."

"You do?"

"Yeah. And, anyway, it got me noticed. Or I think it did." He looks over at Heather again. I guess she talked to him today or something. Which just proves that even in a bad situation, there's always a positive side. Even if you can't see it yet.

☽

An hour later it's still a blast, with the music blaring and Nicole and Danny doing their corny John Travolta *Saturday Night Fever* moves, and even James seems into it. But when Steve and Gloria get here, it hits me all over again. I'm just not ready to see them together yet.

Nicole runs over to me. "Do you want something? There's cookies."

I just stand there, staring at them.

"Or . . . juice?"

I so want to be over it already. Too bad that can't happen overnight.

Then someone's arm is around my shoulders and I know it's James. It's amazing how he has this way of knowing right when I need him, even before I do.

"Hey," he says. "Wanna go?"

"Yesterday, if not sooner." I glance at Nicole. "Coming?"

"No, you guys go ahead," she says. "I'm staying with Danny."

I smile at her. "Oh?"

"I'll call you tomorrow."

"Ready?" James goes.

"Yeah," I tell him.

James keeps his arm around me as we walk out. But when we get outside, Danny comes running up to us. "Wait up!" He looks back and forth between me and James. He's like, "Where are you guys going?"

James shrugs. "I don't know. I guess . . ." He glances over at me. "The pier?"

"Yeah," I say.

Danny looks disappointed.

James goes, "What?"

"You guys," Danny starts, "are always doing the same things. You go to the pier. You take walks. You play games. You get cupcakes."

I look at James to see his reaction to all of this. I had no idea he told Danny everything we did.

"It's time to break out of that tired routine!" Danny shouts. "Where's the excitement? Where's the spontaneity?"

I can't answer him. I don't know where those things are.

"That's it," Danny decides. "We're going out."

James is like, "We are?"

"Absolutely."

"When?"

"What do you mean *when*? Now! Right now! *Carpe diem*, yo!"

"Where?" James says.

Danny flaps his hands around in front of his face. "Who cares? It doesn't matter! What matters is that we take advantage of all of this and just *go*!"

"I'm in," I decide.

James is like, "You're *in*?"

"I'm in."

"Sweet!" Danny says. "I'll go get Nicole."

By the time we're at this rad bar that's having an under-twenty-one thing, I'm having so much fun that I start to remember what it feels like to be happy. We're all chilling on this comfy furniture and listening to this awesome band and drinking root beers. Although Danny somehow managed to score a real beer for himself. And I'm all squooshed up against James on this tiny love seat and for the first time ever, I notice he's wearing cologne.

"Are you wearing cologne?" I yell.

"What?!" he yells back. Because you can barely hear a person talking to you right in front of your face, the music is so loud.

"Are you wearing cologne?!"

"Who's Ramón?!"

I shake my head to forget it. It's obvious that he is, anyway. He's probably just too embarrassed to admit it.

☽

So of course we still walk to the pier after. Nicole and Danny went somewhere else together. I'm all hyped up on the adrenaline rush from the bar and the music and just the whole night. Being wild and free. The city energy.

The moon is so bright. And the sky is really clear, so I can see some constellations. The stars make me feel better. They're reassuring. I'm going to be okay.

I love how everything feels so perfect here. The pier. The view. The gorgeous night. The moon.

"Look." I point at it. I jump up and down like I'm five, all excited.

"I know." James smiles.

"What?"

"Just . . . you and your moon."

We're standing at the edge of the water. Only a few other people are here. It's so nice out. All the lights are reflected in the water and there's a warm breeze. Plus, the moon is so bright. But it seems like there's something wrong with James. Like he's nervous or something.

"What's wrong?" I ask him.

"Nothing. Well . . . I guess there is something. Since you're asking and all."

"What?"

"There's no light show."

"What?"

He points to the building in Jersey City with the slanty top—my favorite building across the water that has the light stripes. But tonight, there's no light show. The building is all dark.

"Oh. That sucks."

"Big-time."

"Maybe it'll start later."

"It better."

He's so cute when he does that. He acts all interested in the things I love like he loves them just as much. I always thought he was kidding. But now it kind of feels like he's serious.

I want to sit here and watch the moon and wait for the lights to start. "Do you want to sit?"

"Um . . . I was thinking of . . . not sitting."

"And doing what? You want to walk more?"

"Not exactly." James takes his iPod out of his pocket.

"What are you doing?"

"You'll see."

He takes one earbud and puts it in my ear. I reach up to fit it into my ear better. Then he puts the other one in his ear and rubs his finger against the iPod dial.

My stomach feels gurgly all of a sudden. The vibe between us is instantly different.

James selects a song and puts his hand out for me to dance with him. We've never done anything even remotely like this.

"Look What You've Done" starts playing. I can't believe he remembers this. I always listen to this song whenever I feel bad. It's like my theme song for starting over again.

I move against him. It makes me feel safe. We dance. James puts his hand on my waist. I lean my head against his shoulder. We turn slowly.

Usually, I cry when I hear this song. It's like a healing thing. But for the first time, I don't cry. I feel strong. James makes me feel strong. He twirls me halfway around and pulls me against him so my back is pressing up against his chest.

I get that blurry sensation of slow motion like I had yesterday. But this time, in a good way. My arm falls backward around his neck.

And that's when everything changes.

I sort of lean back into him. Like I'm melting into him. And in that instant, I finally know what it feels like to be whole. I've been wishing for my life to get better. Now I realize that James can take me to a place where everything's the way it should be. He can definitely take me there.

So when I turn around to face him, I don't think about it at all. I just kiss him. And he kisses me back.

And everything I knew about the world, everything that was so familiar to me, is suddenly different.

And the lights come on.

And the music plays.

And the night moves.

And then I hear wind chimes. Which is my text ringtone. Dang phone has to go and ruin everything. Why didn't I turn it off before?

"Let me turn this off," I say, reaching into my bag.

"It's a text?"

"Yeah. Sorry." I flip my cell open. "It's from Nicole. Why is she—?" I press VIEW. "Oh my god."

"What?"

My heart sinks. Something horrible just happened.

Because Nicole's message says: **help me.**

CAN I JUST say that if I'm still going to have days like this when I grow up, I should kill myself now?

I look alarmingly fat in everything I've tried on, I'm majorly PMSing, and my mood is type nasty. And all for no apparent reason, which is the funnest part of all. But watch. Half an hour from now? I'll probably be feeling excellent. Which will at least make some sense. But not now. Now I feel crusty.

It's just a bad morning. A bad morning where nothing is going right which had to start off, naturally, with no hot water for optimum suckage. Which P.S.? Never happened when we lived upstate, but for some sketch reason happens in the city a lot. I think it has to do with corroded boilers or some such. There was even a day last week when Jessica didn't come to school because she didn't have hot water until like four o'clock and she couldn't take a shower.

And I'm noticing the worst of everything. Like waiting for the subway? How no one looks like they want to go to work. Everyone seems less than thrilled to be breathing. And then there's this guy who always has to spit on the tracks every morning. And it's not just normal spitting. Not that spitting in public is ever normal, but he does it so loud you can hear it halfway down the platform. Just hacking up a major loogie like he's alone in the privacy of his own bathroom or something. It's like, *Don't mind us. We're just here.* And those American-flag decals they stuck on all the subway trains after September 11 are all dingy now with tunnel dirt and . . . just everything.

Sometimes it takes all the energy I have not to scream.

❀

It goes like this.

Before math I go out to the courtyard and the sidewalk message is all smudged and you can hardly even read it anymore and I knew we should have taken a picture of it last night. And there are some kids hanging out who I know are seniors, but I ask if they're seniors anyway. And this one girl is like, yeah. So then I ask if they know what happened to the message.

And she's like, "That was *you*?" And she's kind of looking at me like I'm Madonna or something.

So I say, "No, I was just wondering who smudged it."

And she says that's how it was when they came out. But then someone else says the word on the street is that Steve erased it. And it looks like it's going to rain any second, and I feel so bad for Rhiannon.

❀

"Okay, let's take out the homework!"

You can totally tell who did their homework and who's trying to front like they did but actually has no idea what topic we're even on. It's all about the body language. The kids who did their homework are sitting all casually and yawning and looking unconcerned, while the kids who didn't are trying to look all competent and alert and like they actually know what they're doing so maybe Mr. Farrell won't call on them. Too bad for them he has excellent slacker radar.

He's wearing my favorite shoes today. And I know from feeling how the expression on my face probably looks that I'm drooling over him like he's a glass of water and I've been stranded in the Sahara all week. But I can't help myself. I never can.

Mr. Farrell's calling on people to answer specific questions about the homework problems while I'm spacing out. All these images are racing through my head, like a million a second, and I'm looking at the clock and seeing these images, and it's like someone is editing a film in my brain and the reel is on fast-forward.

The clock goes tick. *Tick* I see us holding hands walking down the hall with everyone noticing us *tick* eating lunch together in the teachers' lounge *tick* us taking the subway home together every day *tick* me doing homework at his place on the couch while he grades papers *tick* me talking to him on the phone in bed *tick* me going over to his place with some magic square cookies I just made for him *tick* we're in his bed going to sleep and he's spooning me *tick* we're at the beach this summer in the water and he's splashing me *tick* we're kissing on the street as the whole world walks by *tick.*

"Nicole?" he's saying.

I look up in a daze. He's staring at me. Everyone else is staring at me. Like they all can tell what I was thinking. I'm gripping the sides of my desk like it's a life preserver and I'm floating out to sea. It's obvious he asked me a question but I don't know the answer, don't even know what the question was, so I'm like, "Yeah?"

But instead of drilling me for not paying attention the way he would with anyone else, he just goes, "Can you tell us how you got your answer for seventy-three?"

My mouth is all dry and I let go of the sides of my desk and blood rushes back into my fingers and I turn my paper over and I read it out.

And then after we go over the homework, we're doing these problem sets in pairs and there's no way I can stay in this chair. I have to go up there. I have to talk to him. And there's a way to do it that might even pass as vaguely legit.

It's like ever since this obsession with Mr. Farrell started, I've been compelled to do things that I know must look totally strange and hyper, but the inevitable embarrassment doesn't stop me from doing them anyway. It's like my body just starts moving and I have to go along with it because I don't have a choice, something else has control over me. Something's pulling at me, like I'm a magnetic shard and he's due north.

So I stand up even though I don't really want to, with my legs feeling all wobbly, and I walk to the front of the room. Then I go up to his desk and stand there like a total and complete dweeb. That's the heinous thing about having no control. There's no time to plan out what you're going to do once you get there.

He's like, "Yes, Nicole?" and it's so obvious after yesterday that he wants me. I mean, the things he said to me after school when he was supposed to be tutoring me but we just sat around talking for like two hours instead were not the types of things you say to someone you're not interested in.

So yeah. I'm all stammering like, "It's—my pencil ran out."

And he's like, "So you'd like to borrow another one?" As if he doesn't know why I'm really here or what I really want.

And all I can think to say is, "Yes. Please." And I must sound like the biggest nimrod alive.

But he just says, "Here you go," and holds out a new pencil and smiles at me and everything is way obvious, but at the same time we have to pretend like it's not and the whole thing is so ridiculous and juvenile.

So I say thanks.

Then he's like, "By the way, I've been meaning to ask you something."

And I'm all, "Oh?" But I'm thinking, *Doesn't he know that the kids in the front row can totally hear?* But he just wants to know if I ever figured out this super hard problem he gave me yesterday. I tell him that I haven't gotten a chance to figure it out yet, and he says, "Be sure to let me know when you do." And he smiles at me again. That's two smiles in less than a minute.

So I take a risk and smile back and hope that everyone can tell what's going on, because I want the whole world to know that there's something between us. Not like I have to advertise. It being so obvious and all. So we're just kind of chilling there, smiling at each other, and then he says, "Is that all?"

And I'm like, "Hmm? Oh! No, yeah it is. I'll just be going back to my seat now."

So I'm walking back and I pass Ree and she's looking at me queerly and I mouth, *What?* But whatever it is she's thinking, she doesn't say.

❀

I need some serious recovery time from math even though it was two periods ago. It's like every time I'm even in the same room with him, every part of my body is wired. Plus I heard about what happened with Ree at lunch. And how Gloria was such a mega bitch, all shouting her out like that. I tried to call Ree's cell, but she had it turned off. I don't even know where she went for the rest of lunch. And now she's in English, so I can't exactly barge in there and demand to talk to her.

When I push open the bathroom door, there's Gloria. She's at the mirror doing her makeup. Apparently, no one has ever told her that matching your eye shadow to your outfit every day is just plain wrong.

So I'm standing there staring at her like, *Who the fuck does this skank think she is?* And her eyes meet mine in the mirror and she's like, "You got a problem?"

And all I want to say is you're my problem and everyone else's problem and how can you just steal someone's boyfriend like it's nothing? And humiliate me in front of everyone? In *math*?

But I don't want to get into it with her like this, so what I actually say is, "Not really."

And she's like, "Then why you all up in my grill?"

It's obvious she's trying to provoke a fight and I'm not having that. So I just wash my hands and she's all, "That's what I thought."

The thing about Gloria? Is that she comes off all polished and smooth on the outside, but she's got this badass gangsta attitude like you can't believe. I mean, we all know it's there because we have the pleasure of experiencing her evil ways, but sometimes it still surprises you how intense she is. Like the time she got in a fight during the racial-tolerance assembly last year. Scary, yo.

She's doing eyeliner and not even looking at me and she goes, "Loser."

Gloria is so wrong I just can't with her. There has to be a way where she can finally get how nasty she's being to everyone. But it has to be something intense or else she won't care. Gloria only cares about Gloria. So it has to be something that involves her in some way for her to even pay attention. I just wish I knew what that something was.

And I don't want to just walk out of here without doing anything. I want to tell her to stop it with Steve. But it's not like she's forcing him or anything, so what can I really do about it? I can't make Gloria transform herself into a person with an understanding of ethics just like I can't force Steve to feel something he doesn't feel anymore.

So I pull open the door and walk away. The same way I wish I could walk away from all my other problems.

❀

It's raining so bad outside that it looks like we're on a movie set and the prop guys are OD'ing with the rain machine. So they better reshoot this scene or else no audience will ever take it seriously.

I rummage in my bag for my umbrella and I actually find it. But it's one of those mini collapsible ones and this is basically a monsoon-type situation. So when I get the umbrella open and step outside, the wind immediately whips the umbrella around and the underside flips up and I try to grab the edge and pull it back down but it's not working. And then Danny comes up next to me with his huge umbrella that could fit like five people under it that's hardly even flapping in the wind and goes, "Nice umbrella."

So I'm like, "Thanks."

And he's all, "Can I walk you to the subway?" And I'm not exactly interested in having my clothes totally soaked, so I say okay.

At first we're walking with space between us, but my bag is getting wet and Danny sees. So he puts his arm around my waist and it feels really nice, all pressed up against him. And I ask if he's seen Rhiannon and he says no, but he heard that she left early. And I'm like, "Are you sure?" Because Rhiannon would never do that. And he's like, "No, but that's what I heard." And my sneakers are totally soaked and the puddles on the sidewalk are unreal and if Danny hadn't shown up when he did, I just don't even know.

But then I start to feel weird, like this is how we used to be when we were going out and now we're just friends so what does it mean? I'm like super aware of our hips touching and everything. And I guess Danny is noticing that my vibe has changed or something because he's like, "What's up?"

So I tell him about what Gloria said in the bathroom and what she did to me in math and how she can't keep treating people like this. He's all, "I wish I'd been there."

I'm like, "What would you have done?"

He goes, "I would have defended you. It makes me so freaking pissed that she said that stuff to you."

And I can tell he really means it. Danny would have definitely protected me from her evil ways.

He's like, "And Gloria's so fake. That whole Jackson thing? How's she gonna front like she's above it?"

I'm all, "Huh?"

He's all, "You know. How she liked Jackson."

And then I step right in this huge puddle. I'm like, "Jackson *Smith*?" Because there's no way an image-obsessed prom queen like Gloria would ever be into anyone even remotely geeky. And especially not Jackson, mega-geek extraordinaire.

It's really raining hard and plus it's windy, so even with Danny's huge umbrella we're still getting wet.

He goes, "Do you want to get a coffee?"

We're passing Joe, which usually has zero free tables. But since it's a weekday afternoon and most people are at work, there's an empty one. And my whole sneaker is soaked and the subway is half a block from here and I want to hear about Jackson. So I say, "Sure."

After we get set up, Danny tells me this whole thing about how when he used to hang with Jackson freshman year, Jackson and Gloria went out. On the DDL, of course. So Danny's in Jackson's room one day while this is going on, and Jackson's sworn to secrecy by Gloria not to tell anyone. But naturally Jackson's giving Danny the play-by-play because, hello, if you were Jackson and Gloria liked you, wouldn't you be renting a billboard about it?

And then Jackson told his parents about Gloria after she was over one time. They just assumed he was helping her with homework, and even after he told them they didn't really believe him. Supposedly, Jackson's parents don't care about anything if it doesn't have to do with school. And there's all this pressure for him to get into Harvard like his dad, and he never wanted to be such a nerd. He wants to be badass and edgy, because that's how he really feels inside and that's the part of him he wants everyone to see. Plus, it's like the only way his parents would pay attention to him as a real person is if he acted like a real kid.

Danny's like, "Maybe if he got in trouble like normal kids, then his parents would wake up. Realize how miserable he is, just studying all the time."

I'm all, "That's heavy."

"Yeah. Um. So how did I get on this again?"

"You were talking about how his parents didn't believe it about Gloria—"

"Exactly! So a few weeks ago, we were sitting next to each other in the computer lab." And then he says how this note falls out of Jackson's binder but he doesn't even notice. So after Jackson leaves, Danny picks the note up off the floor, and it's this total love letter from Gloria! It's from back when everything was going down between them. And it's all mushy and like how Jackson is so special and she loves him so much and what they have is too personal to share with the world and yadda yadda hoo-ha.

I'm like, "Whoa."

And Danny's like, "Seriously."

"Do you still have it?"

"I'm not sure. Maybe." He thinks about it, and then he goes, "Wait. Yeah, maybe I do. Because I remember using the back of it to take notes on this stuff about Easter eggs."

"Um . . ."

"No, DVD Easter eggs. They're like these hidden clues where you can click on different things when a DVD is playing to get special features."

"Really? Like what?"

"You can get Memento to play backward."

"Word?"

"No lie."

"Wow, so . . . you might still have it?"

"I have to check."

"Can you bring it in tomorrow if you find it?"

"Yeah. Why?"

"I think we could use it."

"Oh!" Danny grabs his head like his brain's about to explode. "Oh, that is *so* righteous! You're on fire!"

And then there's this kind of awkward silence, because did he mean I'm on fire like I'm just having really good ideas? Or I'm on fire like I'm hot?

But I guess it's the idea one because then he's like, "You know what? I think I still have it! Because I think I found it the other day when I was going through this pile of papers."

So I go, "Yeah. I can definitely relate about piles."

And he's like, "I know."

And then there's another awkward silence while we just sit there, looking at each other for a while. Trying to figure out what the other person is thinking.

Then we finish our coffees and the rain is a little better, so Danny walks me the rest of the way to my subway stop. And I just feel like I miss him. I miss him not being a bigger part of my life, the way he used to be, when I could never imagine my life without him.

❁

The first thing I do when I get home is flip open my laptop and look up his address. And of course he lives like seven blocks from me. And of course I have to go see his building and figure out what window apartment 1B is and hope it's facing the street.

So I put on my black hoodie and escape without Mom trapping me for a round of Twenty Questions I Really Don't Feel Like Answering Now But Thanks Anyway. And on the walk over my heart is pounding really hard and my hands are getting sweaty and I'm so nervous that he'll see me and I'm so nervous that he won't and if he sees me I will die of embarrassment because when am I ever on his block?

When I find his building, it has two apartments facing the street on the first floor. The window on the left side of the front door is lit, but the window on the right is dark. Which obviously means that the dark window is his, and he's not home because he's out with his girlfriend at some upscale bar, and later they'll come back to his place and do it all night. And then tomorrow I'll have to look at him knowing that he was up all night having sex with some lingerie model or one of those gorgeous businesswomen I see walking down the street around five thirty in their expensive suits and shiny hair and four-inch heels because they're all 5'4" and 100 pounds. And I'll have to look at him all inferior and lacking and knowing I'm 5'7" and probably 1,000 pounds, considering all the crap I was eating until recently.

Okay, but like maybe? That's not his window. Or it is, but he's just not home for some other reason. Like maybe he's out with a friend or at a coffeehouse somewhere grading papers. And I'm trying to remember where there's a coffeehouse around here, so maybe I can walk by the window really fast and check if he's in there.

But maybe that's not even his window. What if it's the other one and he's home and he's been peeking at me in between the blind slats this whole time? How long have I been standing here? He probably thinks I'm a freak!

I go up the stairs and look at the names on the doorbell list. And there it is. My heart thumps fast. *Farrell 1B.* In the middle of this city, in the serious moonlight, right down the street from where I've lived all this time, he's here. He walks down this street and he climbs up these stairs every day and he lives right here.

So I'm trying to figure out what to do (like obviously, I'm not about to ring his bell or hang out across the street and see if he leaves or comes home) and then suddenly someone is climbing the stairs and I have to make an executive decision. Do I follow her in as if I live here and I'm looking for my key? I start moving things around in my bag in case I decide on that option. Or do I leave and hope she doesn't see me, so if she sees me again she won't think I'm stalking? But she just says excuse me and I say sorry and step to the side and I have to make a decision.

And she gets the door open and kind of glances back at me like she knows I don't live here and why am I loitering, so I decide to leave. Like, what am I going to do inside anyway? But then the door swings closed and right at that instant I realize I should have gone in. Because then I could look for his name on the door and see which apartment is his and why didn't I think of that before? I can't believe how stupid I'm being.

But whatever. I have a ton of homework I haven't even started and it's getting late and there's this huge English paper that's due tomorrow and of course I haven't even started it, because what have I been doing? Fantasizing and spending too much time on math homework trying to get everything perfect to impress him and completely not focusing on anything that doesn't have to do with Mr. Farrell for more than three consecutive seconds, and now I'm screwed. At least I'm ready for the math test since I've been studying for it all week. Except unfortunately there's other stuff going on in the world.

❀

When I'm at home on my bed trying to read this seriously dull book for English, I'm wondering for the bazillionth time why they give us such boring books to read. The only thing that's kept me awake this long was Danny calling to say he found the note. And then we planned tomorrow, which is so perfect it's insane. He called James after to tell him about it.

The highlight of my night is when I go down to the deli and I'm bending down for snack cakes, and all these thoughts come rushing in at me. Like being with Danny today and how good it felt. And the weird thing is? That I even have room to think about him when all I've been obsessing about is Mr. Farrell. But also about Brad's brother and what he said. And the Sheila situation. I tried IMing her, but she's never online anymore. And she didn't call me back after I left three voice mails about how she should call me if she feels like talking.

It's all too much right now. And then there's the whole thing about seeing Dr. Ribisi tomorrow. . . .

There's this grungy deli cat that's always half-covered in sawdust or something. He creeps around the bottom shelves with his tail swiping up against all the stuff there. Somehow, this seems immensely unhygienic. I try to walk around him on my way to pay, but he suddenly takes a spaz and darts in front of me. Not that's it's a black cat, but it *is* the grungy deli cat, so I'm hoping it's not a bad omen and he's trying to tell me something.

By the time it's three in the morning, I'm only half done with the paper. Because I can't stop thinking about tomorrow, which is already later today. And how I'm finally going to know if he feels the way I hope he does.

CHAPTER 17

Thursday

SO OF COURSE there's this humungous zit right on my chin. Since I'm planning to stay after math and talk to Mr. Farrell and all. This zit could not be bigger. There's no way I could hide it if I tried. I mean, okay, so I tried for half an hour with my special concealer-and-Q-tip-combo technique, but it looks worse now than when I started.

I dash into the bathroom before math for a last-minute face check. The results of which are heinous and I wish I never looked, because there's no way I can go to class looking like this. So I go into a stall and sit on the toilet and put my feet up so no one can see that I'm late for class and possibly snitch because I have to decide if I can let Mr. Farrell see me with this thing on my face. Plus, now I also have to think up an excuse for being late, which I'm going to be in another minute.

The door bangs open and someone starts dialing their cell phone.

She's like, "Hey, it's me," and I immediately know it's Sheila. "Sorry to keep bothering you with all these calls. Everything's been getting so much worse lately." I hear her walking toward the stalls. I can tell she's looking under the doors to see if anyone else is in here, so I hold my breath.

She goes, "I can't do this anymore." Then she starts telling the person on the other end how she finally got a chance to catch up on homework last night because she went to the library instead of to Brad's after school.

"But when I called Brad after, he said he wasn't studying for the math test."

Pause.

"Like I was surprised? He never studies for anything anymore."

Pause.

"Yeah, I tried that."

Pause.

"What do *you* think?"

Pause.

"Exactly. And then I tried to convince him that he's on this downward spiral and . . . like how he's scaring me and everything, but he just blew me off. And then he said he's going to cheat off this kid Jackson during the test."

Pause.

"Not really. If he doesn't pass this test then there's no way he can pass the class."

Pause.

"I know! I would tell Jackson, but there's no way I can do it without Brad seeing."

Pause.

"He's in there already."

Pause.

"No, because he's being all scary, and he sits right next to Jackson. So there's not much I can do about it anyway."

Pause.

"Yeah . . . I know . . . Okay, I better go. Thanks, Max." And she snaps her phone shut.

I'm having this convulsion like, *Max! As in Max from film elective! As in Brad's brother who told me that Sheila should stay away from Brad!*

A tub of lip gloss falls out of my bag and rolls across the floor, under the stall door toward the sinks. I hear Sheila pick it up. Then she knocks on my door.

I'm like, "Uh . . . come in?"

She goes, "It's locked."

And I'm like, "Oh yeah. Right." So I unlatch the door and swing it open, and Sheila smiles a little when she sees it's just me.

Then she holds out my lip gloss and goes, "I think this is yours."

So I go, "Thanks. I'm really sorry I'm sitting here like this. I totally didn't mean to spy on you or anything, I just got caught in here and—"

"It's okay."

"It is?"

"You know most of that stuff anyway."

"Oh." And then no one says anything for a minute. I notice that Sheila's wearing a long-sleeved shirt, so I'm like, "Aren't you hot?" Because it's supposed to be super warm today.

She's like, "Not really."

And I know I told Max I wouldn't tell Sheila what he said, and if I tell there could be consequences I can't even imagine, but I have to at least reach out to her in some way. And I think I'm right about this, and if I'm not then it's no big deal, but if I am it could make all the difference.

So I say, "Sheila."

And she looks at me.

And I say, "I know."

At first I can't tell what she's going to do. Maybe she'll try and act like she doesn't know what I'm talking about, or maybe she'll just leave. But instead she does something I wasn't expecting at all. She pulls up her sleeve, and there are bruises on her arm. Like someone grabbed her and wouldn't let go.

I'm like, "Oh my god."

And Sheila says, "I don't know what to do."

"Was it . . . Brad's father?"

But she shakes her head. And she whispers, "It was Brad."

So that's why Max didn't do anything. And he didn't want Sheila to know we talked. In some weird way, he was probably protecting his brother. Or maybe there's more to it. Not that it matters. The only thing that matters right now is that I can help Sheila. Because this has to stop.

So I say, "I know someone who can help you."

❀

Somehow I managed to only be five minutes late to math, and Mr. Farrell didn't even notice because the whole room was in a pre-test frenzy of sharpening pencils and asking last-minute questions and cramming from the book and Mr. Farrell yelling at everyone to sit down so we can start.

After I gave Sheila the contact info for Dr. Ribisi, she went to the guidance office. All I wanted to do the whole period was kill Brad, but somehow I managed not to. I'm sure I bombed the test.

So now class is over and everyone's gone and Mr. Farrell doesn't have anything this period, so I go up to him and say, "Hey. I have a question."

And he looks up and smiles right at me (and it's like he doesn't even see the zit the way he's smiling) and he goes, "I have an answer," which is so cute in a dorky, teachery kind of way.

I'm like, "Do you believe in karma?"

And he's all, "Absolutely."

So I say, "What if you had the chance to help someone receive the ultimate karmic retribution? Would you do it?"

He's like, "No doubt."

I go, "That's what I thought." Not that I need convincing that what we're doing tonight is the right thing. But in a way, I wanted his opinion. Even if I can't tell him what it's about.

He's all, "What goes around comes around."

I really hope that's true. And then it's like evidence right in front of my face when I see Jackson on the way to my last class. Not just because of tonight, but I know about how Jackson stole Ree's note in English, because she sent me a text during her lunch.

I catch up to him and go, "Can I talk to you for a sec?"

He's like, "About what?" All in this tone where it's obvious he doesn't want to know. I can't figure out why he doesn't have more friends with such great conversational skills.

I go, "About that note you took from Ree in English."

He goes, "What about it?"

I'm like, "Why don't you give it back?"

"It landed on my desk. I can keep it if I want."

"Um . . . she really *really* needs that note back."

"I can see why."

"Are you going to get her in trouble?"

"No. I'll give it back to her tomorrow."

"Or you could give it to me to give to her."

"No. Is she going to the dance?"

"Yeah."

"So I'll give it to her there."

I have no idea what Jackson's up to, but he doesn't have a creepy dangerous vibe or anything, so I sort of believe him. He's just a tad lacking in the social-skills department, is all.

I go, "Okay well . . . see ya."

But he goes, "Can I ask you something?"

I'm like, "Yeah."

And he says, "Uh . . . you know how you used to be . . . like . . . different?"

Which is, like, the biggest understatement of the century. So I go, "Yeah."

"Yeah so . . . I was wondering how you did that. Exactly."

"What do you mean?"

"I don't know. Forget it." So then I'm about to leave again, but he goes, "Okay, like . . . it's obvious you're dressing differently this year. But it's like you came back as a different person, you know?" Which is news to me because last I heard, my personality is exactly the same as it's always been. And Jackson doesn't even know me. Maybe through Six Degrees of Danny because they used to be friends and then Danny and I went out, but that's about it.

I go, "Um . . . I just kind of got some new clothes at the end of last summer, so . . ." And now we're both late for class, and why are we even having this conversation? So I'm like, "I have to go."

But then Gloria passes us and laughs when she sees me standing with Jackson. She's all, "Give it up, Jackson. Nicole would never go out with a loser like you. She only likes boys who are fun to be with. Oh, wait. But then she dumps them because she doesn't know how to keep a boyfriend." And she whisks away like it's a totally normal thing to be a complete bitch to people just for fun.

Jackson's like, "She's such a bitch."

I'm like, "This just in."

He goes, "We used to go out."

So now I have to pretend like I didn't know that, but I also don't want it to look like I'm too shocked because he might take it the wrong way. I go, "Really?"

And then he just starts telling me all this stuff about how she used him and made him do her homework and stuff, and he can't believe how stupid he was to go along with it. And how if people knew Gloria liked him, they wouldn't treat him like such a leper. Because even though she's a bitch, she's smoking hot, and that has more status in the social hierarchy of things. But it's not like he could tell anyone about it now, because who would believe him?

I feel bad for him. He must be really lonely to tell me all this stuff. So I go, "I hear you."

He goes, "Thanks for listening to all that. I don't know what's wrong with me."

I so want to tell Ree what he just said. Because it kind of sounds like he wanted someone to find the note and that would make it way easier to convince her if she doesn't want to do this. None of us want to hurt Jackson. But maybe he'll be relieved that someone put the proof out there that Gloria really did go out with him.

I'm like, "There's nothing wrong with you. Everyone's unhappy. Some people just hide it better."

Jackson smiles and says, "You're probably right."

I go, "Well, now I'm so late for class I'm sure it's already over, so—"

And he's like, "Oh man! I'm sorry, I didn't—"

"That's okay." If there's some way to make sure that what we're doing tonight isn't going to mortify Jackson, I should do it now while I have the chance. "Um . . . what if it came out somehow? About you and Gloria? Would you be embarrassed?"

"Hell no!"

This kid cracks me up. "But don't worry. I'm not going to repeat what you said."

I know what it's like to have secrets. Ones that are way traumatic. Ones that are so awful you can't tell anybody, even though you're dying to. So I'm not going to talk about this with anyone.

It's the right thing to do. Karma and all.

❀

The thing about Dr. Ribisi's office? Is that I could totally live here. It's not one of those intimidating shrink's offices at all. She has all these pillows and a sweet couch that's crazy comfortable and a mini rock garden. Plus there's like twenty plants in the windows and these really cool lamps and everything is in these bold, beautiful colors. Just like Dr. Ribisi's wardrobe.

Today she's wearing a violet shirt and I love it because it has all these flowers. They're green and yellow and red, and maybe I'll even ask her where she got it. Only I guess it's not my style. It's too conservative, the way the buttons are.

"So," Dr. Ribisi begins. "How was your week?"

I'm like, "Okay."

But Mom is all, "I don't think that's entirely true."

Dude. Family therapy *sucks*. Like, if it was just me? I'm sure I'd be talking a lot more. But when Dr. Ribisi suggested I come alone, plus once a week with Mom like we do now, I didn't exactly jump at the opportunity. Counseling scares me. It's not that I don't have things I want to talk about and problems to work through (and yeah, I'm aware I have issues) but individual counseling is too much.

So Mom and I come in once a week. Even though Dr. Ribisi tries really hard to get me to open up, and we have to do these communication exercises, and sometimes she asks me direct questions and won't move on until I've answered them, I still feel like I hardly talk at all.

I wish my life were a movie and I could take it into the editing room and totally cut this part out. And some other parts. Some other parts definitely need to be cut.

Dr. Ribisi goes, "To what do you think your mom is referring, Nicole?"

And I'm all, "I don't know."

So Mom's like, "What about when I tried to talk to you after the party?"

I go, "There was nothing to tell."

Then Mom looks at Dr. Ribisi and says, "I try talking to Nicole, but it's hard when she won't communicate."

I'm like, "Nothing happened at the party!"

And Dr. Ribisi goes, "Why don't we take a step back for a moment?" Which is what she says when she senses an attack brewing and we have to calm that down. She's like, "I'm hearing that you felt your mom was asking about something specific, Nicole, but it sounds like she was asking in a more general way." And then she goes on to explain about how we need to not only listen to what the other person is saying but try to hear the meaning behind their words. But my thing is that if you want someone to understand what you're saying, you should say what you mean.

I don't know. I guess it helps on some level. But we haven't made much progress. Especially considering that the ultimate point of all this is to get me to talk about what happened at our old house in Water Mill. Mom gave up trying to talk about it and hopes this will be the magic formula to make me finally open up and expose my soul. Family therapy is just the latest in a series of attempts to get me to spill.

Mom has tried lots of different techniques over the years. There was the social worker who showed up at our apartment one day and tried to take me to a mental hospital for "evaluation." There was getting out of gym to sit with a guidance counselor, which didn't do much except get me out of gym for two days until the guidance counselor called my mom and told her I refused to talk and she couldn't make me. Then there was scheduling more family time and the self-help books and Mom's alternative-healing kick, when she kept announcing that my aura was dusty. Even the strategically placed hotline numbers, when it finally became obvious that I was totally freaked out and wasn't going to talk to anyone about this. But I never called any of them and nothing made me talk.

So the family-therapy thing has been going on since the beginning of this year—when I started dressing all "out there," as Mom calls it, buying new clothes and accessories with the money I saved from my summer job. Mom thinks this is my way of acting out, when really the only thing that happened was I got style.

Sometimes when Dr. Ribisi can tell there's something under the surface that I'm not admitting and she shouts me out, I feel hostile. It's not her. She's just doing her job and I get that. But it irritates me how she knows everything. Like now she's looking at me in this way where I can tell she knows something's going on with me, and I feel angry but I don't know why.

Dr. Ribisi goes, "Tell me something about your week that was significant."

And I'm about to say that nothing happened, same old story blah-di-blah-blah, but then the image of those bruises on Sheila's arm invade my safety barrier. And I know I have to say something. Because I felt helpless before, but Sheila's not. And I can help her end this nightmare.

"Um . . . well, there was this one thing." But I'm uncomfortable with Mom here, because if she hears this she'll totally overreact and call the police or whatever and I just want to do what's best for Sheila. So I'm like, "Could . . . can I tell you, like . . . alone?"

I guess I thought that Mom would put up a fight and insist on staying, but instead she springs up from the couch and grabs her bag and says, "I'll be right outside."

So when we're alone I'm like, "Something happened to one of my friends. Something bad."

Dr. Ribisi waits.

I go, "It's her boyfriend." And I tell about Brad and how much Sheila has changed and what Max said. And I tell about the bruises and then I say, "Brad is . . . abusing her. Physically."

And then oh my god I start crying. Like all of a sudden it just bursts out of me and I'm crying so loud and my chest is heaving and my whole body is trembling like it will never stop. And Dr. Ribisi picks up the tissue box from the table and passes it over to me and I take tissues and press them over my face and I'm so humiliated. I've never cried here before or said as much as I just did. I don't know where this is coming from. I mean, yeah, it's upsetting about Sheila, but I wasn't crying about it before.

So we spend the rest of the time talking about it and . . . it's like I can feel something shift inside of me. Like something's changing, but I don't know what it is yet.

On my way out, I tell Dr. Ribisi that I gave Sheila her number. I'm like, "I hope that was okay."

Dr. Ribisi goes, "It was more than okay. Don't worry, Nicole. You did the right thing."

And for once, I think that's true.

❁

All I can say is, "Wow."

We just spent two hours hanging all these copies. It's really weird being at school this late, and I'm standing in the hall taking everything in. Copies of the note are everywhere. It's like there's nowhere you can look without seeing one. We completely plastered the entire school. We even managed to keep most of the "Danny for President" posters uncovered, but we had to cover some of them or it would have looked suspicious. Everyone else left already, but I wanted to be here alone for a few more minutes, to take it all in. Since I'm the one who started this and everything.

I'm still thinking about it all waiting for the subway. And then this amazing thing happens. This unbelievably astounding, amazing thing. Mr. Farrell comes out of nowhere. I'm farther down on the platform and he just came through the turnstile, so I walk over to him. He looks as surprised as I feel.

We both go, "Hey!" at the same time.

I'm like, "You're taking the Two train, right?"

He goes, "Yeah. You?"

I nod and try to act normal. But inside I'm freaking out because this is so random! Why is he even here? There's no way he was at school this late. Actually, I know he definitely wasn't, because I looked in his room.

And I guess the whole weirdness of it overwhelms me, and I laugh. So he's like, "Yeah, weird, right? I was getting a drink with a friend nearby, so . . ."

I'm like, "Oh."

We so belong together it's not even funny. Two people at the same subway stop taking the same train at a time when they're never there?

Definitely.

The subway ride is so stressful that I have to seriously pee when we're only halfway home. First off, we're sitting together with our knees almost touching so we can see each other while we talk. Or I can see Mr. Farrell while he talks. He seems to have lots to say, while I can barely mumble responses that are even remotely coherent. I get like this when I'm nervous. It's either this thing where I suddenly forget how to use the English language, or I ramble incessantly until the other person completely tunes me out.

Or sometimes when I'm rambling on the subway, I get all jittery and giggly and I start ripping on all of the annoying subway people. Like, what's up with those guys who sit with their legs so far apart they're taking up three seats? Is it really that big? And the people with rudeness issues who read over your shoulder because they can't be bothered to bring their own entertainment. And weirdo spaced-out people who sit across from you and stare at you the whole way. I can't with them. But I don't point out any of these examples now, because I don't want to come off like a child.

Then my knee touches his knee and he doesn't move his knee

away. He just keeps it there, all pressed up against mine. And the automated subway dude voice comes on and he's like, "If you see a suspicious package, tell a police officer or an MTA employee." The scroll announcement screen says: SUSPICIOUS PACKAGE.

And this whole time Mr. Farrell is talking about random unrelated things—just one idea after another, which I think is called "stream of consciousness" or something—and I'm trying to listen, but I'm not hearing all the words because I'm too busy planning what to do when we get off the subway. Do I pretend I don't know where he lives? Do I just start walking home and hope he walks with me? Or do I ask him which way he's going?

We get to our stop and I bump into him getting off and he smells so good I can't even think straight. And we climb the stairs and he's not talking anymore. And I'm definitely not talking. I still don't know what I'm going to say, and I'm wishing so hard that he walks with me even if it's just for a few blocks.

Out on the street Mr. Farrell says, "Are you hungry?"

And I'm like, "What?"

He goes, "Are you hungry?"

And . . . um . . . I'm sorry, is he asking me this just to know? Or is he about to ask me if I want something to eat? Or maybe that's what he just did. Did he just ask me to get something to eat with him? Isn't two people eating together who like each other classified as a date?

I'm trying to follow this logical thought progression like we learned last month in philosophy, but this is beyond logic. My heart knows what it wants.

He's waiting for an answer. So I go, "Yeah, I am."

And he's all, "I'm getting a slice . . . would you like to join me? My treat." And the way he smiles at me makes me melt all over the sidewalk and I can't believe this is finally happening and I've only been waiting forever for this instant to be real.

So I say, "Sure. Thanks." I'm all proud of how calm and collected I sound.

And we walk and he asks where I live and I tell him and he's like, "We're neighbors," which is not exactly a news flash but it feels good to hear him say it.

Then we get to this pizza place that's standard but good, and we get our slices and sit at the counter. I arrange my stuff and give him some napkins, and he takes a big bite of pizza, and I'm so nervous I could hurl.

But I don't hurl. Somehow I manage to swallow my pizza while Mr. Farrell talks, and I even laugh at some of the corny jokes he tells. By the time we leave, I'm feeling great. Just like Tuesday after school when it totally felt like we were chilling as friends, just hanging out and having a great time, but also with that exciting attraction thing going on. I feel like we've just had our second date. Everything about it feels that way.

So we walk up to West 73rd Street, and I'm like, "Here's my street."

And he's like, "Okay, well . . . see you tomorrow." And it's like time stops or something. We're just standing there, looking at each other, waiting. Waiting for the other one to do something. And I just . . . decide. Right here, right now, I decide to make it happen. Because I'm tried of waiting for him to come to me.

I say, "You know what? I kind of feel like walking."

He doesn't even look surprised. He says, "Oh? Well . . . I'm up here on Eightieth," and so we walk. I don't even know what I'm doing yet. I just know I have to do something.

When we're outside his building and he's like, "Well . . . this is me," I almost say, "I know." But instead I just look at him. And he just looks at me. And we're just looking at each other like we're seeing each other in a different way. And he goes, "So . . ."

I take a step closer to him. And he's not going anywhere, so I take another step. And now we're standing so close, and the streetlight is reflecting off his eyes and I can see these little flecks of gold in them. And I don't want to think anymore. I want this to happen, the same way it's already happened so many times in my dreams, and I don't want to think about it. I just want to do what I've been waiting so long for.

But then he says, "Well . . . good night."

And I'm like, "Oh . . . yeah . . . see you tomorrow . . ." but I'm still waiting in case he changes his mind. But he doesn't and he walks up his stairs and goes in and the door swings shut, and just like last time, I'm all alone.

I see the light go on. I know which one is his.

❁

He says, "Your skin is so smooth."

His face is all close to mine and there's beer on his breath. So I know it's going to be a problem. Because the same thing always happens when he drinks and she's at her friend's house playing bridge. It's the same thing that's been happening for almost a year.

And he's kissing me and touching me and I feel like I'm suffocating and he's all over me and I totally can't breathe and I want to die. And his hand moves up my thigh and under my shorts and my shirt is all pushed up and I can't get away because he's stronger than me.

I wonder why I can't tell my mother. And why she can't figure it out for herself.

And why my father has been getting away with this for way too long.

CHAPTER 18

7riday

HERE'S WHAT IT is with Gloria's note. If you ask me? We definitely did the right thing. But Ree's feeling guilty and like it was too much, and she's worrying that instead of karma it was just mean. So I explained that all we did was take who Gloria really is and put it out there for the world to see. Which was actually flattering in a way, if you think about it. Because if Gloria wasn't really using Jackson and she actually liked him, then that means she has depth and a soul and she's not just some bitchy superficial boyfriend swiper. And I explained how you get what you give, and Gloria's been giving out a lot of muck all this time.

But whatever.

I just heard Ree being called to the principal's office, and it doesn't exactly take a rocket scientist to know what happened. Gloria totally turned her in because Ree is the first chick in line seeking Gloria revenge. And now Ree would be about to take the entire blame for this, because there's no way she's going to tell on us, which is so unfair since she wasn't even the one who thought of it.

Which is why we promised her that's not going to happen.

See, we already predicted it would go like this. So now it's time for Operation Day After. Which is what we all agreed on if Ree got in trouble. We also agreed not to tell her about it, because we knew she'd never let us go through with it.

I'm lurking in the hall waiting for my signal when I see Jackson getting a drink. I whisper, "Jackson!" And he looks around and sees me, and I wave him over.

He goes, "Thanks for the note back."

And I go, "Oh, that. Well . . . someone I know found it." Danny told me how he snuck the original note back in Jackson's bag before first period.

He looks around at all the copies plastered on the walls. He goes, "So. Someone really wanted to get back at Gloria, huh?"

I'm like, "I guess." And the way he's looking at me it's so obvious he knows I was involved in this, but he probably thinks that I did it just because of what he told me yesterday. He has no idea this was planned before.

I'm like, "Hey. You want to do something badass?"

And I swear I've never seen someone look more excited about the possibility of getting in trouble.

❀

Danny is mad gassed. He stops me in the hall before lunch and he's talking a mile a minute about how all these people said they're voting for him and he's gotten really good feedback on his posters and he's already making all these plans for next year when he's president and his speech is in the bag and he's stoked.

So I'm nodding and smiling and listening, but I'm also thinking about the pizza I'm missing. Because today is pizza day and if you don't get there early you miss all the big pieces and the ones that are actually cooked right. But Danny's so excited—and it's not like we're not friends or anything—so I'm listening.

And he's buzzing and smiling all big and rambling, and he goes, "Are you going to the dance with anyone?"

I'm so shocked I'm not even sure I heard him right. Like, is he asking me to the dance? After I dumped him?

So I go, "Not really. I mean, I'm going with Rhiannon . . . so . . ."

He's like, "Would you go with me?"

And looking at Danny with all his passion and excitement and cute new haircut, I can't even remember why we broke up. What was I thinking? There must have been a good reason, which I just can't think of right now. But I still want to go with him, so I say, "Okay."

He's like, "Yeah?"

"Yeah."

"Okay. We're going. Cool."

And all of a sudden I'm going to the dance with my ex-boyfriend, who I broke up with for some reason I'm sure I'll remember any second now. I mean, yeah, he's a good person and all, but it's not like everything was perfect.

It's not like Danny is the most amazing thing ever.

❁

Danny is the most amazing thing ever.

We're in the auditorium for the big student-council assembly, where all the candidates for next year's student council are giving their speeches. So far we've heard all the treasurer and secretary and vice-president speeches, and now Danny's giving his. And I guess in a way I forgot how he is and how intense he gets about things he's into (like politics and winning this election) and all of his energy is like vibrating right across the room into me, and I'm zinging. I forgot how he can be even better than sugar.

I look around and try to figure out if people are interested or bored or if it's mixed. Danny's speech is very antiwar, anti–people being mean to each other because that's what leads to war, which you pretty much have to agree with or else what does that say about you? And suddenly this wave of sadness washes over me, because I can picture Danny practicing his speech with James and working on drafts of it and asking Carl and Evan for advice on what to say, and I feel so left out and like I really missed sharing an important part of his life. His speech is so good, though.

And then he holds up this sign that says PEACE. He just holds it up, standing there, not saying anything for like a whole minute. Which doesn't sound like a long time, but a minute of silence when you're supposed to be giving your speech is like an eternity. And I'm in this daze, just staring at him and the sign and thinking of everything it means to him, to us. And it's like I have this epiphany. Right here in the third row, I have an epiphany.

I still love Danny. I never stopped loving Danny. And all of a sudden, why I broke up with him is crystal.

❀

It's like the worst case of déjà vu ever when I realize that I'm stuck in the bathroom with Gloria again. Except this time, she's crying.

She came in while I was peeing, and I just knew it was her by the way her heels clacked across the floor. You know how some people have this way of walking that you can recognize without even seeing them? Yeah.

So there I was doing my thing, and she clacked over to the sinks and then . . . she just started crying. Like out of nowhere. Which is totally freaking me out, because it's like, *Welcome to me at therapy yesterday* all over again.

And it's not like she doesn't know at least one other person is in here. Especially when I flush the toilet. But it's so wild, because even that doesn't stop her. She keeps crying. I didn't know that Gloria even knew how to cry.

I slide the lock and push the stall door open and walk over to the sinks. I don't look over at her. I just wash my hands and notice that there are actually paper towels today, and wow look there's soap too, it's like a miracle. And this whole time, she's standing two sinks down from me, wiping her eyes and looking in the mirror. And not caring at all that I'm seeing her like this.

If I were a mean person, I could totally attack her right now. Say how she deserves everything she got and how does it feel to be on the other side? But I'm not like that. So I walk over to the door. But just as I'm about to leave, Gloria says, "Hey."

I go, "Yeah?"

"Thanks."

"For what?"

"For not harshing on me. I'm having a bad day."

"No prob. We've all been there."

And that's when it hits me. That Gloria, despite popular opinion, really is a human being.

✿

So we're in Ree's room getting ready for the dance, and I'm fully aware that I've been talking about Danny nonstop since his speech, but I can't help it. And I really want a warm H&H bagel with lots of butter, but at the same time my stomach is in all kinds of knots about Danny. And also how Mr. Farrell might be chaperoning tonight.

So of course that makes me think of the last time there was a party, and how Mom grilled me when I got home, and what would she say if she knew the truth this time? It'd be like, *Yeah, Mom. The teacher I'm in love with was there. But don't worry. He's responsible and he always treats on dates.*

I'm like, "I hope I can go home tonight without an interrogation."

And Ree's like, "At least your mom knows what stuff to interrogate you about."

Then Ree says how she wants to connect with her mom more but she doesn't know how because her mom's too preoccupied with work. And how she never sees her dad anymore, and even last night, when it was Brooke's last night here, he didn't come home early. And I kind of feel bad for her, because her dad can be really interesting.

Like this one time when I was over for dinner? We had just finished eating and her dad brought out this red tin of Italian cookies, except they weren't really cookies. They were more like crunchy, moon rock–looking things. And he said how he wanted to show us something cool, so he unwrapped one of the cookie things. The paper it was wrapped in looked like a square of tissue paper. Then he took the wrapper and rolled it up into a cylinder. And he stood the wrapper up on the table and took out a lighter and lit the wrapper along the top rim.

And I was kind of freaking out, because then there was just this cookie wrapper on fire in the middle of the table and no one was throwing water on it or anything. But right before the flame reached the table, the wrapper jumped up into the air and floated almost to the ceiling, and it was the coolest thing ever. And then the burnt wrapper ash floated down, and when I went to grab it, it crumbled all over the place. So her dad's all right. I mean, who else knows about that kind of stuff?

Then I think of another non-Danny-related item to talk about. So I'm like, "Oh. And Sheila set up an appointment with Dr. Ribisi."

And Ree's like, "Awesome. Let's hope she finally sees what a loser Brad is."

I go, "Totally." And I want to tell her about the bruises, but something just shuts me down and I can't. Like taking it over there is too personal and would violate Sheila in some way.

Ree says, "Thanks for doing that. I was really worried about her."

And I'm like, "I know. Same here."

And then "Fly Away" comes on the radio, which we each liked as our favorite song back in third grade and we didn't even know each other then. So we're jumping all around and singing along, although I guess Lenny is a better singer. And Ree gets her feather boas out of her closet and I fling mine around my neck and she twirls hers around and jumps up on the couch. So she's bouncing around and I'm busting a move on the beanbag, but then I jump off because once a beanbag gets a hole in it it's like game over for the beanbag. Then we both scream the part with the *yeahs* at the same time and we're cracking up and imitating Tony and if the dance is half as fun as this, it's going to be awesome.

☸

We've only been at the dance for ten minutes and I've already spilled a Fanta. Plus, I didn't get a really funny joke Danny told, because my brain is on spin cycle and I'm currently unable to process incoming information like a normal person.

Danny's like, "What's wrong?"

So I go, "Nothing," which is true. It's not like anything is wrong. It's just that I'm all jumpy and swirly.

Danny's looking at me strange. He's like, "Seriously. Are you okay?"

I'm like, "Yeah."

And he's all, "Are you sure?"

I go, "Totally."

And he's like, "You're not sorry you came with me, are you?" Which is so far from what's up I can't with that.

So I'm all like, "No!" and it comes out like a yell. So now I'm paranoid that he thinks I'm yelling at him because I'm annoyed. Either that or that I'm denying it too hard, so it must be true. And I know that I could just tell him right now and there's a chance that we'd both feel better. But if I tell him that I'm still in love with him and I want to be with him again, he might say no, and that's just too scary to even consider.

And then one of my favorite songs comes on (it's actually the first song we ever made out to, so of course it comes on now) and I would never think in a million years that Danny would even remember that, but he's looking at me all deep as if he does. And he goes, "Dance with me?"

He puts his arms around me and I press up against him, and it's just like old times. Like nothing ever changed, like our feelings for each other have only gotten stronger. I can't believe I was so stupid and scared. And I guess Danny feels it too because he whispers how nice this feels, dancing all close and being together again. And I know I have to figure out a way to tell him.

We dance to a few more songs and it's feeling more and more intense between us. Then Danny says, "Nicole?"

And I'm like, "Yeah?"

And he just goes, "I miss you."

And my eyes are immediately stinging with tears and my heart is beating so fast and I realize that I've waited so long to hear him say that.

So I say, "I miss you, too."

He's like, "Do you want to . . . I think we should . . ."

And even now, even after all I put him through, he's saving me. I've been trying to find my way into the light for so long, and he just comes along and takes me there.

I go, "Totally." And just like that, he's mine again. The way it always should have been.

Then Ree and James come over and say they're leaving and are we staying? And we tell them that we're staying. And Ree gives me a look like, *What is this?* And I give her a look like, *I'll tell you later.* Because I totally wanted to tell her when I was over at her house before the dance, but for some reason I couldn't. It was like I had to tell Danny first, like he deserved to know before anyone else, even my best friend.

So Ree and James leave, but then a minute later Danny's like, "Don't go away," and he runs out. And when he doesn't come back right away, I'm all paranoid like, *What if he doesn't come back? What if he's trying to tell me that he made a mistake? And that he really doesn't want to be with me?* But just when I'm convinced that he never wants to see me again, he comes running back in and says we're going on an adventure.

So the four of us take this random subway line down to the Lower East Side to this place called Welcome to the Johnsons that's really a bar but totally looks like someone's living room from like nineteen-eighty-whatever. There's a plastic pink flamingo like the kind I've seen in movies on suburban lawns. And then I sort of zone out for a while and imagine what it's like to live in suburbia and drive around in cars and go to the Super Wal-Mart and get cherry Slurpees at 7-Eleven. When we lived in Water Mill, it was such a small area with limited choices. But now I live in the middle of this enormous city with so many choices I don't even know which one to make most of the time. Or I'll make a choice and then spend the next two weeks worrying that I could have made a better one.

There's this twang of feedback, and I snap back to the bar scene and check out the stage. There's this chick in a cocktail dress and glasses with glitter in her hair tuning her electric violin and this punked-out guy with tattoos of angel wings on his back and they're called Unisex Salon. They're so ultra cool they make you feel insufficiently cool enough to be in the same room with them.

Then Danny comes back and flops into the chair with me (which is huge and fluorescent pink and shaped like lips) and hands me my root beer and he goes, "To new beginnings." And we clink bottles and some root beer spills on his shirt. And we turn around to clink bottles with Ree and James and James is like, "I'll drink to that!"

We watch the band. They rock really hard. The lead singer is way cute and his eyes are all intense and you can totally tell they're going to be famous.

Danny leans over and yells in my ear, "These guys are going to be famous!" And the crowd is rocking out and everyone is bobbing their heads around and moving to the beat, and it's like we're all over at someone's house listening to the neighborhood band practice, but in this scenario they're actually good. And Danny's all pressed up against me, and if you didn't know any better you'd think it was just like we used to be. Way back in another life, before I lost control.

It's only twelve thirty on a Friday night and lots of people are still out, but Danny totally wants to protect me, so he insisted on taking the subway with me and walking me home.

So we're standing on my stoop and he says, "Thanks for coming with me. And for everything."

And I'm like, "Of course." And I know that Danny is figuring out if I'll let him kiss me, and I want to but I also know there's something I have to do first. Because I learned the hard way what happens if you don't get the closure you need. So I tell him, "I'll see you soon?"

He's all, "Definitely." And he has his look where he's trying to hide being disappointed, which I think is so sweet because it probably seems like I'm sending him mixed messages but I'm really not.

So I go in, but I just stand in the doorway and wait a few minutes. And I go back out on the stoop and look down the street and he's gone.

I walk fast through the warm night with my heart pounding extra hard like the biggest drum in the drum set, and I don't even think about what I'm doing or how crazy this is. I just know it's something I have to do before I can move on. It's my last chance to do this before I get back with Danny. And then I'm scared that he might be asleep and then what?

But when I get to his building his light is on, so I know he's home. And I'm so nervous I almost faint right there on his stoop. But then I find the courage I need. Because if you take a risk, you just might find what you're looking for.

JAMES
CHAPTER 19
Wednesday

I SQUINT AT the sidewalk chalk like it's going to explain why Rhiannon is being such a numbskull.

There is no possible way she did this.

No possible way.

It pisses me off. Big-time. If she invests one more speck of emotional energy in some dumbass who doesn't even love her anymore, if he ever did at all, I'm going to lose it.

Everyone's standing around. Discussing it. Wondering what it means. Speculating who wrote it.

But I get it.

I read it again. This must have taken forever. Just picturing her here last night, making sure the letters were all even, coloring them in. . . .

I'm so freaking jealous I can't stand to be next to myself. And I'm also pissed off that I got her those flowers.

Maybe the dance thing isn't such a good idea. It's a drag watching this emotional train wreck in action.

How can Rhiannon not know this was the worst possible idea?

On my way to class, I'm relieved I just went to the computer lab for lunch again. But I'm having this evolving conversation in my head that I can't get out of. It's taking place in this alternate universe where she didn't write on the sidewalk. And where she doesn't give a hang about Steve anymore.

The latest version goes something like this.

Me: I can't believe you ever went out with that guy Steve.

Her: I know. I must have been deranged.

Me: That's what I'm saying. No offense.

Her: Steve is the worst.

Me: Steve is a dumbass.

Her: Steve is the worst kind of dumbass.

Me: Word?

Her: Totally.

Me: Nice.

Her: Do you want to move tables and talk about that new computer program you're working on? It sounded fascinating before.

Me: Let's go.

As I pass a poster that says, DANNY TRAGER FOR PRESIDENT. HE STILL LIKES FRUIT ROLL-UPS, a girl coming out of the cafeteria bumps into me. She's talking to her friend about something that just happened at lunch. Involving Steve. And Rhiannon.

And Gloria.

I've heard some rumors going around, but I didn't really believe them. Because how can they be an item already? But now it sounds like they are.

Jeez. The girl moves lightning fast. It's almost like how she approached me last month when I was with Jessica.

For some reason, Gloria and Jessica had a fight. All I know is, it wasn't Jessica's fault. Gloria came out of nowhere, accusing Jessica of spreading some rumor about her. But Jessica had no idea what she was talking about. And no one even heard that rumor, so Gloria definitely made up the whole thing as an excuse to get mad at Jessica. And then she approached me.

I was in the computer lab after school, trying to finish this endless research paper. Gloria came in and sat at the computer next to me. At first I didn't even notice her. But then she started laughing.

So I said, "What's so funny?"

"Nothing," she told me. But she kept laughing.

"I wasn't aware that nothing could be so funny," I said.

"Listen to this." And then she read this joke that someone had e-mailed her. It was actually really funny, so we were laughing at it together. I tried not to look at her breasts.

"Anyway," she said. "I hear you're going out with Jessica."

"Yeah." I focused on the computer screen.

"How's that going?"

"Good. You know. Great."

"Which is it? Good or great?"

"Both. It fluctuates."

Gloria laughed. "I never knew you were so funny."

"Neither did I." I tapped some random keys on the keyboard. I hoped this wasn't going where I thought it was.

But apparently it was already there, because then she said, "Well, if it's ever less than good . . ." And she pulled my hand toward her and wrote her number on my palm.

"I have a girlfriend," I said.

Gloria leaned over and put her lips against my ear. She whispered, "I don't care." And then she just walked out. Like she didn't just disrespect Jessica by trying to steal me away. Like she didn't just disrespect me by dissing my girlfriend.

It's all so messed up.

When Rhiannon comes into Wash World, I almost don't recognize her. She shakes off her umbrella, but it's raining hard and she looks frazzled. And her eyes look different. Defeated.

She sees me sitting on the couch, waiting for a wash to finish. Her sneakers slosh and squeak as she comes over.

"Hey," she says.

"Hey." I'm really surprised she's here. I left her a message, so I thought she'd just call back whenever. I actually wanted to leave her a few messages so she'd know I was worried about her. But I'm sick of playing that game. If she wants to talk to me, she can come to me.

And here she is.

The dryer dings.

Rhiannon's like, "I, um. Are you mad at me or something?"

"No."

"Are you sure?"

"Yeah."

I go over and take the clothes out, piling them on the folding table. I start folding stuff. Rhiannon just stands there, watching me.

The truth is, I'm furious. Which is mad annoying when you combine it with being concerned. But mostly I'm angry. Because why is she doing this to herself? Why do girls always go for the assholes who treat them like dirt?

I'm trying to be strong. Strong and detached. All folding clothes.

But then she comes over and stands behind me and hugs me. I feel her cheek pressing against my back.

"You want me to wait with you?" she says. The clothes are all folded and I'm waiting for another load of wash to finish.

"Yeah."

So we sit on the couch. She rests her head against my shoulder.

And eventually, my anger just melts away.

I notice the rain has finally stopped. "Tell you what," I say. "Why don't I put the clothes in the dryer and we can go for a walk?"

"You can't just leave your clothes like that."

"Why not?"

"It's against Wash World regulations."

"Says who?"

Rhiannon points to a huge sign. It says: DO NOT LEAVE CLOTHES UNATTENDED IN MACHINES.

"Oh," I say. "Right. That's okay, though. I have special permission."

"From who?"

"*That* is top secret information."

"Ah."

Walking down the zigzag streets of our neighborhood, we can see in people's windows with no problem. So we just do that for a while, pointing out the wild palm trees and spiral staircases in all these sick apartments. And then we're standing in the middle of a really quiet street. And suddenly I realize I should do the thing I wanted to do before.

"Hey, so . . ."

"Yeah?"

"About that dance. You know. On Friday?"

"Yeah?"

"I was thinking . . . it might be cool if we go together . . . as, like, a group thing. I mean . . . if you want . . ."

"Oh. With who?"

"Danny and . . ." I can't exactly tell her that Danny wants to ask Nicole. Rhiannon would definitely tell her before Danny gets a chance to ask. "I'm not sure. Whoever he's taking."

"Sure. That sounds like fun."

"Yeah?"

"Yeah."

"Nice."

"Oh!" Rhiannon yells.

"What?" Did she figure out I'm full of it? That the group thing is bogus?

"Check out that stained-glass window!"

I relax. Apparently, she doesn't know how I really feel.

I KNOCK ON the lighting-booth door. Miguel lets me in.

"Dude," I go.

"What's good."

"Everything ready for tomorrow?"

"Yeah. It's all set."

"Nice." I look around at all of the lighting controls. "Just like we talked about?"

"Exactly."

"Okay. So here's how it's going down."

Sheila and Brad are fighting in the hall again.

They're too far away to hear what they're saying. Except for two things. At one point Sheila yells, "That's the last time you say you're sorry, because you're done!"

Then Brad talks all low. You can tell from his body language that he's trying to persuade her about something. A lot of kids are standing around. Some of them are trying to be all undercover about it, but others are blatantly staring.

I hear Sheila say, "It's over." And she storms off.

She rocks. I tell everyone about it at Westville.

"Finally," Rhiannon says. "I can't believe how much he changed her!"

"I know!" Nicole agrees. "How scary was that?"

"I wonder what was really going on between them, you know? Like how a person lets that happen."

Nicole looks like she's about to say something. But then she doesn't.

After we tell Rhiannon about the plan for Gloria's enlightenment, there's a debate about involving Jackson.

"It's not fair to him," Rhiannon worries.

"Are you kidding?" Danny says. "Do you have any idea how much it'll improve his street cred when everyone finds out a hottie like Gloria was into him?" Then he cringes. "Sorry."

But Rhiannon just says, "No, I get it."

"And think about it," Danny pushes on. "Why was Jackson carrying around the note in his binder like that?"

"What do you mean?" I say.

Danny goes, "It just seems like . . . I don't know, maybe he wanted someone to find it. Like what—it just falls out of his binder? And he doesn't even notice when he gets up?"

"Hey yeah," Rhiannon says. "That was sort of weird."

"If I had a note like that and I wanted to keep it a secret, there's no way I'd bring it to school," Nicole adds.

"What are you saying?" I ask. "That Jackson wanted someone to find it?"

Nicole goes, "I don't know. Maybe."

"Oooh," Danny says. "Scandalous."

We keep debating about it. I can't tell yet if Rhiannon will go for it, but I think she will. Because I get the feeling she wants to finally stand up for herself, too.

There isn't a lot of time before I'm supposed to pick up Rhiannon and get back to school by seven thirty. So I tell Danny to hurry up with the master copy.

He thought it would be more effective to title the note instead of just copying it. Something to get people's attention. Something that summarizes what this is about. So Danny, the relentless Beatles fan, decided to title it INSTANT KARMA! He's typing that now. Then we're going to arrange that page with the note on the copier glass.

"Done," Danny announces. He snatches the paper from the printer. "We're in."

"Let's just get this copied and get out of here."

"What's the rush? Got a hot date?"

I glare at him.

At this Kinko's, two out of the five copy machines are usually out of order. Like they are right now. Which of course would happen when we need them the most. Just my freaking luck. We should have gone to the other Kinko's. But that one's farther away and we didn't really have time. And we can't make the copies at Carl's dad's place, because his dad can't know what we're doing. There's a chance we could sneak it in, but it's not worth the risk. Even if he offered to do them for free.

There's a middle-aged guy in a suit hogging one of the machines. Who should obviously be doing these copies at the office. The other two machines have girls on them.

Mr. Inappropriate Alert Guy should be here to tell everyone to get the fuck off the machines.

"Should we go to the other Kinko's?" Danny asks.

"Let's just wait. One of them should be done soon."

The girls are laughing over some story they're yelling between them. Which is making everything take way longer, because they're not paying attention to what they're doing. They copy a page, and then they're all talking and laughing so they don't notice the copy is done, and at this rate we'll never get a machine. Plus it looks like they're copying entire notebooks. As if that weren't annoying enough, I notice someone else was waiting before us. He gives us a look like, *I was here first. So don't even think about it.*

I shift from one foot to the other.

"How many copies are we doing again?" Danny says.

"A thousand."

"So that's like . . ."

"A hundred bucks. I got it."

"Since when? You're Mr. PermaBroke."

"Yeah well. Not today." The truth is, I took the money out of my savings. Which is supposed to be exclusively for college. But drastic times and all.

I shift onto my other foot.

Now the girls are laughing so hard one of them drops her notebook. It smacks onto the tiles. Random pages spill across the floor. This makes them crack up even harder.

"Dude," Danny says. "We need to stage an intervention."

"Now would be a good time for that."

The thing about Danny is that brainy chicks love him. When he goes into flirt mode, no girl with at least half a brain cell stands a chance.

It doesn't exactly suck to be him.

I watch as he approaches the girl who glanced at him when we came over. His strategy is flawless.

As soon as he says something to her, she's hooked. He has her laughing harder than she was with her friend in under ten seconds. Then he tones it down a little, moving closer to her. I see him touch her arm. A minute later, she moves over to the other machine with her friend. Danny waves me over.

The guy who was in front of us gives me the evil eye. I smile and shrug like I had nothing to do with it. He scowls. For a second I worry that there's going to be some major confrontation. But then the suit finishes up on his machine, so we're saved.

"Incredible," I tell Danny.

"As always." He lifts the cover of the copy machine and lines the note up evenly on the glass.

"What did you say to her?"

"Not much." Danny pulls out the paper drawer. I hand him a ream of colored paper I bought before. "Just how you're desperate to make a certain girl really happy. And how making these copies is essential for your somewhat questionable success." He rips the cover off the paper. "And how it would mean a lot to me if she could help us out." Danny looks over at her and winks. She giggles.

"Thanks, man."

"Don't mention it."

The copies look great. With a thousand of these, we're going to cover the entire school with no problem.

After we put the second ream in, the girl comes over. She goes, "Danny, right?"

"Right. Kim."

"You remembered!" She giggles again. She attempts to pull her T-shirt down. Which is pointless since it barely covers her belly button.

"Of course I did," Danny says, all smooth. "What do you think I am?"

"I don't know!" She looks over her shoulder at her friend. Who's trying desperately not to crack up. "Yeah so . . . where do you go?"

"Eames Academy. And this is James. He goes there, too."

"Isn't that the design school?"

"Yeah. Well, it's supposed to be. You know how it is."

"Totally. We go to Environmental Studies? And it's so not for that."

"Word?"

"Yeah. It's so lame. There's, like, two environmental electives and that's it."

"Drag."

Kim looks over her shoulder again. Her friend apparently finds the whole thing so hilarious she can't even look at us anymore. "Um, so, anyway . . . I'll just . . . be over there."

Danny's all, "I'll be watching."

I check the screen. The copies are almost done.

"You interested?" I ask.

"In?"

"Kim, yo."

"Nah. Just having fun."

"She's cute."

"Yeah, but I think she has a boyfriend."

"She told you that?"

Danny shakes his head. "Just a feeling."

But I know the real reason. All he can think about is Nicole.

That's the thing about being hooked on a girl. You see what else is going on around you. You notice other girls. But it doesn't register the same way it used to. You only care about one thing, one goal. And sometimes, being so focused on what you want, you can't see what everyone else does.

"I'm doing it," Danny says. He tapes a copy of the note on the wall above the water fountain.

"Doing what?"

"Asking Nicole to the dance."

"Nice."

I tape copies on some lockers. Danny moves to the other side of the hall to get the lockers over there.

"So here's my angle. Tomorrow night's all about doing this like a casual thing."

"Copy that."

"And after I blow away the entire school with my unbelievably impressive speech, I'll be getting some definite attention."

"Affirmative."

"But I won't push it too far. You know, keep it real light. See if we can hang as friends first. And then we'll get back together."

We tape up more copies.

Danny's like, "And I'm calling that chick from Millennium for you."

I stop taping. "No."

"Dude. What's the problem?"

"I told you I didn't want to be fixed up."

"Why not?"

"I don't want to get into a whole thing with some other girl right now."

"But that's such a lame reason."

I glare at him.

"She's hot," he says. "You'll see."

"No I won't, because you're not calling her."

"Why not?"

If I just come right out and tell him I asked Rhiannon, he'll still want to set me up. But there might be a way to work this so Danny drops it.

"You're playing this off like a casual friends thing, right?"

"Yeah . . ."

"So what if you ask Nicole as a group thing?" I say. "Then it'll be even more legit."

"I feel you. But then who else is in the group?"

"Okay well, me. And . . . it can't be that girl you want to set me up with."

"Why not?"

"Because then it will look like a double date. You setting me up? The four of us going together?"

Danny nods. "Okay. So who else?"

"Rhiannon," I tell him.

"Sweet. Let's do it." He scans the hallway for a surface we didn't cover. There are none.

We stand there, surveying our work. The copies are everywhere. Karmic retribution is almost complete.

I see the swirling ambulance lights from all the way down the street. I start running. When I get to my building, there are EMT people and a couple police officers on the stoop.

"What's going on?" I ask everyone in general.

An EMT turns to me. "Do you live here?" he says.

"Yes."

"What floor?"

"Third."

"Do you know Mrs. Schaffer?"

My heart stops beating entirely. Then it starts again, extra fast. "Yes."

"It seems she had an accident."

"Is she okay?" This is the one thing I've been so worried about lately. Mrs. Schaffer hasn't been herself. I've been afraid that one day I'll come home and she'll be gone. Permanently.

"She'll be all right," the EMT says. "But apparently she fell."

"Is it serious?"

"Hard to say. She may have fractured her hip. We won't know until she's taken in."

A police officer comes over to me. "James Worther?"

My mouth gets all dry. "Yes?"

"Will you be riding in the ambulance? Or would you rather ride with me?"

"Uh." How do they know my name?

"I'm afraid you'll have to come with us. She's in no condition to fill out the necessary paperwork at the hospital and"—he consults his tiny notebook—"do you have a copy of her insurance card?"

Why would I have a copy of her insurance card? "No. I—why would I?"

The officer analyzes my face. "Are you aware that Mrs. Schaffer has you listed as her In Case of Emergency contact?"

My mouth gets even drier. She never told me that. Did she? "Uh . . . no. I didn't know that."

"My apologies. It shouldn't take that long. We just need you to answer some questions at the hospital."

"Questions?"

"A social worker will be meeting us there. We need to determine if Mrs. Schaffer is healthy enough to live in an unsupervised setting."

"Are you—do you mean like putting her in a nursing home?"

"It's a possibility."

I can't believe this. Mrs. Schaffer would die if she had to live in a place like that. And it's not like she has money. If you're a regular person, you can't get quality care. And she'd be all alone. At least here she has me.

"I don't think she'd like that," I tell him.

"I'm sorry, son. But it's not up to her."

CHAPTER 21

Friday

THE PA SYSTEM broadcasts, "Rhiannon Ferrara to the principal's office."

That's my cue.

I cough.

Mr. Martin is waxing rhapsodic about the importance of air and light in stimulating worker productivity. Which is why you have to design office spaces with as much air and light as possible.

I cough some more.

Mr. Martin stops. He zeroes in on me, the source of this rude interruption of his profound thought process. He asks, "May I help you, James?"

"Can I get some water?" I gasp. *Cough, cough.*

"I don't know," he says. "Can you?"

It's one of those ancient teachers' jokes they all think is still hilarious ten generations later. I wonder if they'd still tell those jokes if they knew how tired we think they are. Probably.

"May I? Please go get some water?"

Mr. Martin has this smug expression. "You may," he informs me.

I walk calmly across the room. But the second I hit the hallway, it's showtime. I zip down the halls, round corners at lightning speed, and hurl myself into the main office. The secretary barely looks up. She's seen it all.

"He called me," I tell her.

She nods me in. Doesn't even question me. Because why would someone voluntarily show up at the principal's office and want to go in?

I burst through Mr. Pearlman's door. Rhiannon's already sitting there. They both stare at me.

I say, "I did it."

They're shocked.

"You?" he says.

"Yes."

"*You* did it."

"Yes. I take full responsibility."

He turns to Rhiannon. "You're free to go, Ms. Ferrara."

Rhiannon is about to blow it. I can tell from the horrified look on her face. I send her a telepathic message to stay quiet.

She goes, "But—"

"So you should go," I say.

She gets up. I'm nervous about doing this, but there's no way Rhiannon's taking the blame. And nothing's getting in the way of my MIT scholarships or I'm toast. My public-speaking phobia has prevented me from saying a lot of things I wish I said. Now's my chance to speak up and make a difference.

This better work. If it doesn't, we're all going down.

Rhiannon shuts the door behind her. Time for phase two.

"Care to explain yourself?" Mr. Pearlman asks.

"It's like I said. I did it."

"What are you telling me, James?" The guy knows all about me. Second in my class. Computer geek who can fix any problem with the school's system. Science League state finalist. Moral. Reliable. Which is why I can tell he's having a hard time believing me. "That you made all those copies? That you hung them up last night?"

"Yeah."

"How did you even get in?"

"Not all the doors were locked."

"Oh? Which one was open?"

"It was . . . the side one."

"Which side?"

"Uh . . . the left?"

And then Nicole busts into the office. She says, "I did it."

"Actually," I say, "I did it."

"No, *I* did," Nicole argues.

"What's going on here?" Mr. Pearlman demands. "Is this a game to you? Do you know what the punishment is for this?"

We watch him.

"Do you?"

We shake our heads. I don't even think he knows what the punishment is for this.

"Sit down, Nicole."

She sits in the chair next to mine.

"So both of you did this?" Mr. Pearlman says.

"No," I clarify. "Just one of us."

"Well if both of you are telling me you did it, then both of you will be punished."

"But we didn't," Nicole says. "James wasn't even here last night."

"When you put up all these copies."

"Exactly."

"By yourself."

"Uh-huh."

"I see." Mr. Pearlman has one of those four-color clicky pens. He goes *click click* with the pen. "And how did you get in?"

"Window."

"Excuse me?"

"There was a window open."

"Which window?"

"To the physics lab."

"That's on the third floor."

"Really? Wow."

And then Danny busts in. He says, "I did it."

Now Mr. Pearlman looks really mad. He doesn't like Danny. But Danny's had to take three years of crap from him so he's been ready for this.

"All me," Danny goes on. "Not that you're surprised to hear it. I know you think I've been a nuisance and all."

Mr. Pearlman doesn't respond to that.

"And even if these guys said they did it, you can't punish anyone without absolute proof, can you?"

"Admitting to a misdemeanor is proof."

"Even when the person is lying?"

And then Jackson busts in.

"I did it," he says. "And I have proof."

It's a good thing we don't get searched when we come in for assemblies. Like some schools with their metal-detector crackdown or psycho security officers. So I have no problem smuggling in the remote control. It's this trigger apparatus I spent all week rigging. Definitely my best work yet.

Rhiannon finds me and picks a seat to the right of the stage. I sit next to her the same way I did all those other times. But this time, everything is different.

Danny doesn't even look nervous, sitting onstage with the other candidates. There are two other kids running against him for president, a guy and a girl. The girl is a ruthless Tracy Flick *Election* type who would kill her own mother to win. But the other guy doesn't want it as badly as Danny. He hardly put up any posters, and nothing about him makes him stand out in any particular way. She's some serious competition, though. But Danny's just sitting there, as if he's not about to make a speech in front of the whole school that will be this monumental, revolutionary event.

Rhiannon looks around the auditorium. Kids are still spilling in. "Do you see Nicole?" she says.

I scan the seats. "No." My eyes land on Jessica. Her eyes burn a hole through mine.

I keep on scanning.

"Do you know what Danny's going to say?" Rhiannon asks.

"Sort of."

"Did he practice with you?"

"Nah. You know Danny. He can do this stuff in his sleep."

"Yeah. It must be awesome to be able to talk in front of everyone like that and not even get nervous."

"Big-time."

"Wouldn't you be nervous?"

"Hell yeah!"

"Right?"

"Like you wouldn't believe."

"Attention, please!" Keith yells into the mic. "Welcome to the student council election speeches, guaranteed to provide one solid period of mindless distraction from your otherwise abysmal routine!"

Rhiannon is still looking around for Nicole. I see her sitting up front. I lean over and whisper, "There's Nicole." I point.

"Why isn't she sitting with us?" Rhiannon whispers back.

I shrug. I check the remote control in my bag. The power switch tends to be a little loose. I've got the nervous excitement thing going on. Unfortunately, we have to sit through the mind-numbingly vapid speeches from everyone else before we get to the good stuff. The only good stuff being Danny. So when he finally goes up to the podium and everyone's clapping, I'm stoked. I slip the remote out of my bag.

"In last week's Random Hallway Poll," Danny starts, "eighty-three percent of you told me you think elections are whack. Fourteen percent of you think they can make some sort of difference. And the remaining three percent?" He pauses. "Believe, with unfaltering conviction, that I should absolutely stop conducting Random Hallway Polls."

Cheers all around. Only they're fake cheers. Everyone loves Danny's Random Hallway Polls.

"But seriously, folks," he continues. "What can I, as next year's class president, do for you? I could make promises. But promises can be broken, while actions are the real deal. So the only promise I'll make today is a promise for action. As your president, I will do something every day to inspire you to revolutionize your lives. Even revolutionize the world."

I check the switch again. My hands are shaking.

"I can cut through the bullshit. I can say 'bullshit' when I'm not supposed to."

More cheers.

"And I can summarize the one thing we all want the most— within ourselves, among our friends, and here in school—in one word."

He holds up a sign. It says: PEACE. "Let's have a moment of silence for all of you to reflect on how this word relates to your life, this school, and the entire planet. Because all three of those things are connected." Then he just stands there like that, holding up the sign, not saying anything. No one talks.

After a while, Danny continues. "When I'm president, I won't let you forget about those connections. I want to open your minds to the possibility of something bigger than this, something massive that we can actually have control over. Think about how scared you were on September eleventh."

Everyone is riveted.

"Something like that could happen again. So we need to rethink how we're living our lives. Because everyone and everything on this planet is connected. You matter. And what you do every day, the choices you make, the way you interact with other people, it all matters. And it all can change the world."

Tatyana stands up and cheers. She's wearing a T-shirt with a peace sign on it that she made. Danny's wearing one she made for him, too.

"Think about what you want to do after this part of your life is over. And what kind of person you want to be. Because everything you do now is deciding that for you. There's no excuse for treating people badly. Especially with everything else we have to deal with. So why can't we be better to each other and to ourselves?

"It's about respect. For others. For ourselves. For our futures."

Then he holds up another sign that says: CHANGE THE WORLD. "We're bigger than every one of us. You all have the power to change the world. Every single one of you. So ask yourself this: What does your ideal world look like?"

The lights go off.

Some girls scream.

Then the music starts.

Here's the part where I flip the switch.

Words are immediately projected onto the walls of the auditorium. And the ceiling. And the floor. And even on the deco moldings from when this school was some kind of studio space in the fifties. The words look cool sliding over their brass surfaces.

The way I designed it, each word has a different font and color. Words like REVOLUTION. And DREAM. And RESPECT. And BELIEVE. Words that are connecting with everyone in different ways. They don't realize what's happening. But it is.

It's kind of like a giant mind fuck.

Plus, Miguel is doing this strobe thing with the lighting. And the music is blasting that Beatles song "Because."

At first, everyone's quiet. Reading the walls.

Then the clapping starts. And then everyone goes crazy. They're jumping in their seats, stomping on the floor, whistling.

Of course it works. It's genius.

In the glint of the strobe light, I can barely make out Mr. Pearlman stumbling onto the stage. He grabs the mic at the podium.

He yells, "People! People!" But you can hardly hear him over the music. It looks kind of funny, actually. He's all straining and scream- ing and trying to get us to be quiet, but the resulting volume is mad low. "Can someone check the lighting booth? *Check the lighting booth!*" I see the AP and some teachers running back in that direc- tion.

But it's too late. Miguel is long gone. And the best part is, no one can accuse me of anything, either. That's the cool thing about this program I designed. When they get to the booth, they won't find any evidence that the light projection is running from there. But they won't be able to stop it, either. And the music is programmed along with the lighting. It turns out that the PA system was easier to hack than I thought.

I'm the only one who can make it stop. I'm the only one who will decide when it's over.

And no one can prove it.

When I heard that Brad was suspended, I immediately thought it was because of whatever went down with Sheila. But that's not it.

It was Jackson, man. Jackson is my hero.

People are saying that he felt all empowered by the atten- tion from Gloria's note. So instead of feeling embarrassed about it, which we were afraid might happen, he turned it around. He's like a rock star. And the way he busted into Mr. Pearlman's office? Dude. I did *not* see that coming. Nicole said she was the one who told him about our plan, and he immediately wanted to get in on it. He used Gloria's original letter as proof that he was the one who put the copies up.

And then there's the Brad thing. Brad threatened Jackson's life during a math test. Which was such a dumbass thing to do. Everyone knows that a verbal threat on someone's life could get you transferred to another school. And even if Brad was joking around, it doesn't matter. Intent is irrelevant. So Jackson reported Brad. I'm sure that's why Jackson only got detention for a week instead of being suspended for the note thing. Mr. Pearlman probably didn't want news of Brad's threat to get out. That wouldn't look good for our school.

Righteous. I guess karma really does work.

But this day could not have been any crazier. So I need some tension-release time. And I've got all this pent-up frustration and anxiety rustling around for some reason.

There's only one solution to a crisis like this: playing Halo 2 on Danny's sick Xbox 360. After school, we grab all the food we can carry from his kitchen and park in front of the TV.

Time for some serious action. I'm on fire. I almost rip the controller in half. Nothing can stop me.

Danny watches me make a sweet energy-sword play. He shrieks, "Tasty!"

That's pretty much the extent of our conversation for the next two hours. Here's what we don't talk about:

- Stuff that I'm starting to hope might happen at the dance.
- And after the dance.
- How Danny's going to deal with Nicole.
- How Danny's going to deal with Nicole possibly not wanting to get back together with him.
- The whole thing with Mrs. Schaffer last night.

Not that I'm thinking about any of this. I just want to chill in the year 2552 for a while.

⊞

"You're so in," I tell Danny at the dance.

"It would appear so, wouldn't it?" he yells back over the music. "Not to be an obnoxious prick or anything."

"Of course not."

Voting isn't until Monday, but it's obvious he's got the election in the bag. We were supposed to go back to class for two more periods after the assembly. Which I guess we did, technically. Or some of us did. A lot of kids bailed after. And those of us who stayed didn't exactly get work done. The teachers all had this creeped-out look like it was Columbine Part Two or something. All anyone wanted to talk about was who did it? And how did they get the lights to go off when no one was in the lighting booth? And why wasn't Danny disqualified?

The answer to that last one is easy. They couldn't prove anything. And in New York City the rules about punishing students are really tight. Mr. Pearlman knows that if he disqualified Danny without any proof, Danny's parents would be up his butt so fast he'd wish he kept Vaseline in his desk drawer. They only manage to nail kids whose parents don't care. If Mr. Pearlman accused Danny and suspended him or whatever, Mr. Pearlman would probably be the one to get in trouble.

Example. I remember the best teacher from seventh grade, Mr. Leto. It was the beginning of the year and some kid wasn't doing the Do Now, which is this short assignment you're supposed to do right away. So Mr. Leto goes over to him, and he's like, "Jose! Do the Do Now!" And he tapped his gradebook really lightly against Jose's head. According to Jose, Mr. Leto pounded him over the head with a brick. He ran out of the room yelling, "Mr. Leto hit me!" And the principal came in and Jose was crying. Then Mr. Leto didn't show up for a whole month.

Mr. Pearlman knows that's his reality if he does anything without absolute proof. Works for me.

I take in the scene. Rhiannon by the drinks, talking to Nicole. Tony doing that lame dance he always does. The way the girls standing on the side are trying to look like they don't care that no one's asking them to dance. The boys pretending not to notice them, even the ones they like. It's all such a game. And for some reason, I'm over playing it.

I'm trying to avoid looking at the lead singer's breasts, but it's really hard. She's this cute chick with a tiny shirt cut so low it doesn't take much effort to imagine her naked. But I don't want Rhiannon to think I'm interested. I'm just looking. Kind of like admiring fine art at the Guggenheim.

Ripping my eyes away and forcing myself to notice other stuff, I check out the bar and see that *The Breakfast Club* is playing on TV. The TV is set up with couches and a coffee table around it to look like someone's living room. Actually, the whole place looks like someone's living room.

I point to the TV and yell over to Rhiannon, "Check it out!"

She yells back, "Yeah! I saw!"

"Nice!"

"Totally!"

We watch the band some more. Or, Rhiannon watches and I try to focus on the keyboard. And then she goes, "Are you wearing cologne?"

I'm like, "What?" Even though I heard her.

"Are you wearing cologne?!"

The correct answer is yes. But now I feel like a nimrod because I kind of put it on for her. And if I admit that I'm wearing it she'll probably figure that out, because I've never really worn cologne before. So I pretend that I still can't hear her.

When we're out on the street after and all talking about how sick the band was and how hot the bar is, I'm trying to think of a polite way for Rhiannon and me to ditch Danny and Nicole. This was a blast and all, but I could use some downtime.

Danny's got his own agenda. Eventually he says, "Peace out," and leaves with Nicole.

"Do you feel like going somewhere?" I ask.

"Yeah," Rhiannon says. "I'm not even tired."

"Me neither."

So we get a cab. And then we walk. We end up at the pier. Which we have entirely to ourselves.

Someone's home in the apartment tower across the street. You can see right in, since the tower is mostly glass. It was designed by Richard Meier, this rad architect we studied in mechanical drawing. The people in there are so lucky. Their view is amazing. I wonder how many of them really appreciate what an incredible home they have.

I listen to the water. All this quiet is righteous.

I'm all, "Nice how I reserved the whole pier, huh?"

"It's sweet."

"Yeah. I'm sweet like that."

I think about my new playlist. And the iPod in my pocket.

I'd only known Rhiannon for like a month when we were doing homework at my house and I put a Jet CD on. She said she didn't know who they were. I told her it was total Rhiannon music. I was right. And I haven't been wrong since. So I made a playlist of Rhiannon music.

Then I get that anxious pang again. And I'm still not sure why. But I'm starting to get the picture.

"What's wrong?" she says.

Busted.

"Nothing. Well . . . I guess there is something. Since you're asking and all."

"What?"

"There's no light show."

"What?"

I point to the building across the river. Its slanted top is all dark.

"Oh." Rhiannon looks. "Maybe it'll start later."

"It better." I wipe my hands on my jeans. I should have brought mints.

There are some flowers on the grass. Rhiannon watches them bending in the breeze. She says, "I like those flowers."

"They're nice."

"Those pink ones are so pretty."

"Well, they're not as good as the ones in your locker, but . . ."

She gives me a weird look. "How do you know about that?"

"About what?"

"Did I . . . I didn't tell you about the flowers, did I?"

"What flowers?"

"Those . . . flowers Steve left in my locker?"

"I don't know anything about those flowers. I only know about the flowers *I* left in your locker."

"No way! That was you?"

"Yeah."

"But how did you know . . . ?"

"Remember when we were walking past that house on Charles Street and they had all those flowers outside? And you said how they were—"

"—so pretty."

"Yeah."

"I totally forgot about that."

"Yeah, well. I didn't."

She just looks at me for a while. Then she goes, "Do you want to sit?"

There's that pang again.

"Um . . . I was thinking of . . . not sitting."

"And doing what? You want to walk more?"

"Not exactly." I take out my iPod. I separate the earbuds. I put one in her ear. "I'd rather do this." I put the other one in my ear. I select the first song on the playlist. It's "Look What You've Done."

And then we're dancing. I just made it up. iPod dancing. I'm not exactly the most romantic guy, so this is kind of extreme for me.

There's this feeling I get when we're together like this. It feels calm. All the noise in my head is quiet. And it feels like I've finally found where I'm supposed to be.

So when I kiss her, it's like nothing else exists but this.

But then her cell chimes. It's the worst timing ever.

She says, "Let me turn this off."

"It's a text?"

"Yeah. Sorry." She checks the screen. "It's from Nicole." And then she's like, "Oh my god."

"What?"

"It says, '*Help me*.'"

"That's all it says?"

"Hang on." Rhiannon types back. I move next to her so I can see the screen. She types: **where r u?** and sends it.

A few seconds later, the screen says: **211 W 80**.

That's all I need to know. I remember when he told her he lives in her neighborhood. So it's pretty obvious where Nicole is.

"Is that between Broadway and Amsterdam?" Rhiannon says.

"Yeah. I know where it is."

"Let's go." She types in: **don't move. we're coming**.

On the cab ride over, I tell Rhiannon about overhearing Mr. Farrell and Nicole. And how he said he lived in Nicole's neighborhood, so maybe she's at his place.

"Why do you think she texted instead of calling?" Rhiannon says.

"I don't know."

"I hope she's not, like, trapped inside."

"I'm sure she's okay," I tell her. But images of what could be going down keep harassing me. Maybe I should have said something before.

By the time we're running down West 80th Street, we're both freaking out.

If he did anything to her . . .

We find her across the street. Sitting on the curb. Crying.

"Nicole!" Rhiannon runs over to her. She collapses on the curb and hugs Nicole. "What happened?"

But Nicole is crying too hard to answer. Every time it seems like she's about to tell us, she just keeps taking these big gasping breaths. All she can get out is, "I—I—" It's like she can't get enough air.

"Let's get out of here," I say. I put my hand on Nicole's shoulder. She's shaking really hard. And crying even harder.

She's having a major meltdown.

We get Nicole to her place. Her mom's asleep, so we try to be quiet and sneak Nicole back to her room. Rhiannon gets her into bed and piles blankets on top of her. I pace around, furious at myself. How could I have let this happen?

After Rhiannon brings Nicole some water and the crying slows down, Nicole starts talking. But she's not making any sense.

"She . . . she knew. Maybe not at first. But she knew eventually."

Rhiannon gives me a look like, Who's she talking about?

I shrug. The only thing I want to do right now is ask Nicole if Mr. Farrell hurt her. But when I step forward and go, "Did he—?" Rhiannon shakes her head at me. But I have to know. "Did he . . . do anything to you in there?"

But Nicole says, "No. I never went in."

Then we just listen.

"There was this one night when she came home early. From her bridge game. And I heard her coming upstairs. And then . . . that's when he left my room. So she saw him. She saw him leaving my room."

"Who?" Rhiannon asks.

But it's like Nicole didn't even hear her. She just keeps talking.

"Maybe she knew for a while. Like on some subconscious level. But she didn't want to admit it."

She can't be talking about Mr. Farrell. If Nicole's mom caught him in her place, she would have gone ballistic. Everyone would know.

"After she found out . . . that's when we moved here."

"I thought you moved here because your parents got divorced," Rhiannon says.

Nicole focuses on Rhiannon. She pushes the blankets off. She's not shaking anymore.

And she says, "That's why they got divorced. My dad abused me."

I can't believe it. None of us knew.

"I think I want to talk about it," Nicole tells us.

"Okay," Rhiannon says. "We're here."

So she begins.

EPILOGUE

Excerpt from a screenplay by Nicole Nelson:

INT. THERAPIST'S OFFICE-DAY
CAMERA zooms in on DR. RIBISI and NICOLE near a big window.
DR. RIBISI is sitting in an armchair. She is writing something on a notepad. NICOLE is sitting on a couch, with her
feet up.

                    DR. RIBISI
Let's go back to that Friday night. You were at Mr. Farrell's door, but you didn't ring his bell.

                    NICOLE
I really wanted to.

                    DR. RIBISI
What stopped you?

                         NICOLE
(A pause) Reality. I just realized . . . I mean, I was
still in love with Danny. But I didn't want to deal with
how serious we were getting, so I pretended I wasn't.
But then at the dance, it was obvious that we should be
together.

                         DR. RIBISI
So it was your feelings for Danny that stopped you?

                         NICOLE
It was more like . . . I saw myself inside and what would
happen if Mr. Farrell really liked me. And it reminded me of
my dad. All I could see was this older guy with a way younger
girl, even though that's what I wanted. I guess I stopped
wanting it. Or with Danny, I knew it was real. And with Mr.
Farrell, it was probably just a fantasy.

                         DR. RIBISI
You mentioned that you saw a similarity between your
situation with Mr. Farrell and what happened with your
father.

                         NICOLE
It's weird how stuff keeps repeating. And how you don't
even know it when you're in the middle of it.

                         DR. RIBISI
Why do you think that is?

                         NICOLE
About the repeating? Or the not knowing?

                         DR. RIBISI
Either one.

                         NICOLE
Well . . . I guess if you're not aware that something in
your life is repeating, the cycles keep continuing until
you realize what you're doing.

                       DR. RIBISI
This is a good place to pick up next time.

                         NICOLE
It's time already?

                       DR. RIBISI
(Smiles) Time flies when you're having fun.

     EXT. SIDEWALK IN FRONT OF OFFICE BUILDING—DAY
NICOLE leaves the building. She takes out her cell phone
and dials.

                         NICOLE
Hey, Danny. I'm having an epiphany. Where are you?

CAMERA zooms out. NICOLE walks to the corner. Just as she
gets there, the streetlight turns green. She crosses the
street.

Entry in Rhiannon's journal:

    Question: Where does love go?
    Answer: It doesn't matter. What matters is that love finds
its way back home to you. And when it does, it's stronger
than ever.

♥

Copy of a note found on multiple lockers:

Sexy Jackson Thang,

You were so cute yesterday when you carried my books to class!!! I felt like Sandy in "Grease" or something. Like a girl in a poodle skirt right out of one of those old movies you like.

Hey babe, I just wanted to say that even though you are really special to me and I always want to be with you, I don't think it's a good idea for you to show up at practice like that. It's not that you're not invited, but it's way too distracting for you to be so close! What we have is really special and I don't feel like sharing it with the whole world—I want you all to myself! Like if I could keep you in a box I would. ☺ But a cute, heart-shaped box, you know?

Anywayz . . . love ya!

Kisses forever,
Gloria

Letter to James Worther from Edith Schaffer, delivered after her death:

My Dearest James,

Well, I bet you're surprised that an old lady like me had so much money in the bank, huh? Especially after the way I clipped all those coupons and checked the sales before I made my grocery lists. But you'd be surprised what saving a little money here and there can do after so many years. I've been saving all my life, and now I have this gift to give you. It's my way of saying thank you for all those kind things you did for me.

I've heard that sometimes old people know when they're going to die. They have a feeling a little while before they pass away. And now I'm the one having that feeling. I don't know how much time I have left, but I know it's not long. So I'm writing you this letter, and my lawyer will give it to you after I'm gone.

Now I want to make sure you understand something. This must seem like a lot of money to you. Believe me— I know! You may be tempted to spend it on fun things you don't need. But this money is meant for college. You're only allowed to spend it on that. I know what it's like to grow up always doing without. It's time for you to stop worrying yourself so much.

You're probably wondering how I'll know what you spend it on, being dead and all. I don't know what happens to us after we die, but I have my theories. Maybe there's a way for me to find out what's going on down there. Who knows? Maybe I'll make new friends and not be so lonely anymore.

People sometimes ask me what the secret of life is. I should know this? Looking back on everything now and knowing my time left on this earth is short, I will say this: Enjoy every day of your life. Appreciate everything your life gives you. You'll be surprised how fast it all goes by.

You're a good kid, James. Stay that way. Keep working hard and you will achieve your dreams. Take good care of you.

Remember me to your mom. And carry me in your heart, my dear.

Love,

Mrs. Schaffer

Turn the page for a preview of
Susane Colasanti's next book,

Waiting
for
You

Text copyright © Susane Colasanti, 2009

1

The best thing about summer camp is the last day. Because that's the day you get to go home and live like a normal person again.

Don't get me wrong. Camp was freaking awesome. I spent the entire summer in Maine at a special camp for the arts. My dad gave me his old Nikon camera and taught me how to develop photos last year, and ever since then photography has been my passion. There's something about vintage film that captures the Now in a way digital can't. It just makes everything look softer somehow. And the whole old-school method of developing your own photos exactly how you want them is really cool.

So yeah, I learned a lot more about photography at camp and had a ton of practice. I've also been playing the violin since seventh grade, so I had violin lessons there, too. We even had a concert last night.

I've only been home for like three hours but I've already

participated in the following critical post-camp activities:

- Took a real shower. With water pressure. That actually got me clean.

- Remembered what air-conditioning felt like. Did a little happy dance at the supermarket.

- Put on clothes that didn't smell like mildew. They also did not feel permanently damp.

- Sat on the couch and watched TV.

- Got a cold drink from the refrigerator. Ice rules.

The only thing left on my list is to get together with Sterling for the first time since June, so I'm majorly stoked. I can't wait to see her. Not just because she's my best friend, but because school starts in a week and we're getting psyched for it.

I love the beginning of the year. It's all about renewal and reinventing yourself, becoming the person you've always wanted to be. You can go back to school as a whole new person and have a totally different time. Every year I get all excited about how everything's going to be different, but it never really is. I'm tired of always being disappointed. This has to be our year.

It feels good to knock on Sterling's door with "Wheel" playing in my head. Like I've come full circle after a long journey, even though I've only been at sleep-away camp for two months. But this is such a "Wheel" moment. That song rocks. The best part is where John Mayer says how our connections are permanent, how if you drift apart from someone there's always a chance you can be part of their life again. How everything comes back around again. I have a theory that the answers to all of life's major questions can be found in a John Mayer song.

Sterling flings the door open. Her hair isn't brown anymore. Now it's blonde.

"Oh my god, your *hair!*" I yell.

Then she grabs me and we're hugging and squealing and doing this thing where we're hopping around.

"I know!" Sterling goes. "It was supposed to come out more like yours, but the stylist said your color is complicated."

"Why didn't you tell me you were dyeing it?"

"I wanted it to be a surprise."

"Oh, I'm surprised."

"So, what do you think?" Sterling twirls around so I can inspect her hair from all angles. It's a lighter blonde than mine, since my hair has different shades of blonde mixed in, and I'm not sure if it works with her coloring.

"It's hot," I say. Maybe I just have to get used to it.

She points to my usual stool in the kitchen. "Sit," she says.

Sterling took over the kitchen when she was twelve because her mom can't cook. Plus, she's never here. And Sterling got sick of eating things like hot dogs and Tater Tots and those instant pasta sides every night for dinner. So one day, Sterling announced that she was doing all of the cooking. Now she takes cooking classes and everything. Her mom was thrilled. The agreement is that Sterling puts what she needs for the week on the grocery list and her mom gets everything.

There are four different pots going on the stove. Vegetables in all different colors compete for space on the counter. Two place mats are set out across from each other on the other counter where we always sit, with cloth napkins and schmancy silverware.

"You didn't have to do all this," I go.

"Of course I did. What kind of lame welcome home dinner did you think I was making?"

"Yeah, but it's so . . . extensive." I had to beg my parents to let me come over to Sterling's for dinner since it's my first day back and all, but they finally let me. And we're going to a pier party after.

"Only the best for you, friend girl."

"Wow." Something bubbles in one of the pots. Everything smells so good. "Thanks for doing all this."

"Please. You're the one who's doing me a favor. No one's tried any of this stuff yet. Well, except for me, but I'm not exactly impartial." Sterling picks something out of a bowl and stuffs it in her mouth. "I can't stop eating these," she says. "Try one."

I peer into a bowl of weird-shaped cracker thingies that look like someone cut them out of cardboard. "What is it?"

"Feng Shui rice crackers." Sterling used to have this tone with me when I asked her what something was, like, *How can you not know this?* But now she's used to my culinary ignorance. My family is basically the meat-and-potatoes kind.

Slowly, I stretch my hand into the bowl, as if a rice cracker might bite me. They feel kind of sticky. But I don't want to insult Sterling, so I take a small bite of my cracker. "Hmm."

"Aren't they *so* good?"

I guess I'm not a rice cracker person. "They're . . . different," I tell her. Which I know will make her happy. That's like the highest compliment you can give Sterling about anything going on in her kitchen. She's into the exotic.

"I know." She chomps into another cracker. "I've already eaten like a whole bag of these."

It's hard not to be jealous of Sterling. She's so tiny, but she eats constantly. If I even look at a doughnut I immediately gain five pounds.

Sterling darts to the stove and multitasks between two pans and a massive pot.

"What are you making?" I ask.

"Risotto. Wait, I have to concentrate on this part. It's all about the timing."

While we're eating, Sterling tells me about her new lifestyle plan. She got on the self-improvement train the first day of summer vacay and is riding it right into sophomore year. "Okay. So." She puts her fork down. "Do you need more sauce?"

"No, I'm good." Everything tastes incredible. Sterling could be a professional chef right now, and people eating at her restaurant would never know she's only fifteen. You know, if she stayed hidden in the kitchen and all.

"So," she goes. "You know how I'm kind of high-strung?"

"Pretty much."

"Guess what I'm into now?"

"Uh . . . competitive Ping-Pong?"

"No."

"Auto repair?"

"No! Guess real guesses."

"I give up."

Sterling puts her hands up, like, *Wait for it.* Then she announces: "Yoga!"

"Yoga?"

"Is that cool or what?"

I'm kind of leaning toward "or what." If it was anyone but Sterling, I'd agree that it's cool. But she's the most hyperactive person I know. Her attention span is nonexistent unless a recipe is involved. She can't even sit still for more than three minutes. And now she's doing yoga? How is that possible?

Of course, I can't say any of this. I'm her best friend. I have to be supportive.

So I go, "Is it fun?"

"It's already changing my life! I can *feel* my concentration improving."

"That's awesome."

"Totally. Now you."

We do this every year. We get together before school starts, when all of the electric energy of possibility is zinging around, and make a pact on how we want our lives to change.

"I'm tired of waiting for my real life to start," I go. "Like, when's all the good stuff finally going to happen?"

"Now! This is our year!"

"How do you know?"

"I can just tell."

I really hope she's right. There's only so much waiting a person can endure until they start thinking that maybe nothing exciting will ever happen to them. Like, *ever.*

"Your waiting is over," Sterling insists. "Trust me."

The problem with the last few days of summer? Is that you can't hold on to them. They zoom by way too fast. You live through them in a dream until they're over. And then everything slows down to a glacial pace again.

Usually I'm not nervous until the day before school starts. But today I'm already nervous because we're going to Andrea's pier party tonight and everyone will be there. Or at least the one person I'm extra nervous about seeing will be there.

When we get to Andrea's house, we go around back and find her sitting on the sand. She waves us over.

"Hey, you guys," Andrea says. "How was your summer?"

"Awesome," we both say together. I glance around for him while trying to look like I'm not looking for anyone.

And then I see him.

There's a volleyball game and Derek is serving the ball. His shirt is off and his bathing suit is sexy. It's red and has a thin neon orange stripe along the seam. It's so perfect that he plays volleyball because he's got that classic California surfer boy look. If we didn't live in Connecticut, you'd totally think he was from San Diego or something.

I watch him play. I haven't fully absorbed how perfect his body is yet.

"Hello! Earth to Marisa!"

I snap out of my Derek trance. Sterling and Andrea are looking up at me. When did Sterling spread her towel out? How long was I staring at Derek? And did everyone see me staring at him like a total loser?

Okay, remain calm. Remember: Control your thoughts to control your actions.

I spread my towel out and try to concentrate on what they're saying. As usual, Sterling's drooling over some boy who's too old for her.

"Who's that?" she asks Andrea.

"Who, Dan?" Andrea goes. "He's my brother's friend from college."

"How old is he?"

"Like, twenty-one? Twenty-two?"

"Does he have a girlfriend?" Sterling wants to know.

Andrea gives her a look.

"What?"

"Why can't you like boys your own age?"

"Ew! Maybe because they're gross?"

She has a point. But so does Andrea. Sterling always likes guys who are way out of her age range. And then she complains when all they do is flirt with her.

"I'm just saying," Andrea goes.

"Yeah, well *I'm* just saying that Dan is seriously hot," Sterling says. "Can you introduce me?"

Andrea scrunches her face up.

"What?" Sterling goes.

Andrea's all, "Forget it." But she obviously thinks Sterling's a slut for going after older guys. Sterling's never done anything with any of them, though.

Sterling's like, "Could it *be* any hotter?"

I go, "In hell, maybe."

"The water's great," Andrea says. "You guys should go in."

"Sweet. Coming?" Sterling asks me.

"I'm good."

"I'll go," Andrea says. "I'm completely crispy."

At first, I watch them in the water and talk to some girls I know from orchestra and convince myself that I shouldn't stare at Derek anymore. But that doesn't really work, because I keep sneaking looks at him.

And then something amazing happens. Something seriously life-altering.

Derek looks over at me and smiles.

He's smiling right at me!

I think I smile back, but I'm not sure if my face is working right. He does this little wave thing and goes back to the game.

I wish it could stay like this forever, with the anticipation of everything.

It's always weird seeing everyone when summer's over. There are kids who got tanner. Kids who got thinner. Kids who totally changed their hair. It's interesting to see how people reinvent themselves over the summer. I wonder if anyone thinks I've changed.

Walking home in the dark, I see Nash out on our dock. He's sitting under the lamplight, probably getting a head start on whatever we have to read for English. It's so weird that I don't really know him anymore, because he used to be such a fixture in my life. We played together in third and fourth grades. We practically lived out on the dock all summer, swimming in the river and playing water games. But then everything changed when middle school started. I just didn't feel like hanging out with him as much anymore. The thing is, I can't remember why.

We've known each other forever. Far Hills is one of those small Connecticut towns where everyone knows everyone else. Where you go to school with the same exact kids from kindergarten until you graduate. Plus, Nash and I are neighbors. He lives three houses down, and we still use the same dock for swimming in the summer (our town is on a peninsula, sticking out into Five Mile River).

We actually like using the dock all year. It's a really good place to go when you need some space. It's just that now we avoid using it if the other one's already out there. Sometimes when I see Nash on it, I want to go over and say hi or something, the way we used to do all those years ago. But then it's like he got there first so I should respect his privacy. I know what it's like when you just need to be alone for a while and block out the world.

It's strange how you can live so close to someone and grow up with him without ever really knowing who he is. Or maybe you used to know him, but now you're like strangers. It's weird how time can change something you thought would always stay the same.

2

Can I just say that when you're hoping things will get better but they don't, it majorly sucks?

I really, really thought that today would be different. I imagined getting to school and everyone reacting to me like I'm not such a freak anymore. But that's not how the first day of school is going. It's bad. Like, desperately bad. Because when everyone expects you to be a certain way, it's really hard to escape that image. It's like once everyone decides who you are, you're locked into their version of you and that's it. And everyone decided I was crazy last year. But I'm determined to break out of that. I have to believe that there might be a possible escape route for me.

Sterling seems fine. But she's always fine. She's little and cute and people like her. We don't have any classes together this year and I have no idea how I'll survive lunch. I saw her in the hall when we got our locker assignments and she was talking to people and laughing like she wasn't even nervous. I always have a knot in my stomach on the first day of school that doesn't go away until I get home. Plus, I can never fall asleep the night before, so I'm trying to handle the disaster of my life on two hours' sleep.

I was expecting people to realize that I've changed. I made an effort to smile at people and say hi in homeroom, but I was basically ignored.

Why doesn't anyone want to talk to me? I mean, other than the same people I've been talking to for years. I was sort of hoping to make some new friends. I only have a few friends and I find that to be lame. Lots of kids go out in these big groups. That would be so fun.

Whatever. I can't even deal with this now because we're supposed to be doing a getting-to-know-you activity in chemistry. I hate it when teachers make you sit in a circle on the first day of school and do some activity where you have to introduce yourself. It's like, every nerve in your body is already twanging, which is bad enough. The last thing you want to do is talk in front of people. How can teachers not know that?

So I guess it isn't too heinous that Mrs. Hunter is making us do this activity in pairs. We already got assigned seats. I sit in front of Nash. Then we got this sheet of questions and we had to pick ten that we would most want to ask a potential friend. Which isn't a bad idea if you think about it. Being able to interview your potential friends would rock. Because then you wouldn't get so many nasty surprises later. It's not like you can take back a friendship.

After we pick our ten questions, I turn my desk around to face Nash.

Nash goes first. "If you were a shape, which shape would you be and why?"

I smile at my paper. That was the weirdest question, which is why it was my favorite.

"What?" Nash goes.

"I picked the shape one, too."

"So what shape would you be?"

"Hmm."

I have to seriously think about that. Not only am I sitting in front of this boy for the rest of the year, but we're also lab partners. Which means we have to do every lab report together, plus a few big projects. So if I make a sucky impression and he thinks I'm a reject, it'll be really hard to prove him wrong after that.

Okay, so it's not the first time he's meeting me. But this is the first time we've said more than three words to each other since elementary school and I want to make a good impact on everyone today. I don't just care about how I look (shoulder-length blonde hair with natural highlights, brown eyes that have these green flecks if the light hits them the right way, not fat or skinny, white T-shirt, jeans, black Converse). It's also important to make sure my new personality is showing.

"I'd be . . . a circle," I go. "Within a square."

"I think you're only supposed to pick one."

"Well, I can't be defined by just one shape."

"I see."

"I'm a very complex person," I say, even though I'm not. But I feel daring and wild, saying it. Like I could be anybody and he wouldn't even know the difference.

"I'm getting that," Nash goes. He has this glint in his eyes and a smile where his mouth only turns up on one side.

Don't let that fool you. He's not potential boyfriend material.

Here's why. Nash is totally geeked out. His hair is always messy, his shirts usually look like he slept in them, and he constantly has to correct people when they're wrong, in this annoying know-it-ally way. His social skills are pathetic and I want more friends, so we don't exactly have the same priorities. Plus, I've seen him lick his fingers at lunch when the napkin is like *right there*.

There's just no way.

Nash does have some good qualities, though. I like how he's really shy and sweet. He's not like most other boys who are always acting all doofusy and fifth-grade about everything, where it's like, *Hello, we're in tenth grade now, grow up already.* Nash seems a lot more mature. He's the type of person Aunt Katie would say has an "old soul."

All those good things about him were enough when we were younger, catching fireflies in the summer and making snowmen in the winter. We could be friends without things getting weird. But everything has a different meaning now that we're older. Now there are, like, *implications.*